Lies Like Poison

Also by Chelsea Pitcher

This Lie Will Kill You

lies

like

poison

CHELSEA PITCHER

MARGARET K. McELDERRY BOOKS
NEW YORK   LONDON   TORONTO   SYDNEY   NEW DELHI

MARGARET K. McELDERRY BOOKS
An imprint of Simon & Schuster Children's Publishing Division
1230 Avenue of the Americas, New York, New York 10020
This book is a work of fiction. Any references to historical events, real people, or real places are used fictitiously. Other names, characters, places, and events are products of the author's imagination, and any resemblance to actual events or places or persons, living or dead, is entirely coincidental.

For information about special discounts for bulk purchases, please contact Simon & Schuster Special Sales at 1-866-506-1949 or business@simonandschuster.com.
The Simon & Schuster Speakers Bureau can bring authors to your live event. For more information or to book an event, contact the Simon & Schuster Speakers Bureau at 1-866-248-3049 or visit our website at www.simonspeakers.com.
Also available in a Margaret K. McElderry Books hardcover edition
Interior design by Rebecca Syracuse
The text for this book was set in Iowan Old Style.
Manufactured in the United States of America
First Margaret K. McElderry Books paperback edition November 2021
2 4 6 8 10 9 7 5 3 1
The Library of Congress has cataloged the hardcover edition as follows:
Names: Pitcher, Chelsea, author.
Title: Lies like poison / Chelsea Pitcher.
Description: First edition. | New York : Margaret K. McElderry Books, [2020] | Audience: Ages 14 up. | Audience: Grades 10-12. | Summary: Three years after one secretly backed out of a plot to kill Raven's abusive stepmother, former friends Poppy, Lily, and Belladonna are drawn back together when one of them is arrested for the stepmother's murder.
Identifiers: LCCN 2020020466 (print) | LCCN 2020020467 (ebook) | ISBN 9781534470958 (hardcover) | ISBN 9781534470972 (ebook)
Subjects: CYAC: Murder—Fiction. | Best friends—Fiction. | Friendship—Fiction. | Secrets—Fiction. | Stepmothers—Fiction. | Child abuse—Fiction.
Classification: LCC PZ7.P6428 Lie 2020 (print) | LCC PZ7.P6428 (ebook) | DDC [Fic]—dc23
LC record available at https://lccn.loc.gov/2020020466
LC ebook record available at https://lccn.loc.gov/2020020467
ISBN 9781534470965 (pbk)

For all the kids who snuck out of tower bedrooms
Found their true families
Chose their own names
And learned to conquer giants

PART 1

The Truth According to Belladonna

Killing her would've been easy. That spring we made flower garlands. That spring petals were strewn across her kitchen table, where she drank her tea. If we dropped a petal of belladonna, a petal of poppy, and a petal of lily into that cup, we'd never really know which one of us killed her.

We'd never know which one of us was guilty.

The police wouldn't know either. We were, after all, three scrawny little creatures, no older than fourteen. What damage could we do intentionally? The death of Raven's stepmother would be ruled an accident, and we'd be reprimanded, sure, but none of us would be locked behind bars.

Only the monster would suffer. The woman who made Raven so sick and so scared, he was absent from school more than he was present. He'd been fine before she moved into his house. Bright and shining, like a prince from a fairy tale. Someone to live for. Fight for. Die for.

And that spring I would've killed for him. I convinced the others to go along with it. I picked out a date. I did everything short of picking the flowers, because we each had to bring our own blossoms. One petal of belladonna. One petal of poppy. One petal of lily.

One petal, for each of our names.

But the night before the murder, one of us got cold feet and ruined everything. We all had to poison her together. That's what I thought, the spring we made flower garlands. The spring we spread them out on the table, where she drank her tea.

But three years later, on the eve of Raven's seventeenth birthday, his stepmother was found sprawled out on the kitchen floor. A shattered teacup beside her. It took a little time for the police to gather their evidence, and then they presented their findings to Raven's father. Apparently, someone had taken a cluster of poisonous flowers and stuffed them into his wife's teakettle.

No poppy. No lily. Just belladonna.

Two hours later, they came for me.

1

Belladonna Killed Her

Belladonna Drake was entangled in her true love's arms when a knock came at the door. Slowly, quietly, she inched out of bed. "Don't say anything," she whispered, creeping toward the window.

Red and blue lights flashed below.

"Go out the back door," she instructed without turning around. "I'll stall them long enough for you to get away."

"Belle—"

"You were never here," Belle broke in, pulling a pair of socks from the floor. "You haven't set foot in my bedroom in *years*. All right?"

A nod in the darkness. Then a rustling of clothing as the two of them got dressed. Belle pulled on a soft, fluffy robe. With her hair tousled and her eyeliner smudged, it really would look like she'd woken from a dream. She wasn't hosting company. Everyone was exactly where they were supposed to be.

Taking a shaky breath, she hurried to the first floor. Opened the front door. Blinked up at the officer and said, "Hello? Is everything okay?"

"Belladonna Drake?"

"Ye-yes," she said, managing to stumble over one word. Great. That didn't bode well for the rest of the conversation. But she could lie about who'd been tangled in her arms that night. She'd gotten very good at keeping secrets. Just . . . not from the cops.

"You're under arrest for the murder of Evelyn Holloway. You have the right to remain silent. Anything you say can and will be used—"

"Wait, what?" Belle's vision blurred and the officer's mouth stopped making noise, even though it was moving. "Raven's stepmother is dead? I thought you were here for—"

The man jerked her arms behind her back, sliding handcuffs over her wrists. "You have the right to an attorney. If you cannot afford an attorney, one will be provided for you."

"But I didn't . . . I *couldn't* have—"

"Then let's hope you have an alibi," he said, gesturing to the gaggle of officers standing by the door. They were going to wake her father, but he couldn't account for her. He'd been snoring in his bedroom for hours. There was only one person in the world who could account for Belle's whereabouts that night, and that person was long gone by now.

"Watch your head," the officer said, guiding her into the police car. Belle ducked, sliding into the darkness. Through the window, she could see her adoptive father storming out of the house, spittle flying from his mouth as he raged at the officers. *Typical Edwin*, she thought with a huff. At least some things could be counted on even in your darkest moments.

Some people.

"I need to make a call," Belle said, as the engine turned over. "I get to do that, right?"

"Who you gonna call?" the man asked, in this jovial tone that made her think he was going to start humming the *Ghostbusters* theme song. Everything about this was absurd. Belle wanted to tell herself it was a dream, because none of this could be happening, except . . . the rest of the night had been incredibly vivid. Those lips, trailing across her skin. Those hands, warm and familiar. Bright eyes. Mischievous smile. They'd hardly touched over the past few years, and yet everything was exactly the way it had been the first time they'd held hands.

Like coming home.

Now her actual home was disappearing in the rearview, and the officer was saying, "Look, you don't need to call an attorney. I'm guessing your rich daddy can arrange . . ." A pause as his gaze flicked to the estate in the mirror. The elegant Tudor rose up in the distance, surrounded by a perfectly manicured lawn. The only thing unruly about the estate was the garden, huge and overflowing with dahlias. Bougainvillea. Jasmine. And tucked in the back, in a corner:

Belladonna.

As beautiful as it was fatal. Belle had cultivated that little patch of flowers, telling herself stories about freeing Raven from his wicked stepmother. She'd come up with a plan. Now, three years later, she told herself she wouldn't *really* have gone through with it. She was protective of her ex-boyfriend, but she wasn't a killer.

None of them was.

"How did Mrs. Holloway die?" she asked softly. Every word that came out of her mouth, she analyzed. Did she sound innocent just then? Did she sound guilty? She *wasn't* guilty, she swore to herself over and over again, but it was hard to believe that with cuffs around her wrists. It was harder to believe when the police station came into view.

"You tell me," the officer said from the front seat. "You had a whole cluster of it in your yard. It even looked like some had been pulled recently. We made sure to check before—"

"Pulled?" Belle almost choked on the word. "Which plant was pulled?"

"It had such a pretty name," the man said, catching her eye in the mirror. "You have any guesses, Belladonna?"

The back of the car went silent. It was the middle of the night, so Belle expected it to be quiet, but in that moment, she heard *nothing*. It was as if she were floating in the recesses of space. Everything dark, everything quiet. "They used belladonna?" she said after a minute. "How did you know to look in my yard? Who told—" She really should keep quiet. She had the right to remain silent, after all. Anything she said could and would be used against her in a court of law. Still, she couldn't help but ask, "Did they use any other flowers? Poppies or . . ."

The man pulled up to the station, then climbed out of the car. Belle counted heartbeats as he strode to her door. Five. Ten. Fifteen. She managed to get to seventeen, the exact number of years she'd been on this earth, when the door swung open and the man reached for her. "Why would there be other flowers?" he asked, guiding her out of the darkness. "Belladonna killed her."

Belle lost a bit of time after that. They were in the local police station, but they wouldn't be holding her there for long. She was a minor, so she'd be sent to the detention center up on the hill. It was kind of funny, if she thought about it. Once upon a time, there had been four of them: Raven, Lily, Poppy, and Belle. But three years ago, Raven went away to boarding school on the other side of the country. Lily left soon after that. Poppy didn't split town so much as *totally betray her*, leaving Belle to pick up the pieces of their shattered friendship.

Leaving her alone.

"I hope she has the same number," Belle said when the officer finally let her make a call. "She doesn't even have the same name. She used to go by Poppy but . . ." *She doesn't anymore*, Belle thought, realizing she was rambling. After Raven moved away, Poppy had changed her name to Jack. She'd started dressing in clothes that were typically relegated to the boys' section of department stores, but she still went by *she*, and the cop wouldn't have understood that.

Probably, he wouldn't have.

Within seconds she'd dialed Jack's old cell number, and to her immense relief, the phone started ringing. She prayed Jack would answer. She prayed Jack wouldn't slam down the phone the second she realized who was calling.

"Hello?" That familiar voice came on the line and Belle's hands started to shake. Tears filled her eyes.

"It's, um . . . it's me," she managed, dashing away the tears with her free hand. "Please don't hang up."

"Belle? Why are you calling me from the police station?"

"I . . ." How much should she say? These conversations were probably recorded. But even if they were, they couldn't be used in a court of law without her permission. Right? You had to agree to be recorded or it was inadmissible. She knew this, because three years earlier, she'd studied her rights. She'd prepared to be arrested after she put her plan into action. But the night before the murder, *someone* had gotten cold feet.

Now that someone was listening on the other end of the phone. "Belladonna," Jack said, her voice low and hard. "What happened? What did you—"

"Raven's stepmother was murdered," Belle blurted. "Someone used belladonna to kill her. *Only* belladonna," she added in a whisper.

"No. That's not possible, unless you—"

"I didn't. I swear. But Edwin was passed out in his bedroom all night, and no one can account for me."

"I can account for you." Jack's voice was steady. Calm. "I'm happy to be your alibi, Belle, because I was with you all night. It's not like you're asking me to lie."

Belle counted to five. Ten. Seventeen. "Why are you helping me? You should hate me, after what I—"

"I do hate you sometimes," Jack admitted. "But I love you too. That's how it is with family."

Belle smiled. She was still crying, but she wasn't alone, and it made all the difference. Jack *was* her family. Raven, too, before he went away. For years the three of them had taken care of one another because the world had betrayed them. Their parents had betrayed them.

Together they'd been unstoppable.

"Listen, you don't know how much this means to me," Belle began as the officer stepped toward her. He wanted her to hang up the phone. But she needed to say this before she ended the call. "I thought I understood what happened three years ago, but I never asked you—"

"Don't say anything," Jack interrupted, her voice still calm. "I'm coming down to the station and I'm getting you out of there. Okay? By tomorrow this will all be over. Try to stay positive."

"How can I stay positive?"

"Because," Jack said, and a chill unfurled at the base of Belle's spine, "even though you're innocent, you got what you wanted. Raven can come home."

2

Jack of Many Trades

Poppy Jacqueline McClain was known, to her closest friends and greatest enemies, as "Jack." It was a fitting name. She was a jack-of-many-trades, a talented sword fighter, and a climber of tall trees. She knew how to bring a fully grown man to his knees. Still, of all her skills and talents, Jack had never claimed one particular ability:

Telling the truth.

She sat at the police station, stuffed into a plastic chair, waiting for Detective Frank Medina to return from the field. She'd been there since eight in the morning. When he finally strode through the doors, well after noon, he took one look at her and sighed. "Miss McClain."

"Detective," she replied drily, wrapping her arms around herself. "Call me Jack. Please."

He pulled back his chair, studying her for a minute. He wasn't wearing his mirrored glasses. That would've been overkill in the brightly lit station with the overhead light flickering. Unfortunately, without the glasses, there was nothing to protect her from his shrewd brown eyes.

"Let's start at the beginning," he said, sliding into his seat. He was wearing a blue blazer and jeans, but she could see his gun poking out beneath the blazer's hem. "Where were you between the hours of eleven p.m. Saturday night and one a.m. this morning?"

"I was with Belladonna Drake," Jack said immediately. "I waited for my mom to fall asleep, because she doesn't like Belle very much. Then I snuck out of the house and rode my bike across town. Belle was expecting me, so she let me in through the back door and we spent the night together. So to speak."

A snort from the man in the chair. He was sizing Jack up, taking in the ripped men's Levi's and faded band T-shirt. She was wearing an olive-green jacket that Raven had given her on her thirteenth birthday, a faux-suede number with equally fake fur cuffs. Back then the floor-length jacket had been two sizes too big, but now it fit perfectly.

"So you and Miss Drake are . . . what? Friends? Girlfriends?" the detective asked, and Jack looked down. She was pretty good at blushing on command, if she thought of a certain person in a certain way.

"Let's just say my mother doesn't like us hanging out together. And if Edwin thought someone was visiting Belle in the middle of the night, he'd probably padlock her bedroom door." *On top of everything else*, Jack thought, but she kept that detail to herself.

"Edwin? Belladonna's father?"

"Adoptive father, yeah. He's really overprotective, which is why I snuck into the house after he fell asleep."

Detective Medina sighed. "So no one saw you entering the Drake residence? No one can corroborate your story?"

"The neighbors might've noticed me sneaking out around two thirty." She flashed a taunting smile. "If you're good at what you do, I'm sure you can drum up some evidence."

"I have plenty of evidence."

"What? Some belladonna in Evelyn's system? That's circumstantial. You can't prosecute—" Jack broke off as the detective opened a file on the table. She assumed it was *her* file. She'd been to this station before. But when he pushed the clear plastic baggie toward her, containing a familiar scrap of paper, that surety slipped away. Everything slipped away as Jack read the words scribbled in bleeding, faded ink:

Recipe for the Perfect Murder

One petal of belladonna

One petal of poppy

Drop into a teacup and stir three times.

"This was lying on the table in Evelyn's kitchen," the detective said, his voice quiet now. Tentative. He was trying to coax a confession out of her, but the confession wasn't *about* her. "There are two names on it: Poppy and Belladonna. But I don't think you're responsi—"

"Someone's setting Belle up," Jack interrupted. She forced herself to take slow, deep breaths. "Look at the handwriting! It looks like it was written by a fourteen-year-old."

"I've already found a match for the handwriting," the detective said, glancing at the clock on the wall. It was 12:37. If he'd been up all night, he'd had more than eight hours to investigate the evidence found at the scene of the crime. "Some of your teachers were nice enough to let me borrow your school essays this morning, and it didn't take long to figure out which one of you wrote this." Resting his elbows on the table, he looked into her eyes. "Anything you want to tell me?"

She met his gaze, unflinching. "I didn't do this."

"I know you didn't, Jack. But the girl who did was alone last night, wasn't she? You're just pretending you slept over at her house."

"I'm not pretending."

"You think you're looking out for her, like you always looked out for Raven. Yeah, I remember you," he added, his gaze softening. "Your hair was wilder three years ago, and you called yourself Poppy, but I remember your visit to the station. I remember every story you told."

"I wasn't telling stories," Jack snapped, sinking farther into her jacket. "Everything I told you was true."

"You told me Raven had a wicked stepmother. You told me she was hurting him. But when I brought Raven down to the station, we couldn't find any evidence of abuse, and he swore his stepmother never touched him."

"She didn't have to touch him! She made him want to lie down in the dirt. She made him want to die."

"How?"

"We didn't figure that part out." Jack's heart pulsed against her ribs. She hated talking about Raven, and how sick he'd gotten after his stepmother had moved in. She hated thinking about it. "We just knew that she was scaring him. Making him want to hurt himself. A few weeks after she moved into that house, he started to hear his mom's voice in the middle of the night."

"It's not uncommon for victims of loss to experience hallucinations. Especially someone so young."

"He wasn't hallucinating. One night, I snuck over to his house to see what was happening. I climbed up the ivy that led to Raven's bedroom, and I looked through the window, and . . ."

"What?" the detective asked, his eyebrows knitting together. A wrinkle formed between them. "What did you see, Jack?"

"It isn't what I saw. It's what I *heard*. Her voice was trickling through the room, soft as a whisper. I'd recognize it anywhere. It was Raven's mom, who'd died a year earlier. She was asking him to join her. She was saying she couldn't do this alone, and she needed her little boy." Jack swallowed, taking a breath. "It scared me so badly, I fell into the rosebushes underneath Raven's window. I still have the scars," she added, pulling up the sleeve of her jacket.

The detective frowned, eyeing the thin slashes that laced their way up her arm. "Why didn't you tell me this before?" he asked.

"So you could recommend psychiatric help for me, too? Ship me off to a mental hospital on the other side of the country?"

"Jack, *you* told me Raven was in danger of hurting himself. I had a professional obligation to order a psych evaluation, and after spending seventy-two hours with the boy, Dr. Grimaldi thought it would be best to send Raven to a place where he could process his grief. The Seven Brothers Academy isn't a mental hospital. It's a boarding school for boys who've experienced trauma. Raven has had round-the-clock doctors at his disposal, and some of the best educators in the country."

"I guess I should thank you then," Jack said bitterly. "Except Raven's going to rot in that place until he's eighteen, and then he'll never come back here, since his father threw him away so easil—"

"You don't know?" Medina's eyes narrowed, and Jack's heart stuttered like the wings of a dying butterfly. "Raven's been given a clean bill of health from the Seven Brothers Academy. As of three days ago, he was cleared to come home."

"He . . . What?" Her eyelids fluttered closed, and behind them she could see soft hands and ebony curls. Bright eyes. "Raven's coming home?"

"His flight gets in this afternoon. He was supposed to arrive last night, but his original flight was canceled, thank God. If he'd arrived when he was scheduled to, he might've been the one to find his stepmother. How terrible would that have been, after finding his mom the way he did? Lying in the snow . . ." The detective kept talking, but Jack didn't hear a word. The phrase *his flight gets in this afternoon* kept trickling through her mind. It should've brought her joy. Should've made her hands tremble in anticipation, but instead, dread settled into her stomach, heavy as a rock.

"Does Belle know he's on his way home? Did she know he was coming home?"

"We're working on getting her phone records, to see if she and Raven were in contact around the time of his release. But we have her on film entering the Holloway estate the day Evelyn was killed. There's a camera over the front gate, and Belladonna entered the grounds at five twenty-three in the evening."

"That was *hours* before Evelyn was . . ." Jack trailed off, her mind reeling. "Why would she sneak over so early? Did you ask her?"

"Her lawyer's got her clammed up," the detective said, frowning. "But her father says they had dinner together later that night, so I'm guessing she cased the joint earlier to make sure Evelyn still drank tea."

"Is there video of her leaving?"

He shook his head. "She must've snuck out the back gate, then snuck back in the same way hours later." Medina took a breath, leveling Jack with a stare. "Now do you want to recant your statement about spending the night with her?"

"I . . ." Did she? Once upon a time, she'd have had no trouble believing Belladonna Drake was capable of murder. Fourteen-year-old Belle had been a scrawny, feral creature, likely to scratch out the eyes of anyone who got close to Raven, whether that person was a friend or a foe. But over time Belle's sharp edges had softened to curves, and her anger had softened too, into calm, quiet patience. *Someday* her beloved boy would return to her. *Someday* it would be safe for him to live at home.

But what if Belle found out Raven was being released from the Seven Brothers Academy and decided to make things safe for him? Jack had barely been able to stop the murder three years ago. Now she was sitting in a police station, providing an alibi for a girl who had *definitely* not slept beside her last night.

"If I recant my statement, what happens to Belle?"

Medina leaned in, his voice surprisingly gentle. "The prosecution's case is solid. The flowers were found in Evelyn's tea, just like the recipe says, and Belladonna's history with Raven speaks to motive. If she and Raven were in contact over the past few weeks . . ." He frowned, shaking his head. "It doesn't look good for her."

Jack's chest felt tight. "And if I stick to my original statement? Get up on the stand and swear Belle and I spent the night together?"

The detective laced his fingers together, resting his chin on his hands. "Best-case scenario, the prosecution will use your history of storytelling to get your testimony thrown out."

"That's the best-case scenario?" Jack felt herself sinking, and she hadn't moved from her chair. "Dare I ask what the worst-case scenario is?"

"The prosecution targets you next. Charges you with providing false testimony. Maybe conspiracy to commit murder. If the judge thinks you were involved in the planning of Mrs. Holloway's death, you could be reuniting with your friend sooner than you think. You two could be spending a lot of time together at that detention center."

Jack's stomach dipped. If she was locked up beside Belle, she'd never be able to figure out what had really happened to Raven's stepmother. "Can I think about it?" she asked timidly. It was the first time her voice had wavered since she'd entered the station. The first time she'd been uncertain her stories would keep her out of trouble, protect her, allow her to sleep at night.

Detective Medina nodded, his gaze still kind. Chin still resting on his hands. "Things are going to move quickly," he warned. "Evelyn was loved by a lot of people, and Rose Hollow hasn't seen a crime like this in—"

"Four years," Jack muttered, thinking of Raven's mother. His real mother, the one who'd loved him.

"The trial could be set in a couple of weeks," the detective went on. "And unless you can bring me a suspect who hated Evelyn Holloway *and* wanted to ruin Belladonna's life—"

"I can." Jack sat bolt upright. Blood rushed through her ears. Her battered heart sprang to life. All this time, the answer had been right in front of her. "I have to go." She pushed out of her chair. "I'll be in touch within the next couple of days, all right? I don't know how long it'll take to . . ."

Get to her, Jack thought, her mind racing a mile a minute. There was someone who hated Evelyn Holloway, and that person would've had no trouble at all dragging Belle's name through the dirt. Unfortunately, that person had been locked in a gated facility almost as long as Raven had been locked in a boarding school on the other side of the country.

Could she have broken out?

"I'll have answers for you soon," Jack promised, buttoning her coat. Winter had ended, but an icy chill still drifted through the air, settling on her limbs. Encircling her throat. "I just need to talk to someone first."

"Say hello to Raven for me," the detective said, mistaking the reason for her exit. Raven was coming home. She needed to see him, desperately, but there was someone else she needed to see first.

"I'm not going to see Raven," Jack said, striding to the door. She was going to see the girl who'd stopped eating after Raven had left town. The girl whose *own mother* had dropped her off at a wellness facility, three months later, and had never come back for her.

Lily Holloway, Raven's stepsister.

"I've already spoken with Lily," Detective Medina said, as Jack touched the doorknob. She turned, slowly, to see him holding the *Recipe for the Perfect Murder* in his hand. "When I showed her the recipe, she started stammering about Belle's innocence. I didn't know the two were friends. What was their relationship like before Lily went to stay at the facility?"

Jack swallowed, a pang of fear shooting through her stomach. A pang of warning. "They hated each other."

3

A Kiss Before Dying

When Raven was fourteen, he lay down in a glass coffin in his orchard. Jack stood over him, heart hammering like a fist. There was lightning in her veins. Starlight in her eyes. At fourteen years old, Raven was already so beautiful, she couldn't take her eyes off him.

"I tried to save you," she whispered, tears welling in her eyes. Seeing Raven in that coffin was like looking at a vision of the future. There was no *if* about saying goodbye to Raven Holloway.

Only *when*.

The tears that fell were genuine. The pain in her chest, crushing. After a minute of staring at him, she turned to the girl at the edge of the clearing, the one dressed in head-to-toe black.

"I can't do this," Jack said.

Raven's eyelids fluttered open. He was wearing a black velvet suit, and one of his dark curls had fallen into his eyes. "Are you afraid to kiss me?" he asked, sitting up.

"I . . ." *Yes. No. Maybe*, she thought, her gaze trained on Belladonna Drake. Belle had insisted on playing the witch in this scenario, because the role suited her so perfectly. She had that dark, glossy hair. Kohl-rimmed eyes. A smile that could cut you to pieces, or bring you to life.

"I told you, it's okay," Belle said, flashing that duplicitous smile. "Tonight we're sharing him."

Jack's throat felt tight. She took a long, slow breath before striding over to Belle. "Can I talk to you for a minute? *Out* of character?"

Belle rolled her eyes. Looping her arm through Jack's, she led her friend through a copse of apple trees. Away from the coffin and the dark-eyed boy. "Look, I get it," Belle said when they were a safe distance from Raven. "You'd rather die than kiss a boy."

"That isn't it." Jack wrapped her arms around herself. "You don't understand."

"Then help me understand. Whatever it is, you can tell . . . Poppy, why are you crying?"

Jack wanted to correct her, to say, *My name is Jack*, but she couldn't do that without offering an explanation. And . . . there wasn't one. At least, not one that would make sense to the others. She wasn't changing her name because her identity was changing. It was almost the opposite of that. Poppy had never felt right. But Jack fit, in a way that nothing had before.

"Seriously," Belle said, as Jack slumped against a tree, wiping the tears from her lashes. "It's fine. If I'd known you were going to break down at the thought of kissing my boyfriend, *I* would've played the knight."

"Neither of us is a knight! Raven isn't a prince! Something is really, really wrong with him, and playing some stupid game we loved when we were kids isn't going to stop—" Jack broke off, sliding down the trunk of the tree. Belle knelt in front of her. She must've been starting to understand, because she lifted Jack's chin with her fingers. "You're worried about him in real life."

"Of course I am," Jack said, jerking out of her grip. "He's going to die. He's going to be lying in a coffin *for real*, and no kiss will bring him back. She's going to kill him, Belle."

"She won't. I won't let it happen."

Jack looked up, her eyes narrowing in the moonlight. "How are you going to stop it?" she asked, the fluttering in her chest going still. Belle hadn't sounded angry then, or scared.

She'd sounded determined.

Quietly, Belle reached into her dress. It was a black lacy thing with tons of ribbons and even more pockets. Perfect for a witch. But she didn't pull out a potion, or a bottle containing the wings of a bat. She pulled out a scrap of paper with something scribbled on it.

<u>Recipe for the Perfect Murder</u>

One petal of belladonna

One petal of poppy

Drop into a teacup and stir three times.

"What is this?" Jack demanded. But she knew what it was. Like the changing of her name, this recipe needed no explanation. "You want us to poison Raven's stepmom?"

"She's poisoning him. She's poisoning his mind, all because he has his mom's eyes and his mom's laugh. Every time his dad looks at him, he's reminded of the woman he lost in the snow. The woman he loved more than he'll ever love Evely—"

"Are you two done talking about me?" a voice called from the north. Raven's voice. He was too far away to hear them, but still, Jack took the recipe and crumpled it in her hand. "You should burn this before Raven sees it," she said.

"No time." Belle plucked the ball of paper from Jack's fingers and tossed it into a nearby creek. "The water will wash away the ink," she promised, flashing a grin. *A wicked grin*, Jack thought, because Belle had always loved playing the witch. Jack had never been happier than when she was playing the knight. She'd rescued Raven from his third-floor bedroom, and from the tallest branches in the orchard.

Now he needed her to rescue him one more time.

"When?" she murmured as Raven tromped loudly through the orchard. He was doing it on purpose. Raven could sneak up on you in the dead of night, and Raven could walk through a pile of leaves without making noise.

He wanted them to hear him.

"I don't have all the details yet," Belle said, pulling Jack to her feet. "But we need to keep him distracted, *playing* dead instead of actually hurting himself. All right?"

Jack nodded, and then Raven had joined them by the creek. Just like it always did, the moonlight *found* him. Cut a pathway to his face. His skin was pale brown, his hair as black as midnight. Lips as red as a rose—at least, they were after Belle was done planting a kiss on him.

"I figured someone should do it," she said with a laugh, and Jack slunk away from them. Into the shadows where she belonged. Once Belle had Raven all to herself, she wrapped her arms around his waist, standing behind him.

He is mine, her stance seemed to say. *Try to take him, and I'll drop a poisonous blossom into your tea.*

Jack shuddered, turning away from them. The night had been unseasonably warm, but seeing her closest friends entangled was making her feel cold. Lonely. At Jack's prompting, the three of them made their way back to the great stone manor, where Raven lived with his father and stepmother. *His wicked stepmother*, Jack thought, and she wasn't playing a game anymore. Ever since Evelyn Holloway had moved onto Raven's estate, he'd grown pale. Gaunt. People blamed it on the death of his real mother, but the truth was, months after his mother's funeral, the color started returning to Raven's cheeks. Light had sparkled in his eyes again. Then *that woman* had moved into his house, and Raven had started to whisper about joining his mother in the dirt.

A few weeks later, he'd snuck into his father's bedroom and stolen a bottle of sleeping pills from the bedside table. When Belle had discovered the pills under Raven's pillow, she'd simply shrugged, tossing three into her mouth. "Let's sleep together," she'd challenged. Then she'd held the pills under her tongue until Raven flushed the contents of the bottle down the toilet.

And earlier that night, when Raven had found a massive aquarium at a yard sale, Belle had helped him carry it into the orchard in front of his house. Together they'd adorned it with roses from his mother's garden, and then Raven had climbed inside, his dark eyes closing. Jack had watched from the edge of the clearing as Belle leaned over him, cackling the way she had when they were scrawny sixth graders playing make-believe in this same orchard.

"Finally!" Belle had shrieked, gliding her fingernails along Raven's cheek. "The precious prince is mine, to have and to hold, for all eternity. Unless you'd like to wake him up?" She'd turned then, catching Jack's eye, and Jack had blushed furiously. She hadn't wanted to *kiss* Raven. Raven was her oldest friend. For years, the two had lived as brothers, dangling from the tall trees of the orchard or wrestling in the rose garden. The thought of pressing her lips to his was shocking. Appalling. But also . . .

"Someone's watching us," a voice whispered, pulling her out of her thoughts. Jack slammed into the current moment like she'd fallen from a tree. Her lungs struggled to take in breath. Her cheeks were blazing, and she wondered if Belle could see it in the light of the full moon.

But Belle was watching someone *else*. Jack turned, and Raven turned too, their eyes finding the girl spying on them from the back of the orchard. Fourteen-year-old Lily must've had a com- plicated relationship with clothing, because she always wore multiple layers under her bulky sweaters. Amidst the pale blos- soms of the apple trees, her white-blond hair made her look perfectly at home, like she belonged there. Like she'd been *born* there. In reality, Lily had moved onto the Holloway estate a few months earlier along with her mother, and in Belle's mind that made her an interloper.

A trespasser on sacred lands.

"Raven," Belle cooed, her voice as sticky as maple syrup, "I'm feeling a bit parched from bringing you back to life. Would you get me some cider?"

Raven eyed her a minute, wary of leaving her alone with his new stepsister. "Play nice," he told her, hand lingering on the door. "If I come back here to find her hanging in the orchard by her feet—"

"She'd deserve it after sneaking into your bedroom," Belle snapped, turning to Jack. "Raven found his stepsister hiding in his closet. How's that for ominous?"

Jack's head swiveled toward Raven, her mouth agape. "What? Lily's been sneaking into your bedroom?"

"Almost every day." Belle cocked her head to the side, touch- ing Raven's cheek. "Do you think she's looking for something? Or . . . *hiding* something?"

"I think she's hiding from her mother," Raven replied, striding through the door.

"You're probably right." Belle watched him disappear into the house. "Or she's hiding something *for* her mother," she murmured, softly closing the door behind Raven. "Something that will scare him. Make him want to disappear."

"Belle," Jack began, a warning.

"If Lily heard us talking, our plan will be ruined," Belle pointed out, jogging down the steps of the wraparound porch. Then she was off. She darted through the orchard, racing toward the girl with white-blond hair. Poor Lily had barely pulled herself into the branches of a tree when Belle grabbed her by the ankle, yanking her toward the ground.

Lily fell.

She screamed, scrabbling to escape, but Belle pounced on her, pinning her arms above her head. "What did you hear, you creepy little spy? Are you going to tattle on us to your mommy?"

At this, Lily stopped struggling. At this, Lily *smiled*. "It isn't what I heard," she said, just loud enough for Jack to pick up the words. "It's what I read. One petal of belladonna. One petal of poppy."

"Shit." Belle scowled, heat flooding her cheeks. "Where is it?" she demanded, tightening her grip on Lily's wrists. The smaller girl, to her credit, had not stopped squirming against her.

Now, against all odds, she managed to shrug. "Where is what?"

"The recipe for our witches' brew," Belle said calmly, her dark eyes revealing nothing. "It was part of the game. The potion I used to kill Prince Raven."

"Raven doesn't drink tea," Lily taunted. "The recipe called for dropping two petals into a cup of tea, and *she's* the only one who drinks tea in this household."

"She?" Jack asked innocently, because Belle's recipe had not included that word. No "he" or "she," no "stepmother" or "Evelyn."

"You know who I mean," Lily said, blowing a white-blond strand out of her face. "The one who loves torturing my stepbrother."

Jack's stomach dipped at the words, and she knelt beside the two girls. "Have you *seen* her hurt Raven? Do you have proof?"

"There will never be proof," Lily said, an edge in her voice. Her arms trembled where Belle had them pinned. "The wickedest monsters know better than to leave footprints."

"*You* think she's a monster?" Jack's gaze shifted to Belle as the moon slipped behind the clouds. "Maybe—"

"She's lying," Belle snarled, leaning down to whisper in Lily's ear. "I know you've been spying on Raven for weeks."

"I've been trying to help him! To find out what she's been doing!"

"Jack may fall for that, but she sees the best in everyone." Belle pulled back, still holding Lily's wrists. "I see the truth. The second I let you go, you're going to run right to your mother."

"I'm not!" Lily squealed, kicking out her legs like a rabbit. "I can prove it. Next month is the Apple Blossom Festival, and half the girls in town will be wearing flower garlands. If you wove a couple of belladonna blossoms into yours, no one would think anything of it."

Belle narrowed her eyes but said nothing.

"And you," Lily added, turning to Jack, "could add poppies to your garland. I could add lilies. They're poisonous too, you know. If we leave blossoms all over her kitchen table, where she drinks her tea, everyone will think it's an accident if a few petals fall—"

"You hardly even know Raven," Jack broke in, the blood rushing through her ears. This plan was getting too specific. Too *possible*. "Why would you choose him over your own mother?"

Lily chuckled, and Jack felt fingers tickling her spine. "I'm not doing this for Raven. I'm doing it for myself."

Jack swallowed, searching for bruises on Lily's hands and feet. Cuts. Scars. "Is your mother hurting you, too?" she asked, as Belle leaned back on her haunches, letting go of Lily's wrists.

Lily slid out from under her, clambering to her feet. "You could search me with a magnifying glass and you wouldn't be able to find my wounds," she said, striding toward the house.

"Wait!" Jack hurried after her. Belle followed more slowly, a wolf studying a rabbit she was saving for later. "What did you do with—"

"The recipe?" Lily asked cheerfully, and it was funny, how innocent that word sounded. Like they could talk about it in front of Raven, and he'd never know what they were planning. They could talk about it in front of his stepmother, the woman they were plotting to poison.

To kill.

"Oh, I tucked it somewhere safe," Lily said, waving a hand. "It's my protection, in case you decide to blame me for the entire thing. It *has* to look like an accident, and we *have* to be equally guilty."

"We don't need your help," Belle said, joining them in the yard. The orchard sat at their backs; the great stone manor sprawled out before them. And on the wraparound porch, Raven held a tray of four drinks in his hands, one for each of them.

Including his stepsister.

"We *do* need her help," Jack murmured, linking her arm through Belle's. From a distance, they must've looked like a couple of school kids, gossiping and sharing secrets. And they were. "People in town know that we're Raven's best friends, and they might've heard us talking about his stepmom. They might suspect us if poppy and belladonna are the only flowers in her tea. But lilies? Named after her flesh and blood?"

The girls turned to Lily then, stopping her before she reached the steps to the porch. "Why are you helping us?" Jack whispered, her back to the house, and to Raven. "You could've let us take care of the problem. You could've kept your hands clean."

Lily swallowed, staring at the dirt on her fingers. "If you'd grown up with my mother, you'd want to do more than get your hands dirty," she said, as the moon broke free from the clouds, painting her a specter against the darkness. White hair. White skin. White teeth. "You'd want to bury her alive."

4

Callous Lily

In the light Lily had withered, but in the darkness she *bloomed*. Hidden away in this gated place, she'd eaten to her heart's content, never worrying about who was looking over her shoulder. No fingernails dug into her arm. No voice whispered in her ear to play the game a little longer, do as she was told, be a good girl.

Lily was not a good girl.

Being *good* led to obedience, and obedience led to being hurt. For the past three years, Lily had lived free of rules and free of pain. Well, there were some rules in the Rose Hollow Wellness Facility, but they were centered around *not* hurting people, and Lily was fine with that. She didn't want to hurt anyone, didn't want to lie or deceive.

But sometimes she didn't have a choice. Like this evening, for example. Lily was sitting on the lip of a fountain, waiting for Jack to arrive at the facility. Jack had been calling her all day, but places like this restricted cell phone usage, so Lily had pretended to be unavailable for most of that time. Her phone had lit up at one o'clock. Three o'clock. Five. Finally, at seven thirty, Lily had answered.

Then she'd gone to wait in the courtyard.

Now she trailed her fingers through the water of the fountain's pool, twirling the water lilies that floated on the surface. This courtyard had been her solace over the past few years. She'd come out here as often as possible, tending to the flowers or letting the coolness of the water soothe her skin.

It was unfortunate that she'd had to leave it behind.

There was a tinkling sound to her left, as someone pushed through the back door of the facility. Lily turned in time to see Jack approaching. Her old friend was hesitant, worry lining her face.

Or was it fear?

Lily pushed to her feet, racing toward her. Before Jack could even react, Lily had ambushed her with a crushing embrace. Jack's auburn curls were wild and they tickled Lily's face. Those curls took on a tinge of gold in the summer, and a tinge of red in the autumn. The sight of them was so familiar, tears welled in Lily's eyes.

That was good. She'd be expected to cry. Her mother had, after all, just been murdered. "I'm so glad you called," she said, pulling out of Jack's embrace. "I'm sorry it took so long for me to answer, but I only have my phone for a couple of minutes each day. Everything's supervised here."

"It's okay." Jack's voice was softer than Lily had ever heard it. She *was* scared. But Lily was good at soothing people's fears, and she took Jack's face in her hands, smiling through the tears.

"You look good. The same, but . . ."

"Different?" Jack suggested, no longer swimming in the long green coat Raven had given her in middle school. Lily caught a hint of a T-shirt and jeans underneath, loose fitting and comfortable. For years Jack had been stuffed into her mother's flashy hand-me-downs, and she'd always squirmed and tugged at them, never seeming to relax.

This was better.

"Thanks," Jack said, following Lily to the fountain. They sat on the edge as the sun sank below the horizon. "And you look like . . ."

"I've been eating? Sleeping?" Lily smiled, glancing down at her no-longer-bone-thin frame. She'd come into this place hating her body, but now, three years later, she was comfortable in her own skin.

Still, she sniffled, because she was supposed to be devastated. She was supposed to feel anguish and grief, and if anyone found out how quiet it was inside her, she might be locked in a scarier place. A place that hurt her instead of helping her heal.

"Things have been good here," she admitted, gaze flicking to the great wooden structure at their backs. One side of the roof sloped lower than the other. The windows were all different sizes. The building was nothing short of ugly, and the second Lily had entered its wood-paneled walls, she'd felt perfectly hidden from the outside world. Tucked away. "At least, things *were* good here, before I got the call about my mother and learned Belle had been arrested."

"And why do you think she was arrested?" Jack asked, a shadow crossing her face. "Did it have anything to do with the recipe the detective found on Raven's kitchen table?"

"I have no idea how it got there!" Lily's cheeks flushed with heat, and she fought to keep her voice steady. "I hid it in the orchard years ago. Then Raven went to boarding school, and I never went back for it."

"Well, that's convenient." Jack shook her head, her jaw tight. "How lucky for you that *your* name wasn't on it. Just poppy and belladonna, which means the police could come for me next."

"It wouldn't be the worst idea to go through your things," Lily admitted, catching Jack's gaze. "Clear out your computer, in case you and Belle emailed about our plan. They could use that stuff against you, even now."

"And you want me to look innocent?"

"Aren't you? I know Belle is."

"How can you be sure?" Jack pressed, her green eyes narrowed. There was a brightness to them. There had always been a brightness to Jack, as if she'd swallowed the sun and was glowing from the inside.

For years Lily had wanted to be close with her. She'd wanted to be Raven's sister. Only one person had stood in her way, and now that person was out of the picture. "I know what you're thinking," Lily said. "Belle came up with the plan to murder my mother. But

we were scared little middle schoolers then, and we were convinced Raven was going to die. We somehow convinced ourselves
we were characters in a fairy tale, taking down a monster."

"A wicked stepmother," Jack murmured.

"Yes! But we wouldn't have gone through with it. I know we
wouldn't have, and besides, why wait three years to commit the
murder? If someone had done it sooner, Raven could've come
home, and I could've . . ." Lily trailed off. She didn't want to
remind Jack that Raven wasn't the only victim of Evelyn's wicked-
ness. Lily had been her earliest victim. The first and last person to
be hurt by her. "Someone else must've killed her. Someone with a
reason to hate her *now*."

"Someone like you?" Jack asked, cocking her head to the side.
Clearly, she hadn't forgotten any of it. Lily's veiled hints. Her desperation. "You hated your mother more than anyone, and you kept
the *Recipe for the Perfect Murder* after all this time. If Belle's not the
killer—"

"I didn't hate my mother," Lily corrected. "I was scared of her,
but I always thought, once I got out of here . . ." She broke off,
frowning. For a moment, she thought she'd felt something stir in
her chest, something like sorrow. Something like loss. "Now that
she's gone, I'll never get to make peace with her. I'll never know
if it was possible."

Jack took her hands. She was warm, and Lily reveled in the
feeling of it. She'd been touched so rarely in this place, and
only when a certain someone had come to visit. But romantic entanglements were forbidden at the Rose Hollow Wellness

Facility, so even then they'd had to steal their kisses. Clasp hands under tables and squeeze for the briefest of seconds. It had been enough, until it hadn't anymore. Now Lily was desperate to get out of here and truly *be* with the person she loved.

But first she needed to tie up some loose ends.

"The police took my mother's phone," she said, as the last of the light disappeared and someone inside the facility waved at her. She wasn't allowed out here after dark, even now. "They took her laptop, too. But my stepdad told me they haven't gone down to her office yet, and if we sneak in there tonight, we can search her computer for suspicious emails. Maybe someone sent her a threat—"

"We?" Jack asked, her brow furrowing. "Are they letting you out?"

"My stepdad's on his way to get me. He and Raven had to stop by the mall first, because apparently my mother got rid of Raven's clothes after he left town. She threw them in the trash or something. Can you believe that?"

"She . . . what?" Jack wrapped her jacket around herself, pushing out a laugh. "She really wanted to erase him from that house, didn't she?"

"She succeeded," Lily said, eyeing the blush in Jack's cheeks. In the weeks before Raven went to boarding school, Jack had started blushing at the sight of him. Or the mention. "But Raven's back now, and as soon as his wardrobe issues are taken care of, he and his dad are coming to get me so I can help plan this Saturday's funeral. That gives me six days of freedom."

"Do you have to come back here after? If your mom locked you in this place, maybe—"

"It's up to the doctors." Lily pushed to her feet, straightening her loose-fitting sweater. Even now there was a part of her that wanted to stay hidden. Unremarkable. The opposite of pretty. "I just went through a review last week, and they seemed really happy with my progress, so . . . keep your fingers crossed."

Jack nodded, glancing at the back window of the facility. "Maybe I should break into your mother's office alone. If you get caught, you'll end up back in this place, no matter how well you've been doing. Or you'll end up at that detention center with Belle."

Lily's breath fluttered at the thought. Her stomach tightened. "Who says we're breaking in?" she whispered, pulling Jack to her feet. "I know where my mother keeps her key."

After that, the two walked into the facility together, where Jack signed out. A boy named Cade was working the front desk. Lily knew him well. He smiled politely as Jack scribbled her check-out time in the visitors' book, and watched in silence as Lily led her to the door. It wasn't until Lily returned to him, resting her elbows on the counter, that he spoke.

"How'd it go?" he asked with a conspiratorial smile. Cade smiled easily. Laughed easily too. Lily had always liked him, and she was going to miss sharing these moments together. He'd been like a brother to her, a stand-in for the family she'd wanted for years.

"It went perfectly." She leaned in, clasping his hands. "Thanks for not telling her I checked out last night."

"She would've had all kinds of questions," Cade said, his violet hair sweeping into his eyes. "And I know exactly where you were last night. But you can't come back here again, pretending you're still a patient."

"I can't visit you?" Lily teased, poking him in the cheek. Siblings did that, didn't they? They tickled each other without feeling danger. They slept side by side without fear.

"You've earned your freedom," Cade said after a minute, pinching her arm. "Don't waste it on me."

Lily nodded, then walked to the doors. She didn't wait for her stepfather to come pick her up. As the doors whooshed open, bringing with them the scent of flowers, she turned back to the boy at the front desk. "I'm not going to waste a second."

5

Jack Be Nimble, Jack Be Quick

Jack entered her bedroom through the window. It was less likely to creak than the doors, and her brothers would come running if they heard someone entering the house after dark. Their ears were finely tuned to the near-silent comings and goings of their mother. Bobbi McClain had a tendency to sneak out at odd hours to meet some boyfriend or another, returning days or even weeks later. Once, Jack had come home from a double shift at the local convenience store only to find her youngest brothers lined up in front of the door, their eyes brimming with hope. Then, when they'd realized their *sister* was creeping into the house at two a.m., they'd tried to mask their disappointment.

After that, Jack had started entering through her window, determined to let them sleep through the night. This night, however, she had an ulterior motive. She hurried to her closet, flinging open the doors. The smell hit her, soft as a feather trailing across her skin, and her stomach clenched at the thought of destroying the only connection to him she had left. Then, after plucking two pillowcases from the floor, she began yanking clothes from their hangers, stuffing them inside.

It took about ten minutes. Ten minutes to eliminate all traces of him from her closet. Ten minutes to empty her dresser drawers. Even the floor had been strewn with Raven's pajamas, and her room looked oddly clean without them. Emptied. Stripping the clothes from her back, Jack stuffed his T-shirt and jeans into the second pillowcase before knotting it closed.

She threw on her floor-length jacket. Wearing nothing but her underwear beneath it, she slipped out of her room, both pillowcases in hand. Next stop was her mother's bedroom. As much as she hated to do it, she pulled on some ridiculously low-waisted jeans and a billowy top, which her mother had no doubt worn to some concert or another. Bobbi McClain loved loud music and loud men and nights that came back to her in flashes the following morning. Right about now, she'd be stumbling into a seedy motel room with a beautiful bass player or a photographer with a wicked smile, and she'd be having the time of her life.

Riding high.

Then, in a couple of weeks, she'd return home with track marks on her arms and no light in her eyes. She'd sit in the kitchen and stare at the wall for hours. Or she'd lock herself in her bedroom and sob. Even now, the room reeked of stale cigarettes and tears. Jack left as quickly as she'd entered, creeping quietly toward the living room. The squat green house was a ramshackle affair, with creaking doors and peeling paint and two tiny bedrooms that weren't big enough for her family. On her eleventh birthday, her brothers had surprised her by moving into the attic, so she could have one of the bedrooms to herself. It was the nicest thing anyone had ever done for her, before Raven offered her more.

Jack swallowed, her throat as scratchy as sandpaper. She would not cry. These clothes were only a memento of dark eyelashes and soft hands, and soon she'd be staring into those eyes. Maybe even holding those hands, if she hadn't ruined everything the last time they'd seen each other.

She entered the living room and knelt in front of the fireplace. Checked the flue. Struck a match. She was just holding the tiny flame up to the logs when she heard a sound at her back. There was a soft gasp, followed by the rustling of clothing.

Jack's heart sank.

Her mother was home. She must've brought some stranger into their house, which she was *never* supposed to do again. Jack had made sure of that. She'd thought she had, but as the fire sprang to life, she wondered if she'd have to take things further this time.

Her heart hammered as the flames grew, casting pools of light in an otherwise dark room. Two people sprang away from each other on the couch, and Jack's breath caught in her throat, her hands instinctively pushing the bags of clothing behind her. The figure on the left was familiar. He had auburn curls, just like she did, and his green eyes were filled with shock. Fear. Shame.

As Jack's gaze trailed to the right, she understood why. He'd thought their mother had come home. He'd thought she'd caught him with this person, and he was preparing himself for the attack. For all their mother's recklessness, there were certain things she wouldn't allow. She'd never liked Raven, though she wouldn't admit it was because of his pale brown skin. Belle's mysterious parentage had made her nervous. And if she'd walked in to find her eldest son tangled on the couch with a bright-eyed, brown-skinned *boy*, she would've started screaming.

At the very least.

Jack waited for her brother to relax. She waited for reality to sink in, as he realized she wasn't their mother and wasn't going to humiliate him. She kept waiting. But Flynn's eyes were trained on the ground, his hands shaking so badly, she thought he might cry. He never cried. Not when their mother taunted him, reminding him that his daddy hadn't stuck around to witness his birth. Not when she disappeared for weeks on end.

When his eyelids started to flutter, Jack strode toward the kitchen, asking, "Anyone hungry? I was going to make a sandwich."

The boys were silent a minute, and then Flynn stammered, "No, thanks," just as the other boy said, "I could eat."

Jack chuckled, tossing him a glance. The kid was stick-thin. In fact, everyone in the room looked like they'd skipped their last three meals, and her own belly grumbled at the thought of a night-time snack. She needed to get the boys out of the living room so she could burn the bags of clothing. But first she needed to take care of her family. "Turkey, ham, or chicken?" she asked, the bags swinging behind her back. "Or, let me guess, all three? That's how Flynn likes his."

The boy nodded, a shock of dark hair sweeping across his face. He was wearing a midnight-blue button-down shirt and jeans, but they hung off him, like they'd been handed down from a much older sibling. "Thanks," he said softly. "I'm Diego, by the way."

"I'm Jack." She tossed the words behind her, disappearing into the kitchen. Before pulling three plates from the cupboard, she set the knotted pillowcases on a chair, hoping they would pass for laundry. Then she started arranging bread on plates.

She'd just applied the cheese slices when she heard footsteps behind her. She didn't have to turn to know who they belonged to. "Your guest is here kind of late," she said, as Flynn approached the counter, still refusing to meet her gaze. Sometimes their mother waited until their muscles had relaxed and their breathing had slowed before she reared up for an attack. Was he waiting for the cutting words? The brittle laughter that could make you curl into yourself, wanting to disappear?

"I had kind of an emergency," Flynn said, helping her with the deli slices. He always put the chicken first, then the turkey, then the ham, and even though there was *no reason* for it, it made her heart squeeze. "Diego's parents kicked him out of the house."

"Oh, yeah? How come?"

He swallowed. "He told them some things they didn't want to hear."

Jack nodded calmly, but the tightness in her chest was overwhelming. She'd spent her life trying to protect people, but there was always some new danger lurking around the corner, some new rug to be pulled out from under her. "Does he have a place to stay?"

"Yes. Here."

"Flynn."

"It would only be for a couple of weeks! Just until he works things out with his mom and dad. Sometimes people react badly at first, but then they come around. You know? But right now he doesn't believe they'll ever talk to him again, so of course I said he could stay here." A pause, as he shot her a sidelong glance. "It's what you would've done."

"Oh, good move," she said, her lips twitching toward a grin. "Flattery, this time of night? You know I'll be helpless against it."

"I thought so." He shrugged, so casual. But his lips were curving up on the left, just like hers were. "So it's cool, then? He can stay for a little while?"

"If he sleeps on the couch," she said after a minute of silence. Flynn was blushing again, badly. "And *you* sleep in your room."

"But—"

"No buts, Flynn. I wouldn't let my boyfriend sleep in my bed."

"What boyfriend? You've never even dated anyone, and now you're telling me what I can't do? He just got kicked out. I want to *stay* with him, not hook up while my siblings sleep a few feet away." There it was. That fourteen-year-old fierceness. That fire. Jack remembered it well, and everything it had led to.

The good and the bad.

"You're too young," she said softly. "You might think nothing's going to happen, but you'd be surprised at how quickly things can—"

"What are you talking about?" He was practically shouting now, his exasperation plain. Jack couldn't blame him. For all the world knew, she hadn't touched anyone in the three years that Raven had been gone. And before that, Raven had been Belle's, so nothing could've happened between them. Just like his clothes couldn't be sitting on a chair beside the table.

When Diego appeared in the doorway, his eyes alight with concern, she took the opportunity to remind herself of what was at stake. Her freedom. Her ability to spend moments like this, tucked away in a tiny kitchen with the people she loved most in the world.

"Sandwiches are almost ready," she said, forcing a smile. "Why don't you boys pick some lettuce from the garden?"

"Oh my God. That freaking garden." Flynn threw back his head dramatically, and Diego raised his eyebrows, amused at their theatrics. "She's *obsessed*," Flynn said by way of explanation, and then he and Diego were slipping out the side door, into the darkness beyond.

Jack waited three beats before racing back to the living room, stuffed pillowcases in hand. She found the poker beside the fireplace. It only took a moment to get the fire blazing, and then she was feeding the red, ravenous flames her best friend's clothing. She'd told herself this wardrobe was all she had to remember him by, but that wasn't really true.

She had the garden.

It had begun with a story. Back when Flynn was ten years old, and their younger brothers were three and four, Jack had gotten her hands on an old book of fairy tales. Flynn had rolled his eyes at the sight of the book, but he'd still curled up beside his little brothers in their attic bedroom and listened as Jack read them stories. "Snow White." "Beauty and the Beast." "Jack and the Beanstalk." That last one had been Jack's favorite, and days later, when they'd gone to the store to pick up some canned beans for dinner, she'd gotten an idea. The boys always went to bed hungry. They had so little to look forward to, and the book of fairy tales had made them happy.

What if she could bring the fairy tale to life?

And so, she ignored the aisle of canned vegetables and led them to the store's outdoor garden. There were little pots of dahlias and begonias, but she passed them by, seeking a packet of beans. *Magic beans*, she told the younger boys, who were just little enough to believe it. They were going to plant them in the backyard, and in a few weeks a beanstalk would grow, just like in the story. They wouldn't be able to climb it, but they'd have fresh vegetables all summer without ever having to go to the store. The boys were thrilled by the idea, and the second they got home they raced to the backyard, eager to start planting. Meanwhile, Jack stopped by the kitchen to put away the bread and the milk.

She hadn't expected her mother to be home.

Bobbi McClain was sitting at the kitchen table, staring at the wall. She looked strung out and exhausted, her eyes red and her fingers flicking a lit cigarette. Her gaze swiveled to the left, finding the packet of beans in her daughter's hand. "What the hell is that?" she asked, waving her cigarette in Jack's direction. It seemed to take all her strength.

"I . . ." Jack struggled for an explanation. Something that wouldn't make her mother scream. Something that wouldn't make her mother rage. "We're going to plant a garden," she managed, hating how hard it was to push out the words. "It'll end up saving money, because we won't have to buy beans all summer, and we'll have fresh vegetables, which will be good for the boys—" She might've gone on like that, rambling into eternity, if her mother hadn't cut her off with a sharp sound. But it wasn't a scream. It wasn't even a snarl. Across the table, her tired-eyed, lank-haired mother had started to chuckle.

"Sit down, baby girl," she said, pushing a chair out with her foot. "I want to tell you something."

Jack sat.

Her mother leaned in, and the scent of nicotine and sweat wafted off her, making Jack's stomach turn. "Listen to me, sweetness. I'd love to let you grow a garden out there, I really would. But nothing's going to grow in that backyard. You know why?"

Jack shook her head.

"That yard is shit. This house is shit." Her mother lashed out, catching Jack's chin between her fingers. "And *you*—"

"Stop." Fingernails dug into Jack's skin, leaving little half-moon imprints, but she couldn't break away.

"You are shit. Your daddy took one look at you and ran in

the other direction. My daddy did the same. They left us in this shit hole, so don't go telling yourself stories about turning that weed-infested wasteland into a garden." She jerked back her hand so quickly, her nail sliced Jack's cheek. "Now give me the seeds."

"I . . . no. I bought them for the boys."

"What'd you say to me?" Her mother lurched forward, the chair toppling behind her. Before Jack could even blink, the packet of seeds was out of her hand. Her mother tore it open. Tossed the seeds out the window like they were trash. Like *everything* here was trash: the house, the yard, and Jack herself, still sitting at the table frozen. Afraid to stand up. Afraid to fight back. Even when her mother strode over to her, brushing the hair from her face, she couldn't jerk away. "I did that for your own good," her mother said. "I love you too much to let you lie to yourself, okay? And I will *not* let you lie to my boys."

Jack nodded, voiceless. The boys were calling to her from outside. What was she going to tell them? When her mother ambled off to her bedroom, Jack hurried out the side door to the house, seeking the window where the seeds had fallen. She tried desperately to pluck them out of the dirt. That was how Raven found her. Hunched over a handful of dirty beans, sobbing quietly so her brothers couldn't hear.

He didn't ask her what was wrong. Instead, he knelt beside her, looping an arm around her shoulder. His voice was soft in her ear. "Let's cover them up," he said, scooping dirt into his hands. "Your brothers said you're planting magic beans."

"They won't grow. Nothing will grow here. She's right."

"She's not." Gently, he guided her hand back to the dirt, and she let the seeds fall there. Together they covered them up. Her brothers had come around the side of the house by then, and they quickly noticed the tiny plot of upturned dirt.

"You planted without us?" Dylan asked, tilting his head to the side. His curls were wild. His eyes narrowed. "Why did you—"

"They fell," Raven said, pushing to his feet, "but I think it's better this way. Now they can grow up the side of the house."

"Yeah!" Conner clapped his hands, coming up beside them. He was the youngest and the most likely to believe their stories.

But Jack didn't. She was having trouble breathing, her stomach sinking at the thought of the seeds drying up in this cracked dirt. Even after the boys wove the hose around the side of the house and carefully watered their seeds, she was certain the beans wouldn't grow.

She woke the next day to the sound of excited voices at the back of the house. When she came outside, she couldn't believe the sight in front of her. The entire backyard had been weeded, the grass overturned, and little rows were being dug by two people in the early dawn light.

Raven and his dad.

"I heard you're planting a garden," Dr. Holloway said, squinting in the light. His crisp white shirt was rolled up at the sleeves. He was wearing black slacks and dress shoes, and Jack wondered if he even owned clothes for gardening. "We thought we'd help."

Jack looked at Raven, then back to his father. Honestly, this was a *brilliant* move. Dr. Holloway's family had helped found the town, and due to his wife's recent passing, he was one of Rose Hollow's most eligible bachelors. The man was handsome. The man was wealthy. If Raven had come alone, with that truck filled with flowers and seeds and fertilizer, Jack's mother would've threatened to call the police. He would've been a *trespasser*. But Dr. Holloway was an *opportunity*, and the entire time he was there, Jack's mom preened and blushed and brought him glasses of lemonade.

Meanwhile, her kids planted a garden. It took several hours, but by the end of the day, there were rows of vegetables on one side, rows of flowers on the other. It was beautiful and it was barely even spring. A few weeks later, the first hint of lettuce started to grow, followed by carrots and bell peppers and zucchini. By the time summer rolled around, Jack had almost forgotten about the beans.

Raven had promised her they would grow. Jack thought of that now, as she fed his clothes to the fire. He'd promised, and he'd delivered. Somehow, in spite of the harsh earth, and the weeds all around, a little seedling had sprouted in mid-July. By the end of the summer, a vine had woven its way up the house. After that, planting beans became a yearly tradition, and when Jack's mother brought home a man who liked visiting her brothers in the middle of the night, Jack had put one of her vines to good use.

She exhaled as the last of the clothes disappeared. Flynn and Diego were taking their time returning from the garden, and when they finally burst through the kitchen door, fresh lettuce in their hands, the fire was in full bloom. Jack hurried out of the living room. She could hear Conner and Dylan rustling around upstairs, awakened by the noises in the kitchen. Soon, they were clattering down the attic stairs, and Jack was cutting her sandwich in half, handing it over to them.

"Who's that?" Conner asked through a mouthful of bread and cheese and turkey, staring at the boy on the other side of the room.

"That's Diego. He's staying the night."

"Are we having a sleepover?" Dylan perked up, his half sandwich forgotten for the moment. "We haven't had a sleepover in a hundred years!"

"No, we're not . . ." Jack trailed off, gaze flicking toward the living room. She wouldn't let Diego sleep in Flynn's bedroom. She knew too well what could happen when two people were left alone in a perilous moment, after everything had come crashing down around them. Their future. Their happiness. Their hopes. But she didn't want to quarantine Diego in the living room when his parents had just kicked him out. So before she could stop herself, she said, "Yes. We're having a sleepover, like we did before you moved into the attic. Remember where the sleeping bags are?"

The smaller boys cheered, racing off to get their supplies. Flynn eyed her a minute, a soft smile on his face, like he knew what she was doing. It didn't take long for everyone to settle into the living room, Jack laying her sleeping bag next to the fire so she could stoke it every few minutes. Conner and Dylan huddled up beside her. Diego got the couch because everyone was feeling generous with their bellies full and their eyes drooping, and Flynn curled up on the floor beneath him.

The fire crackled softly, filling the room with warmth. The

boys chattered for a while, and then their voices grew fainter. Eyelids fluttered. Breathing steadied. By the time Jack slipped out of her sleeping bag, Diego's arm had fallen over the edge of the sofa, and Flynn's fingers had entwined with his.

Jack's stomach tightened at the sight of it. She thought she would do anything to protect them. Then, remembering where such convictions led, she crept toward her bedroom, climbed over the windowsill and disappeared into the darkness.

6

Like Mother, Like Daughter

Lily crept away from Jack's peeling green cottage, trying desperately to understand what she'd just witnessed. Jack, burning
clothes in a fireplace. Suits and T-shirts and jeans. When Lily
had learned that Raven's clothes had been stolen, *of course* she'd
assumed her mother was responsible for it, but now she realized
her mother was innocent of that one small crime.

Jack, on the other hand, appeared to be guilty. But of what?
Had she simply *taken* Raven's clothes, or had she done something
unspeakable while wearing them? Lily wanted to demand answers
the second Jack arrived at her mother's office, but she needed to
play this carefully. Protect herself. Trick Jack into trusting her.
That was the only way to get to the truth of what had happened
the night her mother was murdered.

Lily knew some of it, of course she did. But she didn't know the whole story. *That* she would have to earn. And so she jogged up to Jack, running a hand through her pale blond hair. "You came. I thought you might change your mind."

Jack shook her head, looking apprehensive. There was a smudge of black on her thumb, from the ash in the fireplace, but she didn't seem to notice it. She was shaky, which meant she was nervous.

Or she was hungry.

"I brought snacks," Lily said, pulling a breakfast bar out of her pale pink purse. She'd watched Jack kneel beside the fire, feeding Raven's clothes to the flames, but she'd also watched her hand over a freshly made sandwich to her little brothers. "In case we're here a while."

Jack nodded, her stomach growling loudly as if on cue. Lily giggled as she unlocked the door to her mother's practice. She would keep things light, and she would keep offering snacks and encouragement, and she'd learn *exactly* why Jack had tossed Raven's clothing into the fire.

The door clicked open, and Lily ushered Jack inside the little brick house that had been converted into an office. There was an immediate beeping as the security system blared out its siren song, but Lily silenced it by typing the code into the keypad by the door.

Zero-three-zero-four.

Lily's birthday. For the second time that night, she felt a stirring in her chest. Something soft and unexpected, like a trickle inside a well that has been dried up for a very long time.

She didn't flick on a light. Instead, she pulled up the flashlight on her phone, striding over to her mother's desk. It was a white antique affair with roses painted up the legs, pink blossoms unfurling from thorny stems. Lily sat down in the matching chair. She was wearing gloves, but they were as pale as the roses stenciled onto the desk, disappearing under the sleeves of her sweater. In the darkness they looked a lot like her hands.

"Want to check the filing cabinet?" Lily asked, tossing Jack her mother's keys. Jack caught them easily. "We could be here all night."

"What, exactly, are we looking for?" Jack flipped through the keys, looking for one that was small enough to unlock the cabinet.

"Look for anything suspicious." Lily woke up the computer with a brush of her fingers. Within seconds she was poring over her mother's inbox, sifting through a mix of appointment confirmations and messages from Raven's dad. Both were incredibly dull. The confirmations were automated, and the more personal emails contained grocery lists or questions about dinner. Lamb or pork? The Italian place they'd visited a dozen times or the French bistro down the street? Lily sighed, her eyes glazing as she scrolled through the first hundred emails. "Maybe one of her clients got a little too close to her," she suggested to Jack, who was flipping through files at her back. "I know it's a long shot, but—"

"It's not a long shot."

Lily jumped as Jack dropped a file onto the desk. They'd been searching for only a few minutes, but already Jack had found something. The file was fat, overflowing with pages and the edges of photographs. But none of that held Lily's attention. No, her eyes were glued to the name on the side of the file, the name she'd seen over and over again in her mother's emails.

Stefan Holloway.

"My mom was counseling Raven's dad? That doesn't make sense." Lily frowned as Jack sat on the edge of the desk, flipping open the file. "She's not a grief counselor. She's a marriage counselor who specializes in substance abuse."

"Look at the dates of his sessions."

Lily did, silently studying the first few pages. Her mother had kept meticulous notes. She was obnoxiously organized, and Lily had always resented that about her, but at this particular moment, she was grateful for it. "She was counseling him *before* Raven's mom died."

"Yes."

"Because he was having marital problems, and he thought counseling could help."

"Apparently." Jack flipped forward a couple of pages, to the place where an old family photograph was hiding. Raven must've been three or four, and he was cheesing it up for the camera while his parents stood behind him. Laughing and holding hands.

"Why would your mother have this?" Jack demanded, plucking the photo from the file. She held it between her fingers, staring at Raven. "Do you think she took it from their house after she moved in?"

"I think she asked him to bring in mementos of a time when he and his first wife were happy," Lily said. Sometimes, in an emergency, her mother had hosted sessions at their old apartment. If a client needed her in the middle of the night. If they couldn't make it until the morning. The apartment had been tiny, with paper-thin walls, and even if Lily *tried* not to listen, she couldn't help but pick up snippets of conversation. "A lot of the time, when couples are having problems, it helps to remember why they fell in love in the first place," she explained to Jack. "If they bring in old love letters, and family photos like this, it can awaken something that's sleeping inside them. As long as that something isn't dead."

She'd sounded like her mother just then. A shiver raced up her spine. She didn't want to be sitting at this desk, spouting these old familiar words as if a ghost were speaking through her. Her mother was gone, and though it hadn't happened the way she'd planned, the *last* thing Lily wanted was to resurrect her.

"Copy the file and put it back," she instructed, striding over to the filing cabinet. If her mother kept a file on Raven's dad, maybe there were other secrets in these drawers. Maybe there was a file on Lily herself.

But which name would her mother have used?

She slid open the second drawer, searching for a file labeled *Lily Holloway*. Ever since she'd moved onto the Holloway estate, Stefan had insisted she take on the family name. He'd even promised to adopt her in the weeks following the wedding. Then Raven got sent to boarding school, and Lily got shipped off to the wellness facility, and Stefan must've forgotten about his promise, because the adoption never happened.

The second drawer held no familiar names. Lily closed it

quickly, crouching down to ease open the bottom drawer. Her mother's maiden name had been Quinn, but *Lily Quinn* was not written on any of these files. On a whim, she opened the third drawer, quickly flipping through the *K*s, even though she knew her mother wouldn't have listed her under her father's name.

Her biological father, who'd left her at three years old.

Lily was right. Her name wasn't listed under the *K*s, but his was. *Andrew Kane*, third file from the end. Had her mother been counseling her bio dad? It seemed impossible. Lily's mother had gotten pregnant at sixteen, and by the time her parents were nineteen, they couldn't look at each other. Lily had ruined their relationship. They'd been desperately in love, and then she'd come along, screaming and crying and demanding too much.

Her father had left *because* of her. Hadn't her mother told her that, over and over again, until Lily knew the story by heart? But maybe, unbeknownst to Lily, her parents had reconnected. Carefully, she slid the file under the waistband of her jeans, covering it with her oversize sweater. The copy machine was humming happily at her back, and in order to operate it, Jack would have to be turned away from the filing cabinet. It was unlikely she'd seen Lily's delicate movements. Still, Lily riffled through the drawers for another minute, pulling out a handful of other files. Most of her mother's clients had been couples, but a few men had come to see her on their own, just like Raven's father had.

Lily focused on them. They were the ones most likely to have become unhealthily attached to her mother. Maybe she was grasping at straws, but if she couldn't find a suspect in this office, that left only the three of them. Belle, who was already locked up in a detention center. Jack, who'd knelt beside a fireplace and fed Raven's clothing to the flames. And Lily herself, with all her secrets.

She carried her stack of files over to the copier. "How's it coming along?" she asked casually.

"Almost done. She was counseling him for a year," Jack added, tapping Dr. Holloway's file. "He started coming here the winter Raven was twelve, and only stopped the following November."

"Because his first wife died. Then, a year later, my mom married him. Her own *patient*." Lily set her stack of files on the copier, each containing a different man's secrets. Fears. Desires. "What if another patient fell in love with her? Someone who realized he couldn't have her the way he wanted, so he snuck into her house and . . ."

"Poisoned her?"

Lily nodded, not wanting to speak the words. "If we copy these files tonight, we can search through her sessions to see if anyone mentions having feelings for her. Or spending time together outside of the office."

Jack placed a stack of pages in the copier's feed tray. "Even if we find a guy who was obsessed with her, it won't explain the belladonna in her tea. Whoever did this knew about our plan. They're using that against us, because one of us didn't get rid of the evidence."

"I left it in a tree hollow in the orchard! I don't know how it ended up in the kitchen, I *swear*." Lily's gaze dropped to her hands. "After

Raven went away, you guys wouldn't talk to me anymore. I think you wanted to forget everything that had happened, and maybe it was too painful to face what we'd almost done, but . . ." She looked up, and the tears in her eyes were real. There was a sharpness in her throat that she couldn't swallow down. "You left me in the facility to rot."

"I didn't want to! Belle told me to leave you alone. She said what we almost did broke you, and we needed to take some time apart to heal."

"She told you that?" Lily's eyes narrowed. "I didn't want to be alone. I wanted you to come visit me. I wanted Raven to come home. And . . . that recipe was all I had left of you. The only proof that I'd had friends. I kept it because I knew we *weren't* going to use it, just like I knew you weren't coming back into my life."

"I'm sorry. I should've checked in on you. I shouldn't have waited until your mother was—"

Jack broke off and Lily's heart constricted. Just barely. Just for a second. "I want to forgive you, but I need you to help me figure out who killed her. Maybe one of her clients was stalking her. Maybe they broke onto the estate and found the recipe in the orchard. The wind could've blown it out of the tree hollow."

"How likely is that?"

Lily shrugged. "The tree hollow wasn't that deep, and it's nearly impossible that someone searched all the trees in the orchard. The recipe must've fallen out. Then the killer must've planted it in the kitchen, hoping the police would find it." She shuddered, wrapping her arms around herself. "What if the killer comes back? I don't know how I'm going to sleep—"

"I'll come over," Jack said, still feeding pages to the copier. Page after page, file after file, they made their way through the stacks. "After we've finished here, I'll come back with you."

"You don't have to do that."

"I want to—" Jack began, but Lily cut her off.

"No, I mean . . . you don't have to pretend you're coming over for *me*. I know you want to see him, Jack."

"He's my oldest friend," Jack said simply, not looking at her. "Of course I want to see him and hear about the past three years."

"You two haven't been talking?"

Jack stiffened, then shook her head. "You said Belle and I wanted to forget everything that happened? Everything we'd almost done? I think Raven wanted to forget too. First his mom was taken from him, and then he almost took his own—"

"He's been in contact with Belle."

Jack spun around, her breathing gone shallow. Lily could see it in the way her chest jerked up and down. "How do you know that?"

"Belle came to visit me once," Lily said, pulling the last of the papers from the tray. She put half the copied files in her purse, handing the other half to Jack. "She wanted to destroy the *Recipe for the Perfect Murder* so we could finally move on." Lily huffed, returning the original files to their drawers and locking the cabinet. "If I'd told her where I'd hidden the stupid thing, none of this would've happened."

"Belle wanted the evidence," Jack said, her voice a hollow whisper.

"Yes."

"And she's been in contact with Raven this entire time? If she knew he was coming home, she could've searched the grounds for the recipe. We were out in the orchard when you first hid it."

"Belle's not the killer." Lily strode over to the desk, signing out of her mother's email. Jack was still standing by the copier, a distant look in her eyes. Quickly, Lily searched the hard drive for the name Andrew Kane, and when she found a digital copy of her father's file, she deleted it. Then she emptied the trash folder. As far as anyone knew, he'd never come into this building. Never sat in the chair across from Lily's mother and spilled his darkest secrets.

He'd never be a suspect.

The night was dark as they slipped out of the office, but just barely. In about an hour, the sun would rise. "It's almost morning," Lily said, leading Jack across the parking lot, to the place where their bikes were waiting for them. Lily had moved into the wellness facility when she was fourteen, which meant she'd never learned to drive. She'd never gone on a date. And up until recently, her sleepovers had been incredibly tame. "You don't have to come back with me . . . unless you want to sneak into Raven's bedroom," she added, because Jack had the look of someone who'd been trying to be tame for too long.

For all their differences, they had that in common.

"No, it's okay," Jack said, that old familiar blush taking over her face. Not just her cheeks, but her neck and ears, too. "I want to get home before my brothers wake up. Someone has to make sure they eat breakfast."

Lily nodded, struggling to hide her relief. If Jack came back with her now, she wouldn't be able to read through her father's file. As it was, the two parted ways, promising to call each other the second they found a possible suspect. Lily's bike had a basket, and once Jack was out of sight, she set her purse inside it, tucking the original file beside the copies.

She rode off as the sky lightened to gray.

7

The Boy in the Branches

Jack stood beneath Raven's window, asking herself what she was doing. She'd meant what she'd said about going home. But three blocks from her house, she'd remembered that spring break had started, and she didn't need to get her brothers up for school in the morning. They would sleep late, sprawled out across the living room floor.

No one would know if she made one quick stop.

And so she'd ridden her bike to Holloway Manor. She'd slipped through the loose bar in the back gate, like she had a hundred times before. The last time she'd climbed up to Raven's bedroom, she'd been fourteen years old, but her hands remembered the places where the gray stones stuck out just so. The ivy grew thicker at the back of the house. There was less chance of falling to her death, though it was a possibility.

His bedroom was on the third floor. By the time Jack reached his window, she was panting from the climb. Her chest ached. Her heart was a feral creature, screaming louder than her scratched palms, and she was grateful that he'd left the window cracked.

Some things didn't change.

But most things did, and as she swung her leg over the sill, she wondered if Raven's heart had hardened to her over the past three years. Or worse, if he'd forgotten her entirely. She tried to take calming breaths as she stepped into his bedroom, the darkness overwhelming. The moon didn't touch this place. His curtains were too dark, his window too small, and for a moment, she thought he must be sleeping somewhere else, because the bed looked unlived in, just like it had the last time she'd snuck in here.

Two months after he'd gone away.

She approached the ebony bed frame with caution. It was almost six in the morning. He had to be under that black velvet comforter, curled into himself, like always. Lips parted slightly. Eyelashes fluttering. But Jack was nearing the edge of the bed now, and her eyes had started to adjust to the darkness. No one was sleeping there. Had everyone lied to her about Raven's return? Was this whole thing a trap?

Just as she thought it, an arm slid around her waist, a voice whispering in her ear: "Still breaking and entering, I see."

Jack bristled. "Well, if you'd bothered to send me an invitation, I wouldn't have needed to break in. I could've used the front door."

"That doesn't sound like you." His breath was warm on her cheek. He was standing so close, she could feel his heartbeat pressing against her back, soft and insistent, and she spun around, crushing him to her.

"I never thought I'd see you again," she said, her arms wrapping around his neck. She'd sworn she would be calm the first time she saw him. But sadness and elation were ricocheting inside her, sending shock waves through her body. Three years. How had she survived? Wearing his clothes had not been enough. Sitting in his bedroom had only served to widen the chasm inside her, but now he was here.

The person she loved more than anyone in the world was standing in front of her, and he was just like she remembered. He was, and he wasn't. He'd grown several inches over the past three years, and his hair was longer, stopping just above his ears. Those ears were pointed at the top, the tiniest bit. When Raven was a little boy, his mother had called him her elven prince, and she'd chased him around the kitchen with a wooden spoon, pretending it was a wand.

Queen Arianna and Prince Raven. Back then Jack had thought they would always be around. But Raven's mother had died in the snow, three drops of blood trailing away from her. Raven had disappeared over a year later, and Jack had feared he'd never come home.

She pulled back to stare at his long dark lashes. She wanted to touch his lips. She'd done it before, once, and she wondered if they were as soft as she remembered, or if memory had made a fantasy out of him.

"You're home," she whispered, willing herself not to grasp at him. Raven was her best friend. For years they'd lived as brothers, racing through the orchard, or dueling in the rose garden. She wanted to hug him. She did not want to push him onto the bed, rip off his shirt, and lick him from his throat to his stomach.

She didn't. And so she tore herself away from the boy with warm brown eyes, walking over to the window and looking down. The garden used to be filled with crimson roses. But after Raven and Lily went away, Evelyn Holloway had torn up the red blossoms and replaced them with white. "White roses are purer," she'd sworn.

Jack cringed at the sight of them. She missed the wild crimson roses that Raven's mother had nestled in her son's curls. He'd never been so beautiful as the evenings when he'd stood against the jewel-blue sky with red petals falling around him. The first time Jack had seen him that way, she'd wanted to kneel at his feet.

She wanted to kneel now.

Instead, she turned to look at him, with his plush lips and dark eyes, his careful hands toying with the hem of his shirt. Of course he'd be wearing black satin pajamas with velvet cuffs, because Raven Holloway had grown up in the lap of luxury. For all the good it had done him.

"I don't even know where to start," Jack said softly. "Are you okay? Was boarding school terrible?" *Why didn't you call? Why didn't you write? No*, she thought, as he stepped toward her.

Why did you only write to Belle?

"The academy was okay. I liked my professors for the most

part. Some of the guys were all right. Others, not so much." He was looking at his hands. He only looked at his hands when he was keeping secrets. She remembered that about him, even now. "We need to prove Belle's innocence, and then we can catch up on everything else. I know she didn't do this. Belle pretends to be vicious, but underneath—"

"I know you've been talking to her," Jack blurted. "Lily told me, and I don't understand . . ."

"Of course I've been talking to her." Raven stepped up close, and Jack's breath caught in her throat. She was pressed against the window. He was *almost* pressed against her. "I've been talking to you both. You're the one who never answered my letters."

"Your . . . what?" Only Raven could pull the breath from her lungs. Only Raven could make her tremble without a single touch.

"I wasn't allowed to make calls at the academy. I wasn't allowed to email without being monitored, and I didn't want to say anything too personal with someone reading over my shoulder. But I could write letters. I wrote to you for weeks, and when you didn't respond, I thought—"

"I didn't get your letters," Jack stammered, her thoughts racing. Had her mother hidden them? It seemed impossible. Her mother was rarely home. "I thought *you* had forgotten *me*, or you'd gone running back to Belle and never bothered to tell me."

"I couldn't go back to her. I *can* never go back to her."

"But you loved her so much. You two were obsessed with each other."

"Obsession isn't healthy, Jack. And in the months before I left town, Belle started to rant about my stepmother. She said she was going to come up with a plan, and then our problem would disappear."

"Did she give you any details?" Jack swallowed. "Did she say—"

"I don't think she was actually going to do anything. I think she was just trying to make me feel better, but it scared me to hear her talk like that. It made me think I didn't know her. We were so young when we fell for each other. We thought we were going to be together forever, but how can you be with someone when you don't really know them? How can you love them when they haven't become who they're going to be? People grow apart. My parents did, even before . . ."

Jack sucked in a breath. His father's file was *in her backpack*. She could take it out and show him what she'd discovered. But clearly, Raven knew that his parents had been having problems, and if Jack was honest with herself, she'd known it too.

"Do you remember how we met?" she asked, glancing out the window. "I snuck into your orchard to steal apples for me and Flynn. My backpack was overflowing by the time I realized there was a boy hiding in the branches."

It had been after twilight. The trees looked black against the cerulean sky. Jack had made a point to stick to the edge of the orchard, far from the great stone house that rose up like a castle. Her stomach had growled as she plucked her first apple from the ground. She'd wanted to sit there and feast for hours.

Instead, she unzipped her backpack, the same one she wore

now, and began sliding apples inside. When the voice rang out, it came from above her. She thought, for a moment, that she'd been caught by God. How terrible must her luck have been, to sneak into an orchard *one time*, only to be caught by the Almighty himself. That sort of thing would only happen to Jack.

She looked up, prepared to return the apples to the leaf-strewn ground. Or maybe she could bake them into a pie and give them to a homeless shelter. That would be all right, wouldn't it?

Even God would be okay with that.

But God wasn't sitting there, sprawled out like Huckleberry Finn with apple juice sliding down his arm. It was a boy. He looked close to Jack in age, no older than eight, and back then, his hair had been shorn close to his head. His lashes were long and thick. They fanned out over dark, curious eyes, as he peered down at her.

"Hello," he said, half-shy and half-shocked. Clearly, he had not expected anyone to find him out there.

"Hi. Are you stealing too?" she asked, because he was dressed in tatters, just like she was. She didn't know that he had clothes for climbing and clothes for going to school. Clothes for dinner. Clothes for church.

"Not stealing. Hiding," the boy said, glancing toward the house in the distance. It was a mass of gray, jagged stones, with a tower rising from the top. Smoke curled from its chimney, making the orchard smell of campfires in addition to apples.

It was autumn, Jack's favorite time of year. For the next few weeks, the ground would be littered with ripe, juicy apples, too bruised for most people to bother with. But for Jack and her five-year-old brother, Flynn, it would mean going to bed with full bellies for the first time in months. Dreaming of pies and turn-overs and strudel.

"You're hiding? From what?" Jack furrowed her brow, search-ing for trespassers in the orchard. She saw no one, but she could hear the faint sound of voices coming from Holloway Manor.

Shouting.

"My house is under a spell," Raven whispered, leaning down. "A witch cast it a hundred years ago, and it makes my parents for-get they love each other. They shout and I hide in my room, but I can still hear them through the heating vent. Their room is right next to mine, and they get so loud. . . ."

"So you ran away."

He nodded, solemn. Solemnity was Raven's natural state of being. But if you could make him smile, it was like finding the moon on the coldest, darkest night. Fierce and beautiful and bright. Jack learned that after she rounded the tree and lifted a fallen branch from the ground. "Let's break the spell."

Raven looked down at her, his eyes narrowed in confusion. "How?"

"We'll have to find the witch. But we'll need a magical sword if we're going to defeat her, and a map to her lair. . . ."

Raven's lips swept into a grin. Carefully, he slid out of the tree, eager to begin their quest. "How do you know what to do? Have you battled a witch before?"

"Not a witch. A giant," Jack said, leading him through the shadowed orchard. One year earlier, her mother had brought home a quick-tempered man who liked to throw dishes at the wall to emphasize his points. Whenever he'd come around, Jack had led her little brother on a quest. As long as they were searching for the next clue, or uncovering the next artifact, they never had to think about what was going on in that house. If they laughed loudly enough, they could block out the screaming. If they went far enough away, they wouldn't hear the shattering of glass.

Raven surveyed the orchard floor, choosing a branch of his own. "I'll fight with you," he said, but he sounded unsure. He'd come out here to *escape* fighting. Screaming. Sharp words that couldn't be taken back.

"You're the prince." Jack plucked the branch from his hands, tossing it behind her. "I'm the knight, and *I* fight to defend your honor."

"What do I do?"

"Um. Mostly you hide from the witch. And get caught by the witch. And then I have to free you." She brandished her sword, left to right. Right to left. "But I won't let anyone hurt you. I promise."

And she hadn't. Not then, and not for the next three years. From ages eight to eleven, Jack and Raven had lived like wild things, climbing trees in the orchard and battling foes in the garden. They'd feasted on apples and crowned each other with roses. He was her prince and she was his knight.

Then, in sixth grade, Belladonna Drake had appeared. She came out of nowhere. According to rumors in Rose Hollow, Belle had been tossed about in the foster-care system for years. It wasn't until she was eleven that she found a stable home. Edwin Drake had taken her into his elegant Tudor mansion, and he'd built her a library full of books. He'd planted a garden for her in the yard. He'd given her everything she could possibly want, except *friends*, and several months after enrolling in Rose Hollow Middle School, Belle finally chose her first friend.

Raven. The boy with bright eyes and the softest smile. She'd found some boys harassing him under the bleachers of the football field, and she'd threatened to poison them with the flowers from her garden. Just like that, Raven knew they'd found their witch, and *he* introduced Belle to Jack.

After that, the three of them became inseparable.

"Belle snuck over here the day Evelyn died," Jack said presently, her body curving into Raven's window. "The police think she was casing the joint, but there's *no way* she'd go in through the front door if she was planning to poison someone. Did she know you were coming home? Did you write to her?"

"I called her, Jack. After I was cleared to go home, they allowed me to use the phone, so I rang up Belle. I told her exactly when I was coming home, and she offered to make sure Evelyn hadn't hidden anything in my room. Anything that could scare me or—"

"Hurt you." Jack's head snapped up. "Did she find anything?"

"I haven't had a chance to talk to her. The police were here for hours, and the detention center has strict rules about when you can call people." He winced. "I told her not to sneak into my room. I told her she didn't need to worry about me anymore, that I was sorry for making her think I was her responsibility."

"Raven, no. You weren't . . . she loved you. We all loved you, and we couldn't stand to see anyone hurting you. Especially after what happened to your mom." Jack hadn't found him that day, lying in the snow. She hadn't seen him clinging to his mother, refusing to let her go. But she'd seen him grow hollow cheeked and pale after Evelyn had moved into his house, incapable of keeping his eyes open during the day and terrified of closing them at night. "We thought you were going to die."

"I let you think that. I *gave up*, because a part of me wanted to believe my mom was calling to me at night, asking me to join her. If she was here, that meant she wasn't gone. And I know it's messed up. I know I put you through hell, both of you, thinking you were going to lose me, but . . ." He bit his lip, looking down at the black-carpeted floor. "I wanted to see her again so badly. I wanted to tell her that I loved her. And that I was sorry."

"Sorry for what?"

"The day my mom died, I was supposed to meet her at the pharmacy after violin practice. Five o'clock on the dot. But I took the long way around, because it was snowing for the first time all year, and I wanted to walk through the gardens in the center of town. If I'd gotten to the pharmacy when I was supposed to, I would've been there when that man showed up." Raven looked at Jack. "I would've been able to get the gun away from him."

"Or you would've been lying lifeless in the snow, just like she was. Raven." Jack took his face in her hands. "What happened to your mom wasn't your fault. It's the fault of that masked man."

"A man the police never caught. I described his build to them, because I saw him running out of the pharmacy. I described his voice, because he told me he was sorry. But they hardly even tried to find him. I guess some victims are more important than others," he muttered, tracing his pale brown fingers along the sill. "That man is still out there because the police don't *care* about her, Jack. They don't care."

"Come here." She wrapped her arm around him, guiding him away from the window. "When was the last time you slept?"

"I don't know. Before I heard about my stepmom? Before I saw my dad's face, and I tried to get him to look at me, and he wouldn't? He's *gone*, Jack."

"Worry about yourself right now, okay? You never do that."

"You're one to talk," he said, but he let her peel back his blankets and guide him into bed. Let her tuck him in. "Aren't you staying with me?" he whispered, and that boy was back again. The one with the timid voice and bright eyes.

Jack crawled onto the bed, staying outside the covers but curving her body around his. They'd never done this before. They'd never been able to lie in his bedroom, alone, because Belle had always been there. Watching. Now Belle was locked in a detention center on the edge of town. They didn't have to worry about her walking in on them. Still, Jack felt a chill at the thought of what would happen once they'd proven her innocence. If Belle was exonerated, she could climb through Raven's window whenever she wanted. Find them. Learn the secret they'd been keeping for all these years.

"Raven," Jack whispered, leaning over him. She trailed her fingers across his cheek. "Do you remember what you said the night before you left for boarding school? About what would happen if Belle ever found out what we—"

"Yes," Raven murmured, his voice heavy with sleep. He was already drifting. When she wrapped her arm around him, pressing her hand to his heart, he sighed softly, curling into her. "I said she'd kill us."

8

Heartless

Belladonna Drake was going to sleep with her boyfriend. This was what she decided, the night before he left town. She put on a lacy black slip and thigh-high boots, then pulled a black trench over it to complete the look.

Sweet Raven didn't stand a chance.

Still, she checked her reflection in the mirror. Dark waves fell around her shoulders, and her black eyeliner was smudged just enough. Tonight, the witch was going to seduce the prince, which was not in any fairy tale she'd ever read, but so what?

She'd rather write her own story.

And so, she snuck out of her house for the hundredth time, after her adoptive father had gone to bed. She stopped by her garden and plucked a couple of belladonna blossoms, weaving them into her hair. She was poisonous and poised to strike. She was *power*, and though she hadn't been able to save Raven from his wicked stepmother, she could give him something to live for.

Love gave meaning to life. Belle was certain of this as she hurried down the block, turning left toward the nicest house in town. Belle's house was fairly nice. Her father was a philanthropist, drowning in old money, but even he couldn't compete with the grandeur of Holloway Manor.

That elegant, haunted house.

It hadn't always been haunted. Less than two years earlier, Arianna Holloway had lived within those stone walls and tended to the roses in the garden. She'd been more alive than anyone Belle had ever met. More like a mother, too, than anyone else in Belle's life. When Belle had first met Raven, she'd told herself stories about moving into that house and living as Arianna's child.

Now *that* had been a beautiful fiction.

Still, she'd bonded with Arianna during school functions, and she'd snuck over to the orchard in the middle of the night more times than she could count. She'd come as close as she could to becoming a part of Raven's family, and someday, when they were older, she and Raven would get married in that orchard.

And Arianna would smile down at them from the heavens.

Belle sighed as she slipped through the back gate of the Holloway estate. Maybe that night, she and Raven could sneak out to the orchard with a blanket, and they could lie down beneath the great, dark sky. The moonlight would reflect in his eyes, and she would trail her fingers over his chest, finding his heart. She'd never slept with anyone before, but she thought it should start that way. With a heartbeat pulsing softly against her skin.

They could never lose sight of their love for each other. No matter how far away he went, the memory of her touch would stay with him, just as she'd always remember the feeling of his heart in her hand. She knew she was taking a risk. The two had only kissed before that night, and there were so many things they could've done before doing *everything*, but . . . she wanted to give this memory to him. She wanted to give it to herself, and if it broke her heart to be so close to him only to feel him wrenched away from her, well, she could handle it.

She could handle anything.

That was what Belladonna thought as she neared the back of the house. The garden was filled with budding roses. They curled out of the ground, tangled and wild, and it was difficult to see movement between them, but . . . Belle did. She heard voices, and one of them was his. It was gentle and teasing, like the wind caressing the petals of a rose.

The other voice was Poppy's. Belle recognized it as she stepped closer, and relief flooded through her. Poppy must have wanted to see her best friend. She must've wanted to say goodbye to him, before everyone was crowded into Raven's driveway, hugging him and crying. Belle. Lily. Raven's dad, who was sending his son to the other side of the country instead of fighting for him.

Belle clenched her fists, stepping closer. Raven was leaning over Poppy, his hand on her shoulder, and Poppy was trembling.

She looked scared.

"What about Belle?" she whispered, and Belle realized that Poppy's fingers were wrapped around the bottom of Raven's shirt, like she'd been pulling on it. Or like she was *about* to pull on it. "If she finds out—"

"She'll kill us," Raven said softly, and for the briefest moment, Belle smiled. They knew her so well. Knew her passion. Knew her power. They knew she would do anything to get what she wanted, because that's what you had to do in a world as wicked as this one.

You had to become a witch in order to survive.

Her black hair swirled around her as she stepped up to the roses and parted them with her hands. It was dark. Her hair would help her blend in with the night, as would her jacket.

They couldn't see her.

But she could see them. Raven's hand was resting on Poppy's neck, and he was gliding his thumb across her skin. Poppy's shaking worsened. "Belle's not going to find out," he promised. "She never wants to speak to me again, because I ended things."

"You broke up with her?" Poppy swallowed, stepping back. There was light in her eyes, the light of hope. It crushed Belle to see it. She felt like her chest was caving in. Poppy was her dearest friend. Raven, her truest love. How could they talk about her like this?

How could they touch each other in front of her?

Of course, they didn't know she was watching. And the really sick thing? Belle felt guilty spying on them. She'd come over here, dressed in lingerie and a trench coat, to be with the person she'd been seeing for *two years*. The person she loved. Who loved her.

Now he was stepping closer to Poppy. His hand, which had been resting on her neck, slid into her hair, and Belle recognized that move. She'd memorized it. Every time his fingers had tangled in her hair, she'd felt a pull deep inside her, drawing her to him.

"I broke things off this afternoon," he said, and another memory flashed in her mind, of Raven, standing in her bedroom.

Raven, telling her goodbye.

Yes, he'd broken up with her. That much was true. But he'd only done it because he was going away to boarding school! He could be gone for years, and he couldn't ask her to wait for him. That's what he'd said, and then he'd kissed her so sweetly.

And Belle had come up with her plan.

She shivered as the wind picked up, slipping under the folds of her jacket. Right now she was supposed to be crawling over him. Teasing him with kisses. Touching him until he gasped. Instead, she watched her best friend whisper, "Why did you break up with her? Is it because you're leaving? And you don't know when you're coming back?"

Yes, Belle thought, but Raven shook his head.

"I told her that was why. But . . ." He swallowed, looking behind him. It was like he knew she was there. Could he feel her, like she could always feel him, whether she was in his bed or her own? At home or at school? In the orchard or in this garden, where they'd kissed a hundred times? "My feelings changed," he said finally, and Belle's gaze shifted to the thorns covering the rosebushes. She could strip naked and walk through those thorns, and they wouldn't hurt her as badly as these words.

They wouldn't cut her as deeply as this betrayal.

Raven leaned in and whispered in Poppy's ear. Poppy shuddered and . . . sank into him. That was how it looked, as if Raven were the undertow, and she was happily drowning in him.

Belle was drowning too. As Raven brought his lips to someone else's mouth, Belle's heart tumbled into the rosebushes. It brushed against crimson petals and sharp thorns, landing in the dirt.

She left it there to wither.

And she turned away from Raven and Poppy, fingers rising to the flowers in her hair. Belladonna, as beautiful as it was poisonous. Once, she'd planned to use those flowers to kill Evelyn Holloway. But that plan was much too small. Too obvious.

Too merciful.

Maybe it would take weeks. Months. Years. But someday, Belle would come up with a plan so brutal, it wouldn't steal the breath from Raven's lungs. It wouldn't poison Poppy's veins. Oh no, they were going to live through all of it. The pain. The ruination. And by the time Belle was through with them, those two would wish for death.

PART 2

The Truth According to Poppy Jack

I never planned to kiss him. I'd only wanted to see him one last time, before he was taken away from me. And so, the night before Raven left for boarding school, I snuck out of my house and rode my bike across town. I hid it in the bushes behind his back gate. Then I snuck onto the Holloway estate, just like I had every weekend for the past six years.

A voice hit my back as I entered the rose garden. "I thought you might come over. I know you were mad— Poppy?" Raven stepped out of the rosebushes, his brow furrowed. "Sorry, I thought you were Belle."

"We look so alike," I said bitterly. I hadn't meant to sound like that. I hadn't meant to feel like that. But my chest had swelled at the thought of him waiting for me there, and as soon as I'd realized he was waiting for her, well, my heart did what it always did.

It shrank under the grandeur of Belle's shadow.

Still, Raven's face was hopeful as he stepped toward me. Maybe even relieved. I couldn't make sense of it, but I didn't want to spend our final moments talking about his girlfriend, so I said, "Are you all packed? How are you feeling?"

"I'm packed. I'm nervous. And I know what you did. Lily told me."

My heart slammed into my ribs, ricocheted off my breastbone, and fell silent. He knew about our plan to poison his stepmother. Knew we'd almost resorted to murder. "We weren't going to go through with it," I stammered. "It was just a story we made up so we could sleep at night. I swear, Raven, I wouldn't have—"

"You didn't go to the police department? You didn't tell some detective about my stepmom and what she was doing to me?"

My throat went dry, but the breath had rushed back into my lungs. My heart had resumed its steady beating, reminding me that I was resilient. I would explain my actions to Raven and he would forgive me.

For this, he would forgive me.

"I'm so sorry," I started, my tongue stumbling over the words. "I shouldn't have done that behind your back. I was in a bit of a time crunch, and everything was snowballing behind me, and—"

"I'm not mad at you."

"You're not?"

A slight shake of the head. He was wearing a black button-down and jeans, his hair glinting in the moonlight. Raven was darkness and light. Red roses and glittering snow. His teeth shone bright as he flashed a sad, regretful smile. "I'm mad at the police for not helping me. I'm mad at my dad for sending me away. And I'm mad at myself for not telling him what was happening."

"You didn't know what was happening."

"I could've told him something. But I didn't, so you swept in to rescue me, just like always. My knight," he added softly, and I swear, everything stopped. The whirring of the wind. The rustling of the trees. The entire planet came to a halt.

And I stepped closer, my bottom lip trapped between my teeth. "I like rescuing you. I've always liked—"

"I know, Poppy."

I cringed, heat rushing to my face. Why was it so hard to tell him my new name? People changed their names all the time, and I wasn't transforming into someone else so much as . . . becoming myself.

"Poppy has never felt right," I admitted, my voice amazingly casual, considering the hammering in my chest. The tightness in my stomach. "I was thinking of going by my middle name from now on."

"Jacqueline?" He raised his eyebrows, his lips twisted as if he'd sucked on a lemon.

"Sure. Or Jack, for short." A shrug, as if it had just occurred to me. As if I hadn't been thinking about this every day for weeks. Months. Years.

"Jack?"

"Uh-huh." I wasn't looking at him anymore, so I couldn't see what his lips were doing. They could've been curving into a frown. They could've been twisting into a sneer. "I don't know, maybe it's—"

"Perfect."

My head snapped up. My cheeks had been blazing before, but suddenly my whole face was on fire, and my neck. My ears. If I'd been Belle, I would've been able to hide my emotions.

Keep the world guessing.

But I was not Belle. I was not Poppy, and I was not Jacqueline. I was Jack, and amazingly enough, it seemed I'd found the only person in the world who understood that.

"I just want to be who I am," I said, forcing myself to look into Raven's eyes. To let him see me, now that I'd started to reveal myself. "Sometimes I think I know what that means, and then it slips through my fingers like the wind through branches. But I know what my name is."

Raven's fingers brushed my shoulder, and somewhere along the line, he started gripping me tighter. Clutching me, like he didn't want to let me go. "Your name is Jack," he said softly, reverently, "and you are a climber of tall vines. A conqueror of giants."

I hitched in a breath. In that moment, I could see him, and he could see me, but even more important, I could see myself. Who I was. What I wanted. I'd never allowed myself to want anything before.

I'd been too busy keeping everyone alive.

But he was here, his fingers gliding across my shoulder, and even with a layer of fabric between us, his touch sent electricity shooting through me. It jump-started my heart. Filled my lungs with breath and drew my body to him. "Raven, I have to tell you something else. Something about us."

"I already know."

I furrowed my brow, trying to ignore the heat in my face. "How could you know? I didn't know—"

"Maybe I know you better than you know yourself."

That couldn't have been true. No one could truly know us better than we knew ourselves, but he'd called me a conqueror of giants. Did he know what I'd done one week earlier, when I'd caught my mother's boyfriend creeping up to the attic bedroom where my brothers slept? Did he know that he hadn't just given me a garden the day he'd found me kneeling in the dirt, a handful of seeds clutched in my palm? He'd given me a vine. He'd given me a weapon. And after it was over, when I lay shaking in my bed, I knew the cost of taking a person's power away. I knew the cost of fighting back. That's why I'd called off the murder of Evelyn Holloway. Lily and Belle didn't know how it felt to take someone's life in your hands, but I did.

I will never forget it.

Still, power flows in two directions. It can be used to destroy or bring people to life. As Raven's fingers trailed from my shoulder to my neck, I wanted him to know how powerful I was. How brave. I reached out, my fingers curling around the bottom of his shirt. So close to his skin. When he whispered, "Jack," a thrill went through me at the sound of my name in his mouth. I wanted to hear it slip between his lips like a sigh.

I'd never wanted such things before, even in the quiet of my bedroom. I hadn't allowed myself to want them, because Raven loved Belle, and Belle loved Raven. When I'd first come into the garden, he'd thought I was his girlfriend. Now his fingers were splayed out on my neck, his thumb gliding over my skin, and I didn't understand it.

"What about Belle?" I asked, when I should've said we can't do this. "If she finds out—"

"She'll kill us," he whispered, confirming my deepest fears. I started to pull away, but his grip on me tightened, his fingers wrapping around the nape of my neck. He drew me near. And he told me a secret, just like I'd told him. Earlier that night he'd ended things with Belle. He'd told her it was because he was going away to boarding school, and he couldn't ask her to wait for him, but deep down he had a different reason.

"My feelings changed," he said, his eyes downcast, as if he was ashamed. "I didn't want them to. I tried to fight it, because I didn't want to lose her, and I didn't want to break her heart but—"

"What?"

He leaned in, his lips brushing against my ear. "I want you. I didn't realize it until I was lying in that glass coffin, and you were supposed to wake me with a kiss, and then . . ."

"I didn't."

He nodded, gaze shifting to my hands. They were still wrapped around the bottom of his shirt. How easily they could slip under it. How easily they could tear the buttons away, leaving him shirtless in this garden of roses. How beautiful that would've been.

"I couldn't kiss you," I told him. "Not if it meant something. It wouldn't have been right to Belle, and . . . you're my best friend, Raven. I don't want to lose you."

"You are losing me. I'm going away, probably for years."

Thorns slid into my heart. I could feel them piercing the delicate flesh, and yet . . . it was amazing what a person could live through. It was amazing that you could slide a vine across the top of the stairs and watch a grown man trip and fall, and hear bones cracking and then . . . just go about your day. Heart still beating. Stomach still growling in hunger and lungs still taking in breath.

I was going to lose Raven. He was going away to boarding school, and he'd probably be there until he was eighteen. If he forgot about me during that time, he might never come back to this place and the father who'd abandoned him so easily.

I might never see him again.

But I couldn't kiss him. He'd broken up with Belle hours earlier, and I'd never kissed anyone before, so it made sense that I'd guide him down to the ground, so gently, and we'd curl up in each other's arms between the rows of crimson blossoms. Hold each other tightly. Wait for the dawn.

And that's exactly what we did. He didn't lower his lips to mine, ripping a shudder from me. I didn't wrap my fingers around the edges of his shirt, tearing until buttons tumbled into the dirt. No jacket slid onto the ground, providing a perfect bed for us on the garden floor. His shirt stayed on. So did mine.

I swear to you, Raven and I never kissed.

9

A Whisper from the Grave

The morning after she broke into Evelyn Holloway's office, Jack slipped out of Raven's bedroom after the sun came up. She'd lain with him for three hours. Three hours of holding her hand to his heart. Three hours of feeling his body pressed against hers as he slept. When she'd untangled her limbs from his, wincing at the light pouring in through his curtains, he'd sighed and reached for her.

"Stay. Please."

"I can't." Two short words, and then she was climbing over the windowsill, heading for the garden below. For the first time in years, that garden didn't flood her mind with painful memories. Raven was home. She could sneak onto his estate every night. Pull him into her arms. And then . . .

Jack froze as she reached the second-floor balcony. She was staring right into Lily's bedroom, which, unlike Raven's, did not have thick velvet curtains covering the window. Lily's curtains were white and fluttery. All it took was the slightest touch of wind to part them, and then Jack was staring into a world of white furniture and painted pink roses.

Just like Evelyn's office.

Lily was sprawled out on the bed. Through the gauze of a pale canopy, Jack saw her poring over the pages of a file, just like she'd promised. But there was something odd about the scene. Something Jack couldn't put her finger on until Lily plucked a folder from beside her, tucking pages inside. They had only stolen *copies* of the files in Evelyn's office. They hadn't taken any of the originals. Why, then, was Lily sitting in the privacy of her bedroom, going through a folder marked *Andrew Kane*?

Jack could see the name clearly as Lily set the file on the bedside table next to the window. She stood from her canopy bed, stretched, and began pulling on a bulky white coat. As she buttoned it, Jack realized she was wearing gloves that matched the color of her hands almost perfectly.

Had she been wearing them all night?

Jack's stomach clenched at the realization that *her* fingerprints were all over Evelyn's office, but Lily's likely weren't. Should she sneak back in? Wipe the place clean? If she did, she might destroy actual evidence, and besides, breaking and entering in the daylight was likely to get her arrested.

Now Lily was tucking the *Andrew Kane* file into a little drawer in her bedside table and covering it with magazines. It wasn't the greatest hiding place, but the police had already searched her house, and Lily's family members had no reason to go poking through her things.

But Jack did. Her heart hammered as Lily slipped out of her bedroom and into the hallway. After the door closed, Jack heard the distinct sound of footsteps retreating on the hardwood floor. Two minutes later, the back door opened, and a blond-haired girl in a white coat slipped outside, eyes darting left and right as she veered toward her bike.

Lily was going somewhere. And she didn't want anyone to know.

Jack had a decision to make, and fast. She could trail Lily to her secret destination, spy on her, then demand answers, or she could borrow the file marked *Andrew Kane*. Lily was so talented at keeping secrets. If Jack confronted her without evidence, Lily might lie right to her face. Or she might lash out. Carefully, Jack reached into Lily's window, her fingers fumbling for the bedside table. Within seconds, she'd liberated the Andrew Kane file and was stuffing it into her backpack, where the copied files were hidden.

Then she climbed over the balcony. Her fingers wrapped deftly around the ivy, guiding her body toward the ground. She'd almost touched down in the dirt when a voice stopped her in her tracks, but it didn't belong to Lily.

It belonged to Raven's mother.

Arianna Holloway laughed brightly, her voice ringing out

through the rose garden. Jack's foot slid off a jagged stone and she fell. The ground came at her hard. She tumbled through the dirt, managing to protect her face from the rosebushes. Scratches laced her hands, but her bones were intact.

She pushed to her knees.

The laugh came again. This time, Jack realized the sound was coming from inside the house, drifting out to the garden through an open window on the first floor. Well, she'd visited Raven in his third-floor bedroom. She'd snuck into Lily's room on the second floor. Why not complete the tour and visit a ghost on the main floor of Holloway Manor?

She slid one leg over the windowsill, then climbed into the house.

Arianna's voice grew louder as Jack crept through the ebony-tiled kitchen, nearing the living room. Pictures littered the black-carpeted floor. Pictures of Stefan and Evelyn's wedding, their honeymoon, their visits to the Apple Blossom Festival. Each year, Evelyn had offered to chair the event, and Jack could remember her standing at a podium, her cropped blond hair adorned with apple blossoms. She wore white in almost all the photos.

Would they dress her in white for the funeral?

Arianna had worn black. Her long dark hair had blended with her velvet dress, and Raven had insisted on placing red roses in her hands. Those roses had always brought her joy, he'd explained, though of course, the greatest joy of her life had been her son. Jack could see it in her warm brown eyes—not just in memory, but in the present moment, because Arianna was in front of her once more. Over on the TV screen, Raven's mother sat at the breakfast table with her son and her husband, laughing over mushroom and zucchini omelets.

Raven's favorite.

For a moment, Jack was mesmerized. Arianna had on a black shirt and jeans, and her dark hair was pulled back into a ponytail. She looked more casual than Evelyn had *ever* looked in her white designer dresses and loud, clacking heels. When Arianna tousled her young son's hair, Jack's heart squeezed. When she lifted a zucchini to her husband's lips, Jack heard the soft sound of a sob.

It had come from the sofa.

She probably should've known he was there, considering pictures had been splayed out across the living room floor like a puzzle he was desperately trying to solve. But she hadn't been able to see him. His head was clutched in his hands, dark curls poking through his fingers. His shoulders jerked up and down as he wept. Jack backed away slowly, leaving Stefan Holloway to his grief, but his head snapped up as she neared the living room's french doors.

"Poppy," he said, his eyes narrowed as if he were looking at a long-forgotten memory.

"I was just leaving. I mean, I was just visiting Raven when I heard . . ." She fumbled for the perfect thing to say. The *helpful* thing, which would drag him out of the darkness. But Jack had spent the morning clutching Raven to her chest, when she wasn't climbing in and out of windows, and her arms were shaking with exhaustion.

She couldn't carry anyone else.

Still, she strode over to the plush white sofa when Stefan beckoned her closer. She sat, stiffly, on the corner. He'd paused the old family video, and Arianna seemed frozen in time, smiling and happy. Jack wanted to stare at her forever. She didn't even ask why Stefan was watching videos of his first wife when he'd only just lost his second. Loss seemed to beget loss in this family, tragedy circling itself like a snake that never tired of devouring its own tail.

Stefan must've been thinking the same thing. He wiped the tears from his tired eyes, still staring at the image on the screen. "Sometimes I think this family is cursed. If anything ever happens to me—"

"It won't."

"But if it does . . ." He clutched her hands. His grip was fierce, and Jack wanted to pull away, but she didn't. She sat there, wincing, as he whispered, "You have to look after my son. You could move into this house, and you could make sure—"

"That isn't going to happen." Jack pushed off the couch, sliding her hands from his grip. "Look, what happened to Evelyn is terrible, and I don't understand it. But you *cannot* leave Raven alone. You can't let anything happen to you and . . ." Here she caught his gaze, holding it as fiercely as he'd gripped her hands. "You can't send him away again."

Raven's father nodded, rubbing at the dark stubble on his chin. He hadn't showered. Hadn't shaved. And while Jack felt for him, she was not about to stand there and watch him push Raven away. "You're the only family he has left. He needs you."

"I know. But I don't know how—"

"Then figure it out." Jack shook her head, her fists tightening in anger. She shouldn't be mad at him. He hadn't asked for any of this. But she was so sick of parents abandoning their children, and maybe she'd never be able to say these things to her mother, but she could say them to someone who would listen.

She strode around the couch, crouching in front of Raven's dad. "I know it would be easier to just check out completely. Blame some witch for cursing your family and never get off this couch. But pretty soon, your son's going to come down those stairs, and he's going to need to know that he still has a father."

"How—"

"Get off the couch. Take a shower. And make him breakfast." Raven's father opened his mouth, as if to protest, but she cut him off. "You don't have to be perfect. You just have to be present, all right? You have to be *here*."

He nodded, slowly, wrapping his fingers around the edge of the sofa. In one swift movement, he'd pushed to his feet. He wobbled a little, as if he'd been hunched over on those cushions for hours, and Jack caught his arm, steadying him.

"Thank you," he said, his voice hoarse.

"Don't thank me yet. I'm going to come check on you to make sure you've done what I said." When Dr. Holloway chuckled, Jack smiled a little too. "I'll bring you vegetables from the garden you helped me plant," she added, as he hobbled toward the stairs. "You can make him an omelet, like you did when he was a kid."

Then she left. She didn't climb out the window like a trespasser, but rather went out the front door like a proper visitor.

Jack had not felt like a proper visitor in a long time. Not since the first Mrs. Holloway was laid to rest in the ground and the second made a home for herself within these stone walls. But things were different now. Raven's father had not only invited her into his home, he'd said she could *live* there if anything ever happened to him. And though Jack had no intention of moving into Holloway Manor, she felt truly welcome for the first time in years.

As if she belonged.

Her heart swelled as she looped around the back of the house, nearing the place where she'd hidden her bike. But as she climbed onto the seat, her stomach tightened in fear. She wished she could return to Raven's room. Wished she could crawl into his bed and sink into the fairy tale they'd invented when they were young, about a knight who rescued a prince from a villainous witch.

But Belle was not really a witch. She was a seventeen-year-old girl locked in a detention center, alone and afraid. If Jack kept avoiding her, she'd be no different from Stefan Holloway, hunched over on the couch.

Avoiding reality.

And so, instead of turning east, toward the little green house where her brothers slept, Jack turned north, pedaling up the hill. It took half an hour to reach her destination. The tightness in her stomach worsened as she parked her bike outside the large square facility, painted the ugliest shade of orange and surrounded by a barbwire fence. A person could rot in this place. There was no garden to tend to and no room full of books, like the library Belle's father had built for her.

She could be in this place if she didn't play things very carefully.

Still, she asked the attendant to buzz her in. Parked her bike outside the door. There was a desk ahead of her, where a woman with dark skin and burgundy ringlets waited to greet her. Off to the right, Jack saw a wall of glass separating her from the visitors area, where family members came to meet their incarcerated loved ones. Soon, she'd be sitting at one of those little square tables, stuffed into a hard plastic chair, and Belle would be sitting across from her.

Jack approached the front desk, breathing in and out slowly. The woman looked up, blowing a strand of burgundy hair out of her face. "I need to see your identification and check your bag." Her eyes narrowed. "Are you under eighteen? You have to be at least—"

"I . . ." Jack's gaze flicked to the wall of glass, and the figures beyond it. She should've instantly recognized the blond girl sitting at one of the tables. But the girl's back was turned to her, and her pale hair blended with her coat. Her coat blended with the white plastic chair. For a minute, Jack told herself it *wasn't* Lily Holloway sitting at the detention center, nervously pulling a thread on her coat.

Lily despised Belle. Belle despised Lily. The two had been at odds since Lily had started sneaking into Raven's bedroom—when she wasn't spying on him in the orchard. Belle had never trusted her, and after Lily had discovered the *Recipe for the Perfect Murder* and hidden it somewhere on the Holloway estate, that distrust had darkened to hatred.

Presently, Belle entered the visitors area. Her dark, lustrous waves were pulled back in a stringy ponytail, and her fierce eyes were rimmed with circles instead of kohl. She looked tired. She looked scared. As she slid into the chair opposite Lily, Lily grabbed her hands and yanked her forward before a guard could intervene. A gasp slipped from Belle's lips. Then a smile lanced across her face as Lily pulled her in for a kiss.

Belle Époque

It took about three months. Three months of missing Raven. Three months of replaying the scene in the rose garden over and over again. By the time spring had bled into summer, and all the roses in town were in full bloom, Belle knew exactly how to repay Jack and Raven for betraying her.

She just needed one thing.

The August before her freshman year, she paid a visit to the Rose Hollow Wellness Facility while her father was at a charity auction. She scribbled her name in the visitors log at the front desk. And then she sat in a rickety wooden chair, bracing herself for the reunion with Lily.

The last time they'd seen each other, Lily had been a wild, poisonous blossom, but as she shuffled into the wood-paneled foyer, it was obvious that blossom had wilted. Her long, lithe arms clanked against her sides, as delicate as glass. Belle could see the outline of her rib cage beneath her paper-thin shirt. There was a common area off to the right, where patients lounged about in street clothes, but Lily clearly hadn't earned that privilege yet.

She ambled forward in a uniform that looked a lot like scrubs. White collared shirt. White pants. She wore tattered slippers, and Belle wondered if it was because shoelaces could be used to wrap around a person's neck. Your own or someone else's. She'd never been particularly fond of Lily Holloway, but in that moment, she wanted to throw the smaller girl over her shoulder and bolt out of there like a villain in a silent movie.

"Is there somewhere we can go?" Belle's eyes darted toward the boy at the front desk, who was watching them through his long violet bangs. He had a kind enough face, but you never could tell who people were by looking at them. As Lily had once said, the wickedest monsters knew not to leave footprints.

Lily eyed Belle a minute, her blond hair shorn into a haphazard pixie cut. She looked like a child who'd taken a pair of scissors to her locks when her mother's back was turned. Finally, she waved Belle through the common area, down a short hallway, and out the back door. They stepped into a courtyard with a fountain in the center. Roses wove around the back gate, curving up to wrought-iron finials, but they were pink, rather than the red roses in Raven's garden.

It didn't break Belle's heart to look at them.

Lily, on the other hand, seemed distrustful of the roses, and it gave Belle an idea. She sat down on the lip of the fountain, trailing her fingers through the water. "You know what this pond needs? Water lilies."

Lily's head snapped up, and there was a spark in her eyes that hadn't been there before. "Lilies? What are you planning?"

"Nothing. I'm done planning. That's why I'm here. I was hoping you'd give me the *Recipe for the Perfect Murder*, so we could put this thing to bed."

Lily sat down close to Belle, keeping her voice low. At present, they were the only two people in the cloudy courtyard, but Belle could see an attendant lingering by the back window, watching them.

They had to be careful of what they said.

"What if I don't want to put things to bed?" Lily asked, her eyes watching the misshapen wooden building. "You just *decided* it was over, but it isn't over for me. I'm still living it."

"What is your mother doing to you?" Belle whispered, her chest tightening at the thought of finally getting an answer to this question. She'd been wondering for months, searching Lily for signs of abuse. Bruises. Cuts. But like with Raven, she'd found nothing. "Why can't we go to the police?"

"The police are useless! They sent Raven to the other side of the country instead of *actually helping him*. They took my stepbrother away. Your boyfriend."

Belle's lips twitched, and she curled her fingers over the lip of the pond. The police hadn't taken her boyfriend away. Jack had.

Jack was going to pay for that. But first Belle needed to destroy the *Recipe for the Perfect Murder*, so no one could link her back to the crime. She'd written it in her own handwriting. She'd never be so foolish again.

"You're right," she murmured, close to Lily's ear. "You told us a hundred times your mother doesn't leave evidence, and that's why we can't go to the police. But maybe you could break out of here."

"And then what?" Lily ran a hand through her shorn hair, and Belle wondered if she'd chopped it off before she'd come here. And *why.* "There's a girl in the facility who looks a bit like me, and she'll be eighteen in a couple of months. She said I could have her ID if I wanted to run, but I don't know where I'd go. And I can't stay here forever." The way she'd said it . . . it was like she wanted to be locked in this place, far away from Holloway Manor. From her mother. From the man who'd promised to adopt her but hadn't had time to sign the papers before she was sent to this facility.

"Lily." Belle touched her hand, and Lily jumped as if she'd been struck. Her cheeks flushed pink. Tears welled in her eyes. "What about your dad?" Belle asked, drawing back her hand. "Your biological—"

"No, he'd never want me. He left my mom *because* of me."

"Did she tell you that?"

Lily nodded, her eyes downcast. "She told me he left when I was three years old. They were so in love before she had me, but I was too much for him."

"She could've been lying. God, Lily, for all we know she *absconded* with you in the night, whisking you away to some far-away state while your dad was sleeping."

Lily's lips twitched, and after a minute, she smiled. "Maybe you're right. Maybe he didn't abandon me. But my mom didn't *abscond* with me either. I was born at the Rose Hollow Medical Center. My mom has pictures of me as a newborn, and you can see signs from the hospital in a couple of them."

"Raven's dad works at that hospital," Belle said, an idea forming in her mind. "If he gave me a reference, maybe I could get a job as a filing assistant. I could track down your birth certificate and see if your dad's name is on it."

"You would do that for me?"

"Why not?" Belle shrugged as if it were no big deal. "You're going to give me the *Recipe for the Perfect Murder*. Right? That way, your mom can never find it. It has my name on it, and if she ever put two and two together . . ." Belle bit her lip, trying to look panicked. Trying to look scared. "You'll keep her from hurting me, and I'll keep her from hurting you. Once we have your dad's name, it'll be easy to look him up online."

"Unless his name is Joe Smith or John Johnson."

"Think positive," Belle said, bopping Lily's nose with her finger. Again Lily flinched, and Belle tucked her hands into her lap. "I'll need a little time to get hired as a filing assistant, and a little more to gain access to the restricted sections of the hospital."

Lily nodded, gesturing to the space around her. The courtyard.

The building. The wrought-iron gate tipped with sharp, twisting finials just waiting to impale anyone who tried to escape. "I've got all the time in the world."

Three months later, Belle returned to the Rose Hollow Wellness Facility with a gleam in her eye and a birth certificate in her purse. "Well, I was wrong about one thing: Dr. Holloway wouldn't give me a reference. He said I'm too young to be considered for a filing position, and 'playing doctor' with Raven doesn't pass for hospital experience. I don't think he likes me." Belle pouted, crossing her arms over her chest. "Too bad for him, the hospital was looking for volunteers."

"They were?" Hope in Lily's voice. Hope on her face, too, as her cheeks flushed pink. "Did you find my dad's name?"

"I sure did."

Lily gasped, leaping from her bed. She threw her arms around Belle. When she pulled back, Belle could see that her pale blond hair hung down to her ears. She was wearing a dab of lip gloss, strawberry or cherry, and her limbs didn't look quite so thin in her sweater and jeans.

"It took a bit of searching, but I tracked down your birth certificate. Looked up your dad online. And . . ." Here, Belle blushed, struggling to explain what she'd done next. Three months earlier, she'd wanted nothing more than to retrieve the *Recipe for the Perfect Murder*. But the closer she'd gotten to finding Lily's father, the more dangerous the endeavor had felt. What if he was just like

Lily's mom? What if he was worse? "I might have called him and told him about you."

"What?" Lily's mouth dropped open, the blood draining from her face. "How could you—*why* would you?"

"I needed to find out what kind of person he was! If you called him up and he told you to get lost . . ." *It would've broken your heart*, Belle thought, brushing past Lily. She sat down on the edge of the bed. Her purse was clutched to her chest like a child, and she wondered if her parents had ever clung to her that way before giving her up. Had they thought of her *once* since abandoning her to the foster-care system? Her birth records were sealed, and it was unlikely she'd ever be able to track them down, but if she did . . . would her parents want to know her at all?

"I asked your dad if he wanted to see you," Belle explained, her throat tightening with every breath. "I figured if he said no, I'd lie and tell you I couldn't find your birth certificate."

"But you did find my birth certificate. You're sitting here telling me you did."

"Yes," Belle agreed.

"Which means . . ."

When Lily broke off, Belle nodded, a smile curving over her face. "He wants to see you. He told me he *did* leave when you were little, but only because he was a hardcore drug addict and he didn't want you around that life. After he got clean, he reconnected with your mom, but she was wary of letting him near you."

"Because she thought he might bail again?"

"Yeah, or he'd relapse and put you in danger." Belle's chest flashed with heat at the words. The entire time she'd known Lily, the smaller girl had *always* seemed to be in danger because of something her mother was doing. Something insidious. Something subtle. The idea that Evelyn had *protected* Lily from her father seemed more than uncharacteristic. It seemed like an outright lie. "According to your dad, your mom demanded that he become one of her clients and agree to random drug testing. He said yes, and for a while it seemed like they were getting along. Maybe even falling back in love. But out of the blue, she started dating Stefan Holloway, and she cut off your dad completely. He was really broken up about it on the phone. He almost started crying."

"He did?" Lily's voice cracked as she sat down next to Belle. "Why are you doing this for me?"

Belle shrugged, her chest warming again. What was wrong with her? She didn't get attached to people, except for Raven. And since that had ended so terribly, she knew better than to feel anything for this strange, broken girl. She'd held up her end of the bargain. She needed to get the location of the *Recipe for the Perfect Murder* and get the hell out of there.

"I want to help you get away from your mom," Belle said, touching Lily's arm. "But I need you to help me get away from her too. If she finds that recipe stashed on her estate, she could have me arrested for plotting—"

"Oh, wow." Lily jerked away from Belle's touch, pushing off the bed. "I was actually starting to think you cared about me, but you only care about that stupid recipe."

"What? No, I just want to move on."

"You're lying! I should've known. You're a liar." Lily shook her head, chuckling grimly. "The last time you agreed to get me away from my mother, you cut me out of the plan, rescuing Raven behind my back. You didn't care that you'd left me with her. You've *never* cared—"

"I never cared? I have your birth certificate in my purse. Do you know how much trouble I could get into—" Belle broke off when she realized her mistake.

"It's in your purse?" Lily glanced at the empty doorway, then turned back to Belle, a smile slicing across her face. Belle opened her mouth to call for help. But Lily was alarmingly fast for someone who'd ambled through these hallways mere months earlier, and before Belle made a sound, Lily had lurched forward, slapping a hand over her mouth.

Belle bit her fingers, but Lily didn't cry out. She didn't make a sound. Instead, she pulled back her injured hand, glaring daggers at Belle, and then she lunged for the purse. Both girls fell backward on the bed. The two went tumbling, Lily on top of Belle, Belle on top of Lily. After much thrashing and flailing, Belle had her opponent pinned beneath her, just like she had in the orchard so many months ago.

She held Lily's arms above her head, leaning down. "You cannot beat me," she whispered, so the attendants outside the room couldn't hear her. If anyone walked in on them now, Belle would be banned from the facility. "The best you can hope for is to strike a deal."

"This isn't a game," Lily snarled. With a burst of unexpected strength, she wriggled her legs free, kicking Belle to the side. Belle went careening off the bed, her purse slipping out of her hands.

Lily clambered forward, plucking it from the floor. "You have a father who loves you," she spat, her hair hanging over her eyes. She brushed it aside, revealing a long thin slash where Belle's fingernails had scratched her. "You have no idea what it's like to live with—"

"A monster?" Belle said from the floor, and her voice was hollow. All of her was hollow. Her broken, battered heart had fallen out of her chest that night in the rose garden, and the *only* thing keeping her alive was her hatred. Her fury. "You don't know anything about me. You don't know anything about my dad."

"Edwin?" Lily reached into the purse, pulling out a folded birth certificate. She didn't seem to notice the packet of poppy seeds Belle had bought earlier that day. "Everyone says he's a saint. When the library burned down at Rose Hollow Elementary, he paid to have it rebuilt, and he donated the children's wing at the hospital." A pause, as she handed over the purse. Belle hugged it to her chest, fiercely protective of the seeds that were an important part of her plan. "Plus, he took you in after everyone said you were too old to be adopted."

"Lovely," Belle said, leaning against the bed frame. She felt defeated. Humiliated. She'd lost her leverage, and Lily had no reason to hand over the *Recipe for the Perfect Murder*.

She might as well go back to the hospital. Edwin thought she was volunteering until six, and if he found out her shift ended an hour earlier than she'd claimed, things could get really ugly at home. She wished she could stay in this place, even as she knew it was a ridiculous thought. No one chose to sleep on a hard bed in a wellness facility when they could be curled up on a four-poster in an elegant Tudor.

No one except Belle.

"What else do people say about Edwin?" she asked, as Lily crouched in front of her. She must've sensed that Belle was trying not to cry. And it was funny, because moments earlier, they'd been at each other's throats, but now Lily's voice was soft. Tentative. "You lived in six foster homes before Edwin came along and adopted you. He built you a library. Planted you a garden. Everyone says he's the nicest man in the world."

"He is," Belle said, her gaze drifting to the window. It was after five thirty, and the last of the light was trickling from the sky, cerulean hues darkening to indigo. "Until the sun goes down."

11

Beauty and the Beast

Belle was eleven years old when she met the man with kind eyes and an easy smile. His hands were wrinkled. His clothes, impeccably pressed. He wore the brown tweed jacket of an English professor, complete with patches on the elbows.

Belle liked him instantly.

It should be noted that, at eleven years old, Belladonna was not prone to liking anyone. She'd been in six foster homes so far, and though no one had thrown her down the stairs or forced her to sleep in the yard like a dog, she had suffered some . . . unusual situations. There had been the woman who, upon returning from work each night, demanded a two-hour foot rub before Belle could climb into bed. One of her so-called "fathers" had snuck Tabasco into her food whenever she disobeyed him. Her most pleasant experience had been with a kindhearted couple whose only flaw was wanting to help too many children, and she'd been stuffed into a two-bedroom apartment with three brothers and two sisters.

Edwin was different. He didn't simply want to foster her for a couple of months and then send her on her way. He wanted to adopt her. Adoption meant *forever*. Adoption meant a stable home and a loving family, and the first time Belle set foot in his grand Tudor cottage, she felt tears running down her cheeks. This fairy-tale cottage was going to be her house. This four-poster bed was hers for the bouncing. There was a bay window in the kitchen that looked out into the backyard, where willow trees trailed long, elegant branches across green grass.

Her first night in the house, Edwin gave her a tour of the Tudor, starting at the burgundy front door and ending on the second floor. Her bedroom was on the left side of the hall and his was on the right. There was an attic above them, but it was locked with actual chains. She wasn't allowed inside.

Belle didn't mind. Who cared about a stuffy old attic when you had a canopy bed and three gigantic windows? She could look out over the street, the backyard, and the side of the house, where a little flower garden had been planted. After the grand tour, and an elaborate dinner of roast duck and potatoes, Belle wanted nothing more than to curl up in one of those windowsills and look out at her kingdom. But the darker the house grew, the more agitated Edwin became. Long shadows draped across the dining room, making him jumpy. When a crow flew in through the window,

Edwin knocked over his wineglass, spilling it on the white table-cloth.

Belle frowned, hurrying to mop it up. "I know how to clean," she said proudly.

A soft, low chuckle. "I'm sure you do. I'm sure they taught you how to cook, and do laundry, and all sorts of things you're too young to worry about." Edwin smiled, pushing back from the table. "But you don't have to take care of me, Belle. I'm the grown-up, and I'm going to take care of you."

He took her hand, leading her toward the stairs. They hadn't even cleared the table yet! Belle thought that was odd. At eleven years old, she knew there was a certain order to things, and clearing the table happened immediately after dinner. Then, scrubbing the pots and pans. Wiping the countertops. By the time she got to bed most nights, it was after ten, but that night the sun had just slipped below the horizon when Edwin brought her up to her room.

"The world is filled with monsters," he said, retrieving a tool-box from under her bed. Belle perched on the purple comforter. "Some will force you to look after them, even though you're just a little girl. Some will sneak into your bedroom at night and snatch you out from under me. That's why we have to take precautions."

Belle flinched as Edwin pulled a hammer from the toolbox. "What are you going to do?" she asked, heart tolling like a bell in a tower. She pulled the comforter up around her like a shield.

"What I have to do." Edwin strolled to the eastern window. The one that looked out into the yard. "I couldn't do it before, because your social worker would've been angry. She wouldn't have let me take you." He pulled out a single nail, pressing it into the wood of the window frame. Belle jumped at the first swing of the hammer.

"I could help," she said in a light, cheerful voice, as if they were playing a game and she wanted to be included. But deep down, she felt the pressing need to protect herself. "If you have another hammer—"

"No, no, no," Edwin said, checking the window to see if it would open. It didn't. In the briefest span of time, he'd nailed the window to the sill. Now Belle couldn't slide it open and curl up inside it, letting the breeze tickle her dark hair. She couldn't fall asleep there, her eyelids growing heavy after watching the stars appear in the sky.

"You'd hurt yourself." Edwin hurried to the second window. "If you hurt yourself, I've failed."

"Failed . . . what?" Belle asked. There was something she was missing, something important, and her mind trickled to the chains wrapped around the attic handle, locking her out. What was up there? She hadn't cared before, but she cared in the moment the second window was nailed to the sill.

Only one window remained.

"You could leave one," Belle said when Edwin didn't answer her question. "I'm on the second floor. Nobody could climb up here."

"They can find you anywhere." Edwin returned to the bed. He crouched down, taking her hands in his. "They have ladders and they have vans. They could pull up beside you when you're walking home from school, and you wouldn't be able to fight them off. They'd be too strong and you'd be too small. Especially someone like you. The second I saw you, I knew I had to take you home. You're too beautiful."

"I am?" Belle's nose wrinkled, the word sounding funny in his mouth. It didn't sound like a compliment at all. It sounded like an insult, like something a witch would curse you with, making your days fraught with danger and peril. If *that's* what beauty was, Belle didn't want it.

"We could chop off my hair," she offered, holding out a strand. She could see her reflection in the mirror on the other side of the room, could see her big dark eyes and olive skin. "Dress me in rags, like a princess before she meets the prince."

Edwin smiled then, a bright, genuine grin that made his eyes crinkle. Belle wanted to like him. She wanted to trust him, and as he moved to the final window, she wondered if maybe he was telling the truth. Maybe the world was filled with monsters and he was doing everything he could to keep her out of their clutches.

As a nail slid into the third window, her heartbeat calmed.

"We're not going to cut your hair." Edwin tossed the words behind him, working steadily. Working with care. "And I'm going to take you shopping for the most beautiful dresses you've ever seen, all right? I'm not going to punish you for your beauty. I'm not like them."

He's not like them, she told herself, and her grip on the blankets loosened. She pushed off the bed, scurrying toward him. He was hunched over the window, tugging on it to see if it stayed closed. He heaved and panted, but nothing shifted.

"You'll be safe here," he told her, his muscles relaxing now that the job was finished. "I'll take you to school every day and pick you up at three on the dot. Sometimes I have engagements in the evening, but we'll keep you locked up tight in the house. No one will be able to get to you, because you'll never be alone out there."

He gestured to the window, and the world beyond. In houses all over Rose Hollow, little girls were sleeping sweetly in their beds, unsuspecting. Pretty girls. Helpless girls. Was anyone going to help them? Some man could slide open their windows in the middle of the night, and then what would they do? They would scream and they would fight, and it would be of no use. The men would be stronger than them.

But Belle didn't have to worry about that. She had a father now, and he was going to protect her. No matter what. All summer Belle slept in a room with nails in the windows and a door that Edwin locked from the outside with a skeleton key. She had her own private bathroom, so she didn't have to worry about being let out during the night. She slept soundly in her four-poster bed, knowing she was protected from the evil of the world. Unharmed. Untouched.

When middle school began, and she asked to go to the birthday party of a classmate, Edwin sat her down and explained that bad things happened at parties. Boys became . . . dangerous. They transformed like werewolves at the slightest flash of skin, and you couldn't be too careful, so of course he couldn't let her attend. Instead, he set to work building a library, so she could read about parties more lavish than her classmates would ever throw. Masquerade balls and dresses the color of glittering jewels. Princes who behaved like gentlemen and monsters who could be defeated. By the time Belle turned twelve, she'd given up on the idea of going to parties in the real world, and she holed up in the library every weekend, reading about other people's adventures.

It was better that way, honestly. She was safe.

But halfway through the sixth grade, Belle started to realize that staying indoors wasn't *solving* the problem of a world filled with monsters. Yes, she was safe, but what about all the others? All the girls being snatched from their beds, or attacked at parties, or plucked off the street? One day, she snuck out of school at lunch and bought a packet of belladonna seeds for her garden. She wasn't planning to poison anyone.

She just wanted to know that she *could*, if she needed to protect someone.

A couple of weeks later, she was crossing the football field when she glimpsed a group of boys huddled under the bleachers, shoving a person back and forth between them. That person had trembling legs. A face so pale, Belle thought all the blood must've drained out of it. In spite of her pounding heart, she stalked over to the group.

"What game is this?" she asked wryly, because one had to be wry with monsters. They didn't understand sincerity, and begging just made them stronger. So did crying. So did screams. "Can I play?"

"Sure," said a boy with golden hair, shoving the person into Belle's arms. Her body sagged under the weight. But this was not some delicate girl she was holding. It was a delicate boy, with bright eyes and dark curls.

"Now what?" Belle asked, neither shoving the boy away nor pulling him closer. "Am I supposed to *do* something with him?"

A couple of boys snorted, elbowing each other suggestively, but the blond, who was clearly the leader, said, "Yeah. Pass him back."

"That's . . . it?" Belle frowned, glancing at the boy in her arms. He didn't look frightened anymore, or even angry. He was watching her curiously, as if he knew this was *her* game now, and the buffoons surrounding them hadn't bothered to look up the rules. "Your game seems a bit dull. How about a different one? I've been growing belladonna in my garden. Tomorrow at lunch, I'll slip a petal into one of your sandwiches, and you'll get to guess whose face will turn purple. Won't that be fun?"

"Yikes," said a boy with brown hair and frighteningly tight jeans. "Let's get out of here, Landon. This girl's a bitch."

"No, I'm a *witch*, and I'll be happy to poison every last one of you if you ever mess with this boy—"

"Get help," the blond, Landon, broke in, rolling his eyes. But his smile was a little watery. His army looked a little shaken. After a minute, he snapped his fingers, waving his boys off the field.

Belle let go of the boy with ebony curls. "Well, that was unexpected. I know they get cranky when they don't get their naps—"

"You shouldn't have done that." Clipped voice. Tight jaw. The boy smoothed his black fitted jacket, stepping away from her. "Now they're going to come after you."

"They won't. I'll leave a couple of petals in their lockers tomorrow. Nonpoisonous petals," she went on before he could interrupt, "but they won't know that. They'll think it's a warning." She grinned, plucking his backpack from the ground. "I'm Belladonna, by the way."

"Raven."

"Oh, the rich boy? I heard you buy your lunch with fifty-dollar bills." A pause, followed by a lift of her eyebrow. "That true?"

"Come over sometime. I'll show you the bathtub filled with hundreds." When he smiled, it was mischievous. There was a dimple in his left cheek, and Belle found her eyes drawn to it. She'd *never* wanted to go to a boy's house before. Not alone. Not accompanied by an adult.

But suddenly her grand library felt small. Suddenly her bedroom felt like a prison, with its locked door and nailed windows. Her heart sank at the thought of returning there, alone, for one more night. "I can't come over," she said. "My dad's really strict."

"I could sneak you out."

"I promise, you couldn't." She looked down. She was never supposed to break eye contact with a boy. Never supposed to show submission. But she couldn't look into those wide brown eyes anymore, because she couldn't understand how they could be so dark and so bright at the same time. Raven Holloway was like the night sky lit up by stars.

"I should go," Belle said, turning to leave. When he caught her

arm, she remembered Edwin's instructions. She wasn't supposed
to lash out. She was supposed to slip out of his grip and run as far
away as possible. Tell an adult. Ask for help.

Belle didn't run. Instead, she turned to find Raven standing
right in front of her. "Are you afraid of me?" he asked, and his
question felt loaded. There were kids at school who would judge
Raven simply because his mom was black and his dad was white,
but Belle would sooner threaten those people with poison than
stand next to them.

Still, she *was* scared of getting close to him. She was scared
of getting close to anyone, and before this moment, she hadn't
wanted to. "I told you, my dad's really strict," she said, hoping
he wouldn't push her to say more. "He nailed my windows shut
when I first moved in."

"Wait. He what?" Raven's brow furrowed, and his voice was
sharp. Angry, even. "Did he think you were going to fall out?"

"I . . . maybe. Just forget I said anything."

"No, I'm not going to forget." He was still touching her arm,
just barely. Skin brushing her skin. "This witchy, weird, *terrifying*
girl appears in my life. I want to know more about her. About
you."

A twitch in her lips. "Didn't your mother warn you about
witches?"

This time he full-on grinned and it was beautiful. It was the
moon slipping out from behind the clouds. Bright and enchanting.
Belle's chest flushed, and her heart felt like it was on a rickety
roller coaster. Was the ground sloping beneath her? "My mother

doesn't talk about witches," Raven said. "But I have this friend, and I think you'd really like her. Her name is Poppy, and she's been looking for a witch. *We've* been looking for a witch since we were little kids, and it started as a game but . . . I think we've been looking for you."

Oh, that was it. The exact worst thing to say to her, because now she was *swooning*, and swooning led to danger. It led to hundred-year curses and girls falling asleep while boys crawled over them, stealing kisses. Sometimes, when she finished her homework early, Belle slipped into the library and pored over the fairy tales Edwin had bought for her, seeking unusual details. How many princes had kissed Sleeping Beauty without waking her? How many lips pressed against hers without her knowing? And since she didn't know, would all of them stop at kissing? It was the kind of question Edwin would be able to answer, but she didn't want to ask him.

She was afraid of what he'd tell her.

"Speaking of fairy tales, what do you think of 'Sleeping Beauty'?" Belle asked Raven, a quick test. An easy one. Raven would say the wrong thing, and all these soft, sweet feelings would be replaced with anger. Then she would be safe again. "It's so romantic, isn't it? Waking your true love with a kiss?"

"I think kissing unconscious girls is demented. So is trapping them in a castle until they fall in love. And what's with all these princesses just sitting around, waiting to be rescued? Tie your sheets together, girls. Rescue yourselves."

A laugh burst from Belle's lips. It was so unexpected, so joyful, she couldn't do anything to tamp it down. Within seconds they were both laughing under the bleachers, and they might've stayed there forever if the bell hadn't rung, lancing through their gaiety like a blade through skin.

"Lunch is over," Raven said, shaking his head in chagrin. "Too bad. I kind of wanted to see Landon and his friends checking their sandwiches for poison." He guided Belle from the darkness. When they stepped into the light, he let go of her arm. "Stay here a minute. Do you mind?"

"Being late for math? Gee, no, I couldn't." A pause. "Take your time."

Raven wasn't gone long. He slipped through the northern entrance of the school, and Belle, being the mischievous rogue that she was, raced toward the door to spy on him. She cracked it open just in time to see him slip into the wood shop, and when he returned a moment later, she was holding the door for him, not even trying to hide the fact that she'd been snooping.

"Well? Did you rig a machine to cut off Landon's finger? Because I'd like to be there when it happens." She grinned, but it fell away as he dug around in his backpack, then pulled out an eerily familiar object. A hammer. "What is this? What are you going to—"

"I'm not going to do anything. If you want to sneak over to my place and hang out in the orchard with me and Poppy . . ." He placed the hammer in her hand. "You're going to have to rescue yourself."

12

Every Tool Is a Weapon

When Lily left the detention center, she thought she was being followed. Her body tensed at every rustling of leaves. She'd spent the past hour whispering with Belladonna, trying to keep anyone from hearing their plans, so she told herself she was just being paranoid as she rode her bike out of the parking lot and onto the street. There was no rush of sound behind her, no blur of movement when she turned her head.

She was alone.

Still, she stopped on Main Street, beneath the white columns of the justice building, pretending she needed to tie her shoe. She stopped again beside the rose gardens in the center of town. There were a couple of stragglers in the garden, but spring hadn't teased open most of the blossoms yet, so it was easy to see the emptiness between the bushes. No one was hiding there. No one was following her.

She couldn't shake the feeling, though. The hairs on the back of her neck stood on end as she pedaled through the east side of town, toward a little blue house with white shutters. She pulled her bike around the back of the house. Her purse was resting in the basket, and she slid the strap over her shoulder before heading for the kitchen. It wasn't until she was safely inside the house that Lily began to relax.

"I'm home," she called, because she knew he was waiting for her. He worked the night shift at a local plant nursery, unloading flowers from truck beds as the sun went down. This time of day, he'd be home. He'd be anxious to see her.

Lily strode past the kitchen table, where a pair of gardening shears sat beside a bouquet of freshly cut lilies. She could see her father sitting in the living room beyond. He was slumped over in his favorite beat-up chair, watching a game show on TV.

He looked up as she entered the room. "Lil. You're back."

"I wanted to check on you. I promised Raven's dad I'd spend the week at the Holloways', to help with the funeral planning, but—"

Her father choked out a sob. "Lily, I'm so sorry."

"Stop. You didn't do anything wrong." She crouched in front of him. His shaggy brown hair was sticking up every which way, his five-o'clock shadow darkening into a beard. She pushed the hair back from his face, forcing him to meet her gaze. "Everything's going to be fine. I got your file from Mom's office, and I'm going to destroy it in my stepdad's shredder. Then I'm going to clear Belle's name."

"What?" Her father pulled away from her, pushing to his feet. "You broke into your mother's office? Why would you—"

"Because of what you did for me. You protected me when the police came to question us. All I'm doing is returning the favor."

"You need to stay out of trouble." He pulled her into his arms, clinging tightly. His flannel shirt smelled of old milk and sweat. "I can't lose you, Lily. I've been trying to get you back for so long. And everything that happened the other night . . . it's my fault. I should've known you would—"

There was a sharp intake of breath on the other side of the window, and Lily slapped a hand over his mouth. She hadn't realized the window was cracked. "I didn't do anything," she whispered to her dad. "You didn't do anything. There's nothing left to talk about, all right?"

He nodded, and Lily strained to hear movement outside the house. There came a slight rustling, like someone backing away from the window in sneakers. The grass would muffle their movements. If Lily didn't act fast, they'd be gone before she could catch them.

"You know what?" she said suddenly, allowing her voice to carry out the window. "There is one more loose end I need to discuss with you. Something the police might figure out, if we're not careful. I left it in the kitchen."

Loudly, Lily plodded toward the kitchen, plucking the gardening shears from the table. But instead of returning to her father's side, she slipped out the back door, creeping around the side of the house. She was the hunter now. She refused to keep up the role of the wounded animal, constantly looking over her shoulder. Waiting to be caught. When she saw the couple crouching in front of the living room window, their bodies half-obscured by a hedge, she tightened her grip on the gardening shears, creeping up behind them. "Hear anything interesting?"

Raven spun around first, his eyes dropping immediately to the dull, rusted shears in her hand. But Jack, well. She didn't even bat an eye at the sight of them. She simply brushed past Raven, placing her body between him and any hint of danger.

Just like usual.

"Hey, *Lil*," Jack said, using the nickname Lily's father had spoken moments earlier.

Great. They'd probably heard everything. Lily would need to be smart if she wanted to turn things around.

"I can explain," she started, shifting into the defensive. Her eyes went wide, her hands shaking a little, like she hadn't even considered using the shears against them. "I asked Raven's dad not to say anything, because Raven just got home, but after the funeral I'm moving out of the Holloway estate. I reconnected with my biological father when I was staying at the facility. Now that my mom's not around to stop us, we're going to be a family."

Shit. She shouldn't have put it like that. *Now that my mom's not around* made her sound guilty, but she'd meant what she'd said to her dad. Once his file was destroyed, there wouldn't be anything linking him to her mother's murder. "The night my mother died, my dad was visiting me at the facility, and we were going over all the paperwork he'd need to get full custody."

"You were together that night?" Jack narrowed her eyes. "At the facility?"

"Yeah. He was there the whole night, which they don't usually allow, but I'm friends with the guy who was working the front desk and . . . he let it slide. I hope he doesn't get in trouble now that the police are sniffing around. He had to tell them he bent the rules for me."

"So the police know everything." Jack looked defeated, or maybe disappointed. Had she been building a case against Lily? Trying to throw her under the bus? Lily bristled, her gaze shifting to Raven, but he was staring at the house.

He looked unwell. He looked the way he had after Lily and her mom had moved into his house. "That's your dad?" he murmured, his eyes never leaving the window. "You just met him and you're going to live together?"

"We've been talking for more than two years. He came to visit me a lot, and I know it sounds sudden to you, but I've been wanting to know him my whole life." Lily stepped up to Raven, taking his hands. But he pulled away from her and he was shaking. She didn't understand it. "I promise, Raven, I was going to tell you. It just doesn't feel right for me to stay with you, now that my mom's . . ." She trailed off, letting the rest hang in the air. Her mother was dead. Her stepdad had never officially adopted her, and Raven had been away for three years. Once upon a time, Lily had wanted them to be a family, but they *weren't* a family.

Her family was here, inside this house.

"So," she went on, swinging the shears casually now. Drawing attention to them as if by accident. "I've told you *my* secret. Want to tell me why you're huddled outside my window? How did you even find me here?"

Jack blushed and it looked genuine. Like she was embarrassed rather than guilty. "I went to see Belle this morning," she began, and Lily's head snapped up. Her fingers tightened on her weapon. "But when I got to the detention center, I saw *you* leaving in a hurry. I thought it might be better to talk to you before I interrogated Belle, so I followed you, assuming you were going home. When I realized you weren't, I texted Raven to come meet me. He took driving lessons at the academy, and his dad didn't even notice that he borrowed the car."

"And then you crept up to the window instead of knocking on the door?"

Jack ran a hand through her auburn hair, smiling ruefully. "Okay, not my finest hour. But we've hardly seen each other in years, and I figured you'd do the same with me. Gather intel and then ask your questions."

They stared at each other a minute, Jack reading Lily. Lily reading Jack. Finally, Lily's lips curved into a smile, her grip loosening on the shears. "So we've all been sneaking around, spying on each other." She chuckled, shaking her head. "It probably did look sinister to see me walking into a strange house and whispering with a strange man. But he's my dad, and he's a really good guy."

"Are you sure?" Raven asked, toying with a thread on his jeans. He couldn't stop fidgeting. Couldn't stop looking at the house.

"Am I sure he's my father, or that he's a good person?"

"Either. Both. I just . . ." He swallowed, chewing on his bottom lip. "I don't get a good feeling from him. I think he might be dangerous."

"You don't know anything about him!" Lily's cheeks flushed with heat, and she told herself to calm down. Raven had been through hell. His mom had been shot in cold blood and a strange woman had moved into his house, torturing him in a way he still couldn't explain. He had good reason to be distrustful of strangers. "After we've laid my mother to rest, I'll have you and your dad over, okay? You can both meet him, and make sure I'm being taken care of. Right now, we need to find my mother's killer."

"She's right," Jack said, touching Raven's arm. "Why don't you come over to my house and we can talk in private? Go over what we've learned?"

Here, Jack's gaze flicked to Lily, and Lily heard everything she wasn't saying. They both had files to go over. Suspects to discover. And Lily in particular had one file to dispose of, *especially* now that Raven was getting suspicious of her dad.

She pulled out her phone and texted her dad rather than returning to the house: Need to go back to Raven's for a bit.

Forgot something. See you at dinner? She knew if she went back inside the house, he would pull her into his arms again and start crying, and she'd have to explain things she didn't know how to explain.

This was better.

"Let me know if you think of anything important," Lily said, as Raven and Jack headed off the grounds, Jack's fingers still brushing Raven's arm. His gaze still darting to the house. "We need to clear Belle's name, and that means giving the police another suspect. A better suspect."

She let the comment hang. It sounded perfectly innocent, but clearly, Jack sensed the threat underneath. Her head snapped toward Lily, and they held each other's eyes for a minute.

Then Jack turned away, wrapping an arm around Raven's shoulder.

It took a couple of minutes for them to reach the end of the street, where Raven had parked his father's car. Once they'd driven off, Lily looped around the house, retrieving her bike. She guided it to the sidewalk. It wasn't until she'd swung onto the seat that she remembered she was still holding the rusty gardening shears. She slid them into her purse, then set the purse in the bike's basket.

She had a feeling she would need them.

Three hours later, Lily was pacing in her bedroom, angry enough to slide those dull, rusted shears over someone's skin. She should've looked for her father's file the second she'd gotten home. Instead, she'd wasted the afternoon poring over the files Jack had copied at her mother's office. She'd found nothing suspicious, *until* she'd gone to retrieve Andrew Kane's file from her bedside table.

The file was missing.

Who could've taken it? she wondered, taking short, sharp breaths. Jack had gone home after sneaking into Evelyn's office, and Raven had no reason to go snooping through Lily's bedside table. Maybe Stefan had found it by accident. Maybe he'd stopped by to bring her some towels or washcloths or *something*, and he'd opened that drawer without thinking.

Maybe she could get the file back.

Lily hurried out of her bedroom. She could hear her stepdad shuffling around in the living room below, but if she was very quiet, she could sneak up to the third floor without him knowing. Her feet were silent on the hardwood. She took soft, careful steps on the stairs. Soon, she'd reached the third-floor landing, and then she was passing Raven's door.

The master bedroom loomed straight ahead. Lily made a beeline for it, her heart thumping. If Stefan had discovered her father's file, he could use it to make her dad look guilty. Even if her dad *wasn't* guilty. Lily knew for a fact that her father had not delivered the poisonous bouquet to Evelyn two nights earlier. And now that she only had one remaining parent, she had to protect him.

She slipped through Stefan's door.

The room was in disarray, which never would've happened while her mother was alive. Lily checked under the mattress, beneath the four-poster bed, and in Stefan's closet. She found no hint of the file. She started to worry that Stefan had hidden it in his study, and that was far too close to the living room for comfort.

He'd catch her if she tried to sneak in there.

Cursing under her breath, she opened the drawer to Stefan's bedside table, keeping her gaze far from the table on the other side of the bed. Her mother's table. Lily felt a twinge in her gut as she realized she'd been avoiding Evelyn's half of the room. She didn't want to see her mother's dresses hanging in the closet. Didn't want to feel the familiar satin or silk. When Lily had been young, she'd loved the cool feeling of the fabric against her cheek when she'd hugged her mother close.

They'd loved each other once.

But everything had changed once Evelyn had started bringing men into their apartment, and Lily didn't want to think about what had happened next. The manipulation. The lies. She shuffled through Stefan's drawer haphazardly, brushing aside a bottle of sleeping pills and a miniature tape recorder, which was empty. Everyone in the house knew that Stefan had trouble sleeping. He probably popped a couple of those pills and then listened to a tape of whale songs before drifting off to dreamland.

Lily closed the drawer, her panic rising. Her grief. Standing in her mother's room was getting to be too much for her, even with their complicated history. Her chest tightened with each breath. Tears stung behind her eyes. And she didn't *know* that Stefan had stolen the file.

He'd simply been the most logical suspect.

Sucking in little gulps of air, Lily barreled out of the room.

Raven's bedroom was only a few feet away, and it was possible that he'd gone searching through her room. Belle was Raven's ex-girlfriend. If he was desperate to free her from juvenile detention, he'd be looking for another suspect.

Lily snuck into his bedroom. His satin sheets were tangled up, as if he'd slept fitfully. His soft black carpet caressed the soles of her feet as she crossed his room. Dejectedly, Lily crouched beside his bed, not really expecting to find anything beneath it. She found a pair of boxers and a wrinkled shirt. She shifted through a duffel bag beside the window. No file hidden there. She was almost crying by the time she noticed the little green thread waving at her from the window frame, the exact color of Jack's olive-green coat.

Heat flashed in Lily's chest. Her face warmed as she realized that Jack had only pretended to go home after searching Evelyn's office. Jack had followed her back here. Jack had snuck in through Raven's window, and she'd probably climbed down the side of the house after her visit, passing Lily's bedroom on the way.

Lily's hands shook with rage. She almost dropped her phone as she pulled it out of her purse, and it took several tries to pull up the video she'd recorded the previous night. The one she'd taken outside Jack's window. The yard had been dark, but the flames were bright inside the house. It was obvious that Jack was burning clothes. Maybe they wouldn't be identified as Raven's, but either way, a woman had been murdered, and one night later, Jack fed potential evidence to the flames.

It would be enough to make her a suspect. Especially since the name Poppy showed up on the *Recipe for the Perfect Murder*. It took less than a minute to attach the video to a text. Thirty seconds later, Lily had typed out a message. All that remained was to enter a number into the contact field, but she didn't send the video to Jack, or to the Rose Hollow Police Department.

She sent it to Raven.

13

The Least Sinister Explanation

Raven couldn't stop thinking about the man's voice. He'd choked out *I'm so sorry* and Raven's entire body had gone still. Then the shaking had started, and he might've fallen down right then and there if Lily hadn't appeared around the side of the house, her eyes blazing and her fingers curled around gardening shears.

The absurdity had saved him.

Things were different now. He was sitting in the quiet of Jack's bedroom, and everything was painfully familiar. The jade walls. The Halloween costumes hanging in the closet, one from fifth grade, when Jack had dressed as Robin Hood, and another from eighth, when she'd gone as Link from The Legend of Zelda. Raven lay down on the green patchwork comforter. He felt the bed shift as Jack sat beside him, placing a hand on his arm. Suddenly his heart was racing and it had nothing to do with the man Lily had been visiting.

Raven looked up. "What is it?" he asked, acutely aware of the silence around them. When they'd arrived at the house, Jack's brothers had been heading to a nearby park, and her mother was nowhere to be found. No one could interrupt them. But the second their eyes met, Jack pulled her hand away from his arm, sending sparks shooting across his skin. He'd never felt about anyone the way he felt about Jack. He'd never wanted someone so completely. Why couldn't he tell her that?

"There's something you should know," Jack began, speaking to the wall instead of to him. "I did something last night, and you aren't going to like it."

He pushed onto his elbows, his eyes narrowing. "Why don't you let me decide that?" She always did this. Always assumed there were parts of herself that he would reject, or actions he wouldn't agree with. But Jack was the most noble person he'd ever met, and he didn't think anything about her would surprise him.

Still, his pulse picked up as she unzipped her forest-green backpack and pulled out a file. The name *Andrew Kane* was written across the tab. "Before I came over to your house last night, I broke into your stepmother's office with Lily."

"You what?"

"Lily had this theory, and I thought it was smart. If Belle didn't kill your stepmother, and none of us did either, who does that leave? Evelyn spent her evenings with your dad and her mornings and afternoons at work. So while Lily went through her mother's emails, looking for anything suspicious, I went through her files."

"That's incredibly illegal, Jack."

"I know." She nodded, color darkening her cheeks. "And unethical. And dangerous. And—"

"Did you find anything?"

Her head snapped up, a smile tugging at her lips. Jack's smile was unabashed, wide and wild, and the first time Raven had seen it, he'd thought he could spend his whole life making her face light up like that. He'd thought he'd never tire of it. Now, almost ten years later, even a hint of that smile made his chest flutter and his stomach dip.

"We copied a bunch of files," Jack went on, running her fingers over the muted yellow folder in her lap. "Evelyn spent all day talking to people in unhappy marriages. If one of them fell for her and couldn't have her, maybe—"

"They killed her?"

Jack nodded.

"With belladonna from our friend's garden?"

"I know!" Jack threw up her hands, almost knocking the file from her lap. "I can't figure out how everything ties together, but if you're certain Belle's innocent—"

"I am," he said, without missing a beat. "Belle spent half of middle school threatening people with the flowers in her garden. There's *no way* she'd be stupid enough to kill someone that way. This is a setup. Someone must've heard her talking about those flowers and decided to frame her."

Jack cocked her head. "I guess that's possible. But Belle

stopped talking about her garden once we got to high school. She said she needed time away from me, after what we'd almost done, but I still had classes with her. We saw each other at lunch. She never mentioned those flowers. I didn't either, except . . ." Jack's eyes went wide, her hands slapping over her mouth. "Oh my God, Raven. It was me."

"What was you?"

"*I* mentioned Belle's flowers in a letter to you. I started walking by her house after school, hoping she'd see me, and . . . I don't know. Call out to me. Tell me she wanted me in her life. That never happened, but one afternoon I saw her sitting in her garden, and I wrote to you about it that night. I told you she loved those flowers more than she loved me."

"That isn't true," Raven said, but his heart was thundering. His mouth was dry. "And if someone stole our letters, they did it *years* ago. It makes no sense that they'd wait until now to pick those flowers. None of this adds up."

"Not yet." Jack looked stricken, opening the file on her lap. "But while I was copying files from Evelyn's office, Lily stole this file from the cabinet. I never would've known if I hadn't seen her reading it in her bedroom while I was climbing down the side of your house this morning." She huffed, shaking her head. "Say what you will about my penchant for breaking and entering. It does have its advantages."

Raven tilted his chin up, smiling softly at her. The sun was pouring through the window, warming up the room. Warming up the bed. Cautiously, he slid his hand across the comforter, nearing

Jack's. But at the last minute, he lost his nerve and plucked the file from her lap. "Why do you think Lily stole this?"

"Isn't it obvious? Andrew Kane has to be her dad. She's planning on living with him, and if there's anything incriminating in this file, he might be deemed unfit to be her guardian." She paused, gaze flicking to the folder. "Well, that's the *least* sinister explanation."

Raven just looked at her, waiting. He already knew what she was going to say, and after the way he'd felt twenty minutes earlier, standing outside that man's house, he was ready to believe her. Too ready.

"Lily said she connected with her dad more than two years ago," Jack reminded him. "Maybe he tried to get full custody during that time, but Evelyn wouldn't let him."

"So he poisoned her with Belle's flowers." Raven nodded slowly, swallowing the bitterness in his throat. "But that doesn't explain the missing letters. Lily already knew about Belle's habit of threatening people with her flowers. She could've just *told* her dad about it, and he could've framed Belle, since she and Lily hated each other."

"Yeah, about that." Jack bit her lip, not looking at him. "When I went to see Belle at the detention center, Lily was already meeting with her. They didn't know I was watching them, and they, um. Well, they didn't seem like enemies."

"What does that mean?"

"I'm still trying to make sense of what I saw. But I don't think Lily's dad was the only one connecting with her while she was in that facility. I think she and Belle became friends. And if her dad knew that, I'm not sure he'd frame—"

"You really think he'd kill Evelyn and then pause to worry about Belle's feelings? Come on. He'd cover his tracks and never think twice about it. Just like the guy who killed my mom." Raven's chest ached at the mention. Even now, four years later, he could hardly think of her without wanting to curl into a ball. Either that or smash his fist into a mirror, fracturing the glass until it matched the wreckage in his heart.

And Jack knew it. Before he'd even sucked in a breath, she'd taken his face in her hands. "We're going to figure this out, okay? We have this file, and we're going to find out exactly what Lily is hiding from the police." She pulled back, brushing her thumbs beneath his eyelashes. There were no tears lingering there, but it was so like her to check.

She was always trying to protect him.

He could sense her hesitation as she pulled a stack of files out of her backpack. When he asked, "Our suspects?" she nodded, flipping through the stack. Slowly, as if it weighed more than all the other files combined, she procured one from the bottom.

"Did you know your dad was going to see Evelyn before your mom died? It looks like he was one of her clients from—"

"Give me that." Raven yanked the file from her hand, flipping through it in a panic. He had that discordant feeling of being in a nightmare, where the walls are closing in on you and the monsters are advancing, but a part of you senses that it isn't real. If you squeeze your eyes shut tightly enough, and shake your head violently, you can wake yourself up.

Raven didn't wake. Not when he turned page after page with a trembling hand, uncovering the secret his father had been keeping from him. He'd been seeing Evelyn for *a year*. He'd been locked up in that office with her, where no one could see them. Maybe they'd used that time to talk. Maybe they'd used that desk to spread out pictures and jot down revelations about his broken marriage.

Or maybe not.

A terrible feeling was unfolding in the pit of Raven's stomach, and it felt so much more dangerous than fear. It felt like *knowing*. Suddenly, so many things made sense. His father had become distant in the year leading up to his mother's death. Fidgety. He could be caught staring off into space halfway through dinner, or sitting in his study in the middle of the night, watching the walls. Raven hadn't been able to understand it, but then his mother had died in his arms, and his heart hadn't had room for anything but memories of her. The way her hair tickled his neck when she embraced him. The way her warm brown eyes mirrored his own, and when the light went out of them, his world didn't simply fade to darkness.

He sank into it.

All that year Belle had tried to pull him back into the light, and when she realized she couldn't, she'd stayed in that dark place for him. They'd lived in his nightmare together. Raven hadn't even realized it until the night Jack stood over him in a glass coffin, her cheeks flushed at the thought of waking him with a kiss. The moonlight had been filtering through the trees and he'd looked up at her through slits in his eyes, pretending to be asleep but desperately, *desperately* wanting to wake up.

Wanting Jack to wake him.

Now, shaking on the edge of her bed, his father's file in his lap, he looked up to find her staring at him. There were flecks of gold in her green eyes. Strands of red in her hair. Looking at Jack was like peering through a portal into a world of glittering light and ancient redwoods, a world everyone told you to stop looking for, because you'd never find it. But Raven had.

He let her take his hands and tell him, "It doesn't have to mean anything. Your dad probably went to talk about his marriage, because he and your mom were having problems. I bet Evelyn started to care about him during that time, and after your mom died, she must've reached out—"

"You don't have to do that."

Jack's brow furrowed, her lips curving down. "I'm not doing anything. I'm just telling you what probably happened, because I know where your mind is going. It's going to the worst possible place."

"I'm okay, Jack. I promise. I know I spent our last year together scaring the shit out of you and Belle, and I'm so sorry for that. But I'm stronger now. I can handle this." He scooted away from her the tiniest bit, because she would always try to take care of him if they got too close. She took care of everyone. Except herself. "Why don't you go over half the files, and I'll go over the other half. We'll see if there's anything suspicious in them. Anything that could explain what happened the other night. All right?"

For the next few hours Raven curled up on one side of Jack's bed, and she curled up on the other. They pored over their individual files. The shadows shifted, growing longer across the room. Jack's brothers came home, along with Flynn's new friend Diego, who was probably more than a friend, but Raven wouldn't make assumptions until Flynn decided to tell him about it. Raven had known Flynn since he was five, and Connor and Dylan since they were born. He loved those boys with a fierceness that made his stomach ache. When smoke drifted into Jack's bedroom, he suspected they were building a fire on their own.

"Should we check on them?" he asked, looking up from his father's file. He'd spent the bulk of his time investigating the other files Jack had copied, but upon finding nothing sinister or mysterious, his attention had returned to his own family's secrets.

"I'll go." Jack glanced at the file in his hands. "Did you find anything interesting?"

"Their sessions seemed normal, for the most part. He talked about his job at the hospital. There was this kid who kept coming in with bruises, but no one could prove he was being abused. I guess he was about my age." Raven took in a breath, blowing it out slowly. "One night the kid came in and he was banged up so badly, he had internal injuries. My dad tried to save him but he couldn't. After that, he started taking pills to sleep, and when his prescription ended, he stole another bottle from Mom's pharmacy. He kept stealing them, and that's why my parents were fighting all the time. Because he wouldn't stop taking them."

"So he went to see Evelyn, hoping to get help."

Raven nodded, but there was a knot between his brows. He could feel it, and the headache forming behind it. "My mom threatened to leave my dad if he didn't get help. And it sounds like Evelyn *did* help him, at first. But toward the end of his sessions, Evelyn started crossing out my mom's name in his file."

Jack snorted, head tilting to the side. "She blacked it out? Like a government document?"

"She attacked it," he said, holding up one of the copied pages. In three separate places, his mother's name had been slashed to oblivion. "She must've used scissors, or maybe a letter opener. I wish I could've seen the original file. Did you notice anything when you were making copies?"

Jack shook her head. "The pages went through the copier so fast." She frowned, peering at the places where *Arianna* had been sliced through with thin, sharp lines. "Why would Evelyn do this?"

"Maybe she'd fallen for my dad at that point. Maybe she wanted him to divorce—" He broke off at the sound of clattering on the other side of the door. "Sounds like the boys are dueling with fire pokers again."

"I'm on it." Jack rose from the bed. She was only gone a couple of minutes, and when she returned, the smell of roast marshmallows told Raven that the boys were making s'mores. He'd taught them that, one late October evening when their mother had promised to attend Connor and Dylan's school play and had failed to make an appearance. Again. By the end of the night, their faces were stained with chocolate instead of tears and their sobs had given way to shrieks of laughter.

Raven's heart hurt when he thought about it. His hands shook at the thought of his father *seeing* someone behind his mother's back. But none of that compared to how he felt when the text message popped up on his phone, containing a video of Jack burning clothes in her fireplace.

The file was accompanied by a threat. As Jack strode back into the room, Raven beckoned to her, all the blood in his body rushing to his heart. Making it hammer. Stealing his breath. They read the message together, hunched over on the bed: Burn the file or the police will find out that Jack burned your clothes last night.

I Will Not Lose You Again

Jack stared at the message for several seconds. She closed her eyes. She opened them again. The words started to blur, but they didn't rearrange themselves, and the accompanying video kept playing over and over on repeat. She could see herself feeding Raven's T-shirts to the fire. His jackets. His jeans. Even worse, she could feel his body tensing beside her with each passing second.

She wanted to bolt from the room and never return.

Carefully, with fingers that wouldn't stop shaking, she guided the phone out of his hand and hit delete. The message vanished but the damage had been done. "Raven, I can explain."

"You stole my clothes?"

A beat, during which she swallowed, but the pain in her throat didn't go away. "I only meant to borrow them. Actually, I didn't even mean—"

"Jack."

"I just missed you, so I snuck through your window one night, like I had a million times when you lived at home, and I walked around your room. Your drawers were open. I saw one of your T-shirts, so I picked it up and . . ." She was practically crying. She *wasn't* crying, because she didn't want him to pity her on top of hating her. She took slow, steady breaths, swiping at her eyelashes as the tears started to form. "I just wanted to feel close to you, at first."

His head swiveled toward her, his brown eyes narrowed. The room had grown heavy with shadows, making it difficult to read the expression on his face. It was almost as if he wore no expression at all. "You did it to feel close to me," he repeated, his voice emotionless.

Jack nodded, not trusting herself to speak.

"At first," he went on, and all his missing emotions seemed to rush into her. She felt the beating of two hearts. The rush of too much blood in her ears. She shouldn't have been so honest with him, but she couldn't take back the words now. He'd already heard them.

And so, like she had with the changing of her name, she tried to brush it off like a casual thing. "You know how it is for me at home. My mom hands me down these ridiculous outfits. Sequined tops and miniskirts. I mean . . ." Jack huffed, shaking her head. All of this was a lighthearted conversation. She didn't want to usher him out of the house, lock the front door, and never open it again.

Stay protected. Stay safe.

"I took the clothes to feel close to you, but once I realized how comfortable they were, I just kept wearing them. You have very nice clothes, Raven." She poked his arm teasingly, as if to remind him that not everyone had cleanly pressed suits and crisp, tailored shirts. Suspenders and belts. Silk ties and pocket squares. "I mostly wore your jeans and T-shirts, because I knew Belle would figure it out if I wore some of your nicer things, but I felt really at home in your clothes."

"Why did you burn them?" Raven asked after a minute. His voice was softer now, not so much neutral as gentle, and she told herself it was a sign that she should keep the rest to herself. He understood things, so far. There was no reason to push it.

"Your stepmother was murdered," Jack explained. "And Belle called me from the police station, freaked out and crying, so I told her I'd provide an alibi—"

"Wait, what?" His head dipped down as if to understand her better. "I don't know what I'm having a harder time believing: that Belle was crying or that you'd falsify an alibi. You could've ended up in a cell."

"I know! That's exactly what the detective said when I claimed I'd spent the night at Belle's. He told me I'd get charged with providing false testimony, or conspiracy to commit murder, and I knew I couldn't figure out the truth if I was locked up, so I bolted out of the station and went to talk to Lily. *She* told me the police were going through people's things, so I figured it was only a matter of time—"

"Before they found my clothes and thought you had something to do with the murder."

"Exactly." Jack nodded, throat tightening again.

"But you didn't," Raven said. He sounded so sure. "And now that the clothes are gone, there's nothing linking you to the murder except that video." He reached across the bed, gathering up Andrew's file. "All we have to do is burn this, and the video won't get sent to the police. Then I'll sneak into Lily's bedroom while she's sleeping and delete it from her phone."

"I can't believe she followed me home. She said she was waiting for your dad to check her out of the facility, which was obviously a lie." Jack strode to her window, peering through the curtains. The glare of the sunset was bright, staining the sky scarlet and gold, and Jack's eyes fluttered against the brightness. She searched for movement in the yard. For eyes glistening back at her. When she found nothing, she closed the curtains tightly, turning back to Raven. "The facility must've released her into Andrew Kane's care after her mom died."

"So Andrew is her father?"

"Definitely," Jack said without missing a beat. "The file proves it."

Raven's gaze dropped to the file in his hand. "He talked about Lily during his sessions?"

"He did more than talk about Lily. He talked about Evelyn. He was clearly in love with her, and he wanted the three of them to be a family. He said he'd do *anything* to get Lily back in his life. *Anything* to prove he could take care of his daughter."

"Then our theory makes sense. He could've poisoned Evelyn to get full custody of Lily."

Jack returned to the bed, sitting beside Raven. "Lily's dad has an alibi. She swears he spent the whole night at the facility." Then again, Lily had claimed she'd hidden the *Recipe for the Perfect Murder* in a tree hollow, and the recipe had turned up in the kitchen. "What if Lily's lying to protect—"

Raven's phone chimed, cutting Jack off. They read the second message together: You have ten minutes to burn the file. Send me a video to prove it's been destroyed, or my video goes straight to the police.

Jack lifted her gaze, peering at her oldest friend. He was resting his head in one hand, his fingers tangled in his curls, and his face didn't look expressionless anymore. His eyes were bright. His lips were set in a firm line. She knew what he was going to say before he said it.

"We're burning this." He pushed off the bed, tucking Andrew Kane's file under his arm. "If Lily was lying about her father's alibi, somebody at the facility will be able to tell us the truth. But if the police see you burning my clothes, I could lose you."

"The video alone doesn't prove I'm a killer," Jack insisted, following him across the room. "If we explain what happened the night before you left for boarding school—"

"The kiss?"

She nodded, finally admitting it to herself. Part of her had truly believed the kiss had been a fantasy. Something she'd conjured out of loneliness and desperation. "We can tell them I was some lovesick kid, missing you and wanting to feel close to you again."

"Lovesick?" Raven's lips curved up on the ends, and it seared her from the inside out. She felt pleasure and pain. Fear and desire.

"You know what I mean," she said, wanting to get the file away from him. "Puppy love. A teenage crush. Adolescent girls are always acting dramatic on TV, and if they think I'm—"

"This isn't a negotiation. You could go to jail while Evelyn's killer walks free." Raven took her face in his hands. If she wanted to, she could yank the file from under his arm and bolt out of the room. Race down to the station. Hand over their evidence. But in that moment, with his fingers brushing against her skin, she was frozen. He lowered his forehead to hers, and she told herself not to get her hopes up. He might not want to kiss her again. He might not want to lose himself in the feel of her, the softness of her breath, the taste of her lips.

But maybe he did. Jack tilted her head up and Raven tilted his head down, her stomach tightening as his lips neared hers. She needed him. She wanted him, and she was struck with the all-consuming power of letting yourself want someone you hadn't believed you could have. All the lies she'd told herself tumbled over her, lies about just wanting to be friends. Of living as brothers in the orchard. Kindred spirits, but nothing more. When he whispered, "Jack," like an incantation that could make impossible things real, she slid one arm around him, pressing her hand into the small of his back.

Drawing him near.

"Yes, Raven?" she murmured, brushing her lips across his jaw.

It was the lightest touch and it was electric. The crackle of energy before the downpour.

"I lost you for three years," he whispered into her mouth. His breath was life giving. Life affirming. "I will not lose you again."

He leaned in. Grazed his lips across hers, so softly. And then he left. One second he was cradling her face, and then his hand slid away, twisting open the door. Jack was too shaken to stop him. Too frozen in that moment and heavy with wanting. Lovesick. Love starved. When she finally realized where he was going, her legs stumbled after him, but it was too late. He'd gotten too far away. She arrived in the living room to find their evidence blackening in the flames. Off to the left, she could hear the boys laughing in the kitchen.

But she had no room for laughter in her shaking frame.

"Why?" she demanded, though he'd already told her, hadn't he? She just refused to believe him. This house was shit. Their yard was shit. And she was just the same—that's what her mother had told her, over and over until she'd believed it.

Until she'd felt it in her bones.

Now Raven was pulling out his phone to record the destruction of the file. "I won't let the police lock you up when you haven't done anything. You would never hurt anyone."

Jack brushed past him, reaching for the shovel that swung beside the fire poker. She desperately tried to fish the burning pages out of the flames. "We'll take pictures of the file," she stammered, stomping on the charred, curling pages. "We'll keep them as insurance."

"Jack, stop. I need to send this video to Lily, and right now you're in the frame."

"I'm not letting you send that video!" Jack dug another pile of pages out of the fire. She had no idea what order the pages were in now, or if any of them were readable, but she refused to give up on the *only* evidence they'd uncovered. The only real lead they had. She took picture after picture, and twenty minutes later, she was sitting on the floor, scanning through the photos.

Everything looked charred and wrinkled. She could barely make out a word.

"The file is destroyed," Raven said, crouching beside her. He scooped up the half-burned pages, dumping them back into the fireplace. "I'll send Lily a video to prove it, and then we can plan our next—"

Raven broke off at the sound of pounding on the front door. Jack's heart skittered into her throat. She told herself it was her mother, drunk and incapable of dredging her keys from the recesses of her purse. It had to be her mother. It couldn't be the police.

Jack took slow, unsteady breaths as Raven strode to the window, parting the heavy green curtains. His phone chimed. He pulled it out of his pocket, reading the message aloud. "'I warned you,'" he whispered as Jack caught a glimpse of flashing lights in the driveway.

"We took too long to send the video. We have to burn the other files before the police find them."

"*You* have to run," Raven countered, bolting back to Jack's bedroom. He returned seconds later, and before Jack could utter a word, he'd hurled all of their stolen files into the flames.

"Raven—"

"Go, now," he said as her brothers hurried in from the kitchen. Everyone Jack loved was in this room. How could she leave them? But the second Flynn saw police lights in the driveway, he put himself in front of the other boys. Raven took Conner's hand. Diego took Dylan's.

Jack backed away from the door, wondering if she should sneak out the back of the house or go through her bedroom window. If she went out the window, she'd have to scale her neighbor's fence. It would be difficult. Painful. But the police might be waiting for her in the backyard. Jack veered right, pushing into her bedroom, her heart beating as loudly as her steps. Each beat sent a jolt of panic through her. She couldn't breathe. Her hands shook as she reached for the window. It took a couple of tries to wrench it open, and then she was slipping outside at the exact perfect moment. The last of the light had bled from the sky, leaving the world not black but *absent of color*. No one could find her in the moment the sun dipped below the horizon, because no one could see anything in that moment, and soon she'd be climbing over the neighbor's fence. She'd be racing to freedom. She'd be—

A hand gripped the back of her jacket, jerking her to the ground. She fell fast. She fell hard. Her cheek slammed into a rock, and pain ricocheted through her, bringing tears to her eyes. She should've kissed Raven when she had the chance. She should've believed in his affection for her, *for once*, instead of doubting that anyone could really love her if they knew who she was.

Now she might never have the chance to tell him. Feel his arms wrap around her. She focused on this image as the officer jerked her to her feet. Handcuffs slid around her wrists easily, as if they'd been made for her, and she heard her mother's voice again.

Hadn't this been inevitable? The man was treating her like garbage, and it felt like a prophecy fulfilled. As if this were her destiny, and she was far from being the hero of her own story. The knight. The man dragged her toward the front of the house, where Raven was arguing with two uniformed men. Jack wanted to bolt over there, because the officers in this town weren't known for serving and protecting boys who looked like him, but as soon as she arrived on the scene, all eyes were on her.

When a man strode over to her, she took a resigned breath. "Detective," she managed through a swollen lip.

"Jack." Detective Medina frowned down at her, his head shaking in disappointment. "I got an anonymous tip on my way out of the station. The caller claimed you'd burned clothing in a fire the night after Evelyn's murder. They said the clothes are the key to finding the killer, and they sent me a vid—"

"You can't arrest me for burning clothes in a fire. That isn't illegal."

"You're right." The detective nodded. "But my boys are going over that fire with a fine-tooth comb, and they've already found a scrap of paper with Evelyn's letterhead on it. Care to explain?"

"I didn't—it isn't—"

"Please tell me you didn't break into Evelyn's office. We swept the place this morning, and there was a fresh set of fingerprints on the filing cabinet. Once I book you down at the station, we'll be able to figure out if those prints are a match."

Jack's eyelids fluttered closed, the muscles in her arms starting to cramp up. She wanted to stretch so badly. To scream. To run. "I want to talk to an attorney," she said, as Medina led her toward a car with blinking lights. "I can explain everything, but you aren't *listening* to me."

"Every time I listen to you, I catch you telling lies." He opened the door to the police car, guiding her inside. "Three years ago, you came to me with a story about Raven's wicked stepmother. Now she's dead. If I find out you had anything to do with what happened to her, I won't be arresting you for destroying evidence. I'll be arresting you for murder."

15

Kill Each Other Over Boys

When Jack arrived at the detention center, Belle was curled up in her cell, reading a book. There was no library within these gray, peeling walls, but donations arrived sporadically, and Belle had laid claim to an old book of fairy tales, not unlike the ones she had at home.

It gave her a small measure of peace.

But when she saw the familiar face peering through the bars, that peace crumbled like a castle long battered by the winds. The cell clanked open, and Jack was nudged inside, dressed in a nondescript gray sweatshirt and matching pants. The standard uniform in this glorified prison for minors. The guard provided a clipped introduction, which Belle did not find necessary, considering her history with Jack. But she thought it might be wise to play it cool and pretend the two were strangers.

Until they were alone.

That quality alone time came swiftly, as the cell was closed and locked once more. Belle watched Jack through the limp strands of her hair. She could live without the curling iron and the hair dryer, the kohl liner, and the dresses of satin and lace. But every time that cell closed, a panic was incited in her chest. She wasn't *like* a caged animal in those seconds. She was a living, breathing creature in a literal cage, and she thought she'd do anything to get out of it.

At the present moment, she had something to focus on, and it loosened the tightness in her stomach. As Jack shuffled into the small gray cell, Belle set her book of fairy tales aside, rising to her feet.

"You look like shit," she said, and Jack's head snapped up.

"Belle."

"You don't get to call me that. You can call me Belladonna, after the flowers you stole from my garden." She narrowed her eyes. "You must've snuck over after I went to bed that night and carried your little bouquet to Evelyn's house—"

"I didn't poison Raven's stepmother! I offered to get you out of here, remember?" Jack shook her head in exasperation. "I went to the cops and provided *your* alibi, but the detective wouldn't listen to me. He said I had a 'history of telling stories.'"

"Man, he has you pegged. Jack the storyteller. Jack the liar."

Jack's face flushed burgundy, and Belle stepped closer. There were no weapons in this cell. The table and chair in the corner were bolted to the floor, and the bedding would've made a pathetic noose. That threadbare fabric could disintegrate in an instant. The charcoal-gray blankets already looked like dust. No, Belle would have to use her words to slice Jack open and leave her gutted.

"When you offered to be my alibi, I had this intense rush of relief and . . . *shame* for how I treated you over the past few years. But then—" Belle huffed, wagging her finger in the air. "Then I realized you weren't providing an alibi for me. You were providing one for yourself."

"I was home that night," Jack insisted, striding past Belle. She sat down on the bottom bunk, curling into herself. "My brothers can account for me."

"Your brothers would lie for you in an instant." Belle stepped up close. "And before you bring up your mom, I need you to remember that I know you very well. I know you better than Raven. I know you better than that detective who thinks you're some sweet little girl who got caught up in someone else's darkness. *You're* the one with the darkness in you, Jack. You lie and you steal, and you never care who you hurt."

"I don't—"

"I saw you," Belle snapped, plucking the book of fairy tales from the bed. She flipped through the old, yellowed pages, landing on an image of crows descending on Cinderella's stepsister. "I went to see Raven the night before he left for boarding school. I saw you wrap your fingers around his shirt and pull him closer. I saw you kiss him, and it hurt so badly, I wanted to summon the crows and laugh as they clawed at your skin."

Belle flipped to another chapter, where a young, beautiful girl pushed a crone off a cliff. "I wanted to kill Raven's stepmother for putting him in danger. But you know what I realized, sitting alone in my library after Raven left town?"

"What?" Jack swallowed, visibly steeling herself against the daggers in Belle's voice.

"I thought I had to punish you for snatching Raven out from under me. I thought I had to poison Evelyn to keep him alive." Belle trailed her finger along the spine of the book, touching the names printed there. "It's what they wanted me to think."

"Who?"

Belle strode over to the desk in the corner. After opening a drawer, she pulled out a crumpled piece of paper where she'd been keeping a tally of every storyteller who'd given her ideas as a child. She could be a princess, waiting patiently for a prince to save her. Or she could be a witch, wicked and powerful and wild.

She returned to Jack, smoothing out the piece of paper before handing it over. "Notice anything?" she asked, pointing to the list of storytellers she'd loved so much. "What do they all have in common?"

"They're old dead guys?" Jack said, brow wrinkling at the list.

"Take out dead."

"They're old guys?"

"Take out old."

"Belle." Jack looked up, shaking her head. "What are you—"

"*They* taught us to hate each other over beauty. To kill each other over boys. They taught us to cut off pieces of our bodies in order to make ourselves smaller—"

"You're blaming fairy tales for what we almost did? We almost killed a person, and we knew exactly what we were doing. I did."

"And you called it off at the last minute because you're the knight. I'm the witch. And Raven's the bright, shining prince that all of us were willing to kill for, if it meant saving him from someone truly evil. But you know what's funny, Jack?" Belle sat on the bunk, her heart racing so fast, it was hard to push out the words. "I grew up with a man who hammered nails into my windows and locked my door from the outside. You grew up with a woman who told you, over and over again, that you were nothing. Garbage. Shit. We could've done any number of things to get away from them—"

"We learned how to creep down ladders and climb up vines. And you found that skeleton key at a thrift shop when we were fourteen, which made it easier to get out of your room."

Belle snorted. "We learned how to hide. To sneak. To lie. But we never fought for ourselves. We only fought for Raven."

"Raven was our family," Jack managed, crumpling the paper. "And sometimes it's easier to fight for other people than to fight for ourselves."

"Like with your brothers," Belle said calmly. Casually.

Jack's ears reddened, her gaze dropping to her hands. "What are you talking about? My brothers don't have anything to do with this."

"I thought so too, at first. When Lily came to visit me here and said you were sneaking around, burning Raven's clothes in a fireplace, I thought there had to be a logical explanation. You couldn't have killed his stepmother and framed me for it, because you were the one who called off the murder. You didn't have a violent bone in your body."

"I don't."

"You do." Belle's smile cut across her face, sharp as a scimitar and equally deadly. "I just had to figure out the connection between everything. You called off the murder so suddenly, just days after your mom's boyfriend fell down the stairs. He swore somebody tripped him. He refused to come back to your house after that," Belle added, and it didn't escape her attention that Jack's breathing had gone shallow.

"I didn't trip him," Jack whispered. "I couldn't have tripped him, because he fell down the attic stairs, and I was in my bedroom sleeping when it happened. My mom came out of her room first, and I came out after her. It would've been impossible—"

"Yeah, I remember what you told the police," Belle broke in. "You recited it to me and Raven like you were quoting from a script. But I have a theory about what happened that night, just like I have a theory about what happened the night Evelyn was murdered. If you don't start telling the truth, I'm going to take both theories to the police."

Jack's eyes were on the ground. She was sinking into her ratty gray sweats, as if she might disappear entirely. But there was no escaping this facility, just like there was no escaping what she'd done. "What's your theory about the other night?"

Belle leaned in as a guard passed their cell, briefly glancing inside. A moment later, she said, "You've been in love with Raven for a very long time. You thought you loved him enough to kill for him, but then your mom's boyfriend fell down the stairs. He claimed someone tripped him, and if the police found a petal of poppy in Evelyn's tea *a few days later*, they might suspect you'd gone all vigilante on the adults in town. So you found a way to protect Raven without risking arrest, and you found a way to feel close to him, even when he was gone." Here, she flicked her gaze to Jack's clothes, and even though they weren't the familiar T-shirts and jeans Jack had been sporting for the past three years, Jack clearly caught Belle's meaning. "Did you think I wouldn't figure out that you were wearing his clothes to school? I went shopping with him for half those clothes. Peeled some of them off him, too."

Jack flinched at that. Her entire body seized up, and in that moment, Belle knew that she really did love Raven. Completely. Desperately. But desperation led to ugly things when little girls were raised on fairy tales, and Jack was not the hero in this scenario.

She was the villain.

"Then you heard Raven was coming home, and you realized you had a choice to make." Belle paused for a beat, then two. "You could let Evelyn torture him again, and you could let me try to steal him back, or . . . you could get rid of both of us in one fell swoop."

Jack's face was pale as marble, her breathing so quiet, it didn't make a sound. She sat still as a statue, as if waiting to be shattered by a hammer.

Belle smiled at the thought. "There's just one thing I don't understand," she admitted. "Sneaking into my garden would've been easy, and getting Evelyn to drink poisonous tea was probably a piece of cake. Catching that man creeping up to your attic, though . . . how did you do it? How did you make it back to your bedroom by the time he'd fallen down those stairs?"

"I didn't—"

"You're lying. You've always been the liar, Jack. But I want to understand why you did what you did. Was he messing with your brothers? It's the only explanation, isn't it? You couldn't have been defending yourself. We've already established that we don't do that. We only rescue boys."

"Stop." Jack's head was bowed, her body trembling. Tears had gathered in her lashes. But she didn't lift her hands from the blankets, where they were digging into the fabric so tightly, her knuckles had gone completely white. "Please don't tell anyone about this. They wouldn't understand. You don't understand."

"Then help me understand! Help me see how all of this ties together. The death of Lily's mother. The police dragging me away from my house in the middle of the night. It all starts with you and the night that man went crashing down your attic stairs. You broke his bones."

Jack's head snapped up, and she wasn't crying anymore. Her grip on the blankets had loosened. When she opened her mouth to speak, there was a curious light in her eyes. "I wanted to break his neck."

16

Jack and the Giant

The first time Jack encountered a giant, she was seven years old. The man towered over her at six foot four. Jack saw his big, meaty fists and thought of glass breaking and bones cracking. She knew what would happen, even before he threw a punch.

He didn't hit anything at first. Most monsters put on a beautiful mask in order to get into your house. They smiled politely and made you dinner, ruffling your little brother's hair. Flynn was four at the time, and Conner and Dylan hadn't been born yet, so Jack only had two people to take care of.

Flynn and her mother.

It was funny, though. The man seemed perfectly happy when it was just him and Jack's mom. He only became agitated when reminded that his bright-eyed, giggling girlfriend had children.

When the first plate was hurled against the wall, and shattered into pieces, Jack simply took her brother's hand and removed him from the situation. She invented a game she would later play with Raven, scouring the neighborhood for swords and magical artifacts that might help them take down a giant. And while they never succeeded in defeating him, they kept themselves out of danger, and it was enough.

For a while.

Then came a man with lazy, drooping eyelids that could barely stay open. When he was around, Jack's mother appeared to be in a permanent state of lethargy, draping her body across the couch or hunching over in a kitchen chair. Jack spent those months making sure her brother ate, and when the new baby came along, she learned how to change diapers and heat formula, and life went on.

One man left and another arrived. Sometimes a wall would get punched, and sometimes Jack's mother would disappear for several nights on end, leaving Jack to care for yet *another* screaming baby, but none of her little brothers were bruised or broken.

She kept them safe.

Then a man arrived in a forest-green baseball cap with the lying smile of a fox. He slunk through the house on gangly limbs, tall and sinewy but not bulky. There was something incongruous about him. He didn't seem particularly insidious, and yet Conner and Dylan started flinching in his presence. Little patterns of bruises appeared on their wrists, as if they were being grabbed when no one was watching. But the bruises faded within a couple of days, and the boys never admitted that anything was happening.

Jack couldn't prove it.

One night, when she was fourteen years old, she heard the creak of footsteps outside her bedroom. Her mother's footsteps were very recognizable, either shuffling or thudding, depending on the amount of alcohol she'd ingested. These footsteps were slippery, as if someone were sliding across the floor in stockinged feet. They were soft as a whisper. Quiet as deception. They paused outside Jack's door, and she tensed, pulling the blankets up to her neck as if that might protect her. All her childhood instincts kicked in at that moment. She made sure her feet were tucked under the covers. Investigated the movement of the shadows, seeking strangeness. She was almost certain she could hear the doorknob twisting, but within a couple of seconds, the footsteps had moved on, and she relaxed. Closed her eyes. And then . . .

A soft creak on the stairs. The squat, ramshackle house boasted only one story, but there was a twisting staircase that led to the attic. The place where her brothers slept. Jack disentangled from her blankets. She stood a little shakily, heart racing and mind spinning and not entirely sure what to think. She had a terrible feeling blooming in the pit of her stomach, but her brain wouldn't allow her to consider the possibilities of what might unfold in that attic.

There was a wall inside her, protecting her from reality.

But her brothers weren't being protected. The three of them were huddled together in one bed, and if someone crept up to them while they were sleeping, they wouldn't be able to defend themselves. They might not even know they needed to until they were already trapped. Some giants stomped around, their heavy footfalls warning of their arrival. But others were surprisingly fleet of foot, and by the time you realized they were towering over you, you had nowhere to go.

Jack tiptoed to her door, as quietly as the giant himself. She twisted the knob, ever so gently. Poked her head outside. No one was in the hallway, and after checking that her mother's door was completely shut, she made her way down the hall, through the living room, and toward the attic stairs.

He'd made a decent amount of progress in that time. Jack had expected to catch him halfway up the staircase, but he'd already made it to the boys' door. With a twist of the knob, it groaned open. He slipped inside. A minute later, he appeared in the doorway again, and Conner was with him. Jack's youngest brother was squirming to get out of the man's grip, but his wrist was clasped as if in a vise. The man loomed over him. Pulled Conner close and hissed about wasteful little boys who didn't finish their dinner. Jack narrowed her eyes, thinking back to earlier that evening. Conner had refused to finish the meat loaf the man had brought him from the diner where he worked because it had mold on the corner.

"I'm doing everything I can to provide for this family," the man snarled, while Conner cowered beneath him. "Your mother would starve without me taking care of her. Is that what you want?"

Conner shook his head, tears streaming down his cheeks. He was wearing his superhero pajamas. It broke Jack's heart to look at him, so little and so terrified. He jerked away from the man for the briefest instant, backing against the window near the top of the stairs.

That was when Jack noticed the vine. One year earlier, Raven had helped her plant that small packet of beans, and now that spring had come again, the vine was climbing up the side of the house. It peeked through the window where Conner was cowering. When the man's temper calmed, and he ushered Conner back through the doorway to the attic, Jack didn't pause to think. She simply crept up the attic stairs, opened the window farther, and pulled that long, twisting vine into the house. She guided it across the third stair from the top, tying the end to the banister, but not too tight. Then she rapped her knuckles against the boys' bedroom door. The man barked at Conner to stay inside the room, and a moment later, Jack heard the whisper of soft, slippery footsteps approaching. She raced down the stairs, out the side door, and into the yard. The door had just closed behind her when she heard the scream.

There came a single thud, followed by tumbling. Groans. An instant later, she heard the sharp cracking of a bone. It was remarkably loud, considering all sound was making its way to her through the window, and when the man started to cry, she crept up to the side of the house, tugging at the vine.

Little by little she gathered it in her hands, and when she was certain she'd pulled the last of it from the attic stairway, she hurried around the house, entering her bedroom through the window. Then she waited. It didn't take long for her mother to wake, and as soon as Ms. McClain had staggered down the hallway, Jack opened her bedroom door. She needed her mother to hear her coming out, so that no one would figure out what she'd done.

And no one did. Not when the police arrived and took everyone's statement. Not when they studied the stairs for signs of foul play. The man insisted that he'd been tripped, but without anything to back up his claim, the police had no reason to believe him.

He couldn't prove it.

17

I'm Good at Taking Things

Belle inhaled slowly, her breath rattling against her ribs like a ghost shaking loose from a skeleton. Beside her, Jack was hunched over on the bunk bed, head clutched in her hands.

"You tripped that man," Belle said, her voice soft and her head close to Jack's ear.

"Yes."

"That's why you called off the murder of Raven's stepmother. Because you almost killed a person, and it scared you to know you were capable of that."

"No." Jack lifted her head, her gaze steely. Unflinching. "I was shaking for days after it happened, and I could hardly eat or sleep, but I wasn't sorry for what I did to that man. I didn't feel guilty." A beat, followed by a breath. "I called off the murder because I didn't want Raven to see what was inside me. I would lose him, and I wouldn't be able to stand it. That hasn't changed."

Belle swallowed, anger slipping off her the way grime slips off a body during a long, satisfying shower. The kind she would take if she ever got out of this place. "You didn't kill Evelyn Holloway."

A slight shake of the head. "Of course I didn't, Belle. I'm not who you think I am."

"Then who the hell did it? I didn't kill her, and Lily was accounted for all night—"

"By her dad."

Belle's head snapped up. "What did you say?"

"Lily spent that whole night with her dad. I guess he went to visit her at the facility, and they spent hours going over the paperwork for him to get full custody." Jack shook her head, tapping her fingers on the blanket. "If both of them were accounted for, then I don't know—"

"Lily wasn't with her dad."

Jack turned to her, eyes narrowed, and Belle told herself to stop talking. She'd distrusted Jack for so long. She'd had reason to distrust Jack *and* Raven, but their crimes felt minuscule in comparison to the horror unfolding around her now. Someone had framed her for the murder of Evelyn Holloway. Now Jack was locked up beside her, but it couldn't have been Lily who was punishing them for their adolescent plot.

Belle knew it for a fact.

"Lily was with me that night," she said softly. "We started talking a few months after Raven went to boarding school, and by the time he was on his way home, she and I were . . ."

"Close," Jack finished, and mercifully didn't ask her to elaborate. For that, Belle was grateful. Belle's entanglement with Lily was nothing to be ashamed of, but for the time being, it was *theirs*. She didn't want to share it. She especially didn't want to detail the greatest night of her life while locked in a dingy cell with the person she'd hated for years.

Those moments had been sacred. Those kisses, life affirming. And that touch . . . no, she wouldn't sully the beauty of what they had just to convince Jack of Lily's innocence.

"She got to my house around ten thirty," Belle said, because this was the important part. The timing. The facts. "According to the police, Evelyn was killed between eleven and one. Lily *couldn't* have done it. She was with me that whole time, which means—"

"She's covering for her dad."

Belle nodded, a heaviness pressing into her chest. "When the cops showed up at my door in the middle of the night, I thought they were there because Lily had snuck out of the facility. I sent her out the back door. By the time I realized they were there to arrest me, she was long gone."

"And you thought she'd gone back to the facility."

"*Yes*. I thought she'd get in trouble if anyone knew she'd broken out. They'd punish her, or drug her up, or send her to a higher-security facility. So I kept quiet when the detective asked about my alibi. I thought I was protecting her, when all that time she could've been protecting me. She could've told the truth instead of claiming she was with her dad."

"Why would she throw you under the bus to protect him?"

"She must not think he's the killer," Belle said, her heart clenching as if a fist had wrapped around it. "At the very least, she's in denial about it. He spent the past year looking for a steady job and a place for them to live. The thought of losing him, after just losing her mom, must be crushing. So Lily started looking for another suspect, and when she saw you burning Raven's clothes, she thought you might've committed the murder while wearing them. She knew you kissed Raven behind my back. I told her, because I'd come up with this plan—"

"About the kiss," Jack broke in, and Belle shook her head, wincing.

"I'm not ready, Jack. I believe you didn't kill Lily's mother, but I'm not ready to forgive you for kissing Raven. He'd just broken up with me. My heart was already so battered, and when I saw the two of you in the rose garden, I swear, my heart tumbled out of my chest. I felt empty for months. And then . . ." Belle closed her eyes, the sweetness of a memory washing over her. She'd been visiting Lily in the wellness facility for more than a year when she'd told Lily what had happened to her heart. The ache of her chest cavity opening and the detached sense of horror when she'd felt her heart, raw and red, slipping out. It had fallen into the dirt, gathering thorns and leaves.

She'd left it there to rot.

"My mother replaced the roses," Lily had said, tucking a pale strand of hair behind her ear. She was wearing her usual bulky sweater, with at least two T-shirts beneath it. "She doesn't visit me often, but we've been emailing a bit, and she told me a story about planting white roses to replace the red. Those are her favorite, you know? They're pure and chaste, like her daughter." A smile, followed by a grimace. "But something strange is happening in the garden. One of the roses keeps growing back red. She's tried cutting it out, and she's tried digging it up, but it just keeps coming back. Belle, I think that rose is your heart."

Belle burst into laughter, because the suggestion was absurd. Impossible. And yet, at the mention of her heart, still alive and causing Lily's mother grief, she'd felt a stirring in her chest that she hadn't felt since Raven had left town.

She strolled out of the facility that day with a spring in her step and a great, buffoonish grin on her face. She didn't care who might see it. For the next few days, Belle was giddy with the thought of her heart surviving the worst thing she'd been able to imagine: the loss of the boy she loved and her best friend.

She didn't visit Holloway Manor right away. Deep down in her gut, she feared Lily's story had been just that: a fairy tale to carry her through dark times. A fable to help her sleep at night. But Belle had never been one for pleasing lies, and by the end of the week, she decided to pay a visit to Raven's estate during her lunch break. She snuck through the back gate. Crept up to the perfectly manicured garden and saw . . . a sea of white roses. No red sprung up among them, and no crimson petals dotted the ground, hinting at a recent pruning.

The red rose did not exist.

Belle started to cry then, big, blubbery tears that filled her with shame. She shouldn't have wanted this. Shouldn't have believed in magical roses or hearts that could be resurrected. Something inside her had died the night she'd watched Raven kiss Jack, and it would never come back to life.

She returned to Lily in a rage. Her friend was sitting in the common area, flipping through a magazine.

"How could you do that?" Belle hissed, sitting beside Lily on the patchwork couch. "How could you lie to me? I found your father for you, and I made sure he wanted to see you before I gave you his name."

"You didn't give me his name." Lily hadn't looked up from the page. Her voice was calm, unconcerned. "I stole it from you."

"Fine, you stole it from me. You're good at taking things and not giving back."

"You're right, I'm good at taking things." Lily pushed off the couch. With a wave of her hand, she led Belle past the common area, down the hall, and through the open door of her room. The bed was unmade. The stack of magazines on the bedside table, arranged haphazardly. Beside the stack sat a vase, and rising up from the clear, elegant crystal was a crimson rose.

"Is that . . ." Belle approached the vase with caution, a softness rustling in her chest. "How did you—"

"My dad cut it for me. We've been emailing for months, and when he offered to come see me, I asked if he could sneak onto the estate and bring the red rose to me. He works the night shift at a plant nursery so he's very good at keeping flowers alive. This one's been here for almost a week." Lily came up behind her, and Belle could feel her presence as strongly as she'd felt Raven's absence in the months after he went away. "You're lucky you came when you did. It's starting to wilt."

Here, Belle's gaze dropped to the smattering of petals already on the table. Living things were so fragile. So quick to wither and die. What would happen to her when the last petal fell?

"You know what I think?" Lily strode past her and sat on the bed. Her fingers brushed the petals of the rose with so much tenderness, Belle swore she felt movement in her chest. Not quite a beat. But a definite pulse. "I think you cast a spell that day, standing in the rose garden and feeling your heart break. I think you let it go because you thought it would kill you to feel that pain. But you're stronger now." She patted the bed, and Belle sat beside her, her stomach tightening in anticipation. Lily turned to her. She turned to Lily. "There's only one way to break the spell," Lily said. Miraculously, her hand was no longer caressing the rose, but rather had come to rest on Belle's.

That time she felt more than a pulsing inside her chest. She felt a thud. "How?" she asked, turning her hand over so they could lace their fingers together.

"You have to kiss someone." Lily looked up, a slight quirk in her lips. "Someone you love. Do you think you can do it?"

Belle sucked in a breath, forcing herself to look Lily in the eyes. "I can try," she whispered, and though nothing happened between them that night, the possibilities unfolded inside her like pathways twisting in a forest. They could have adventures together, and maybe someday her heart would be healed enough to let Lily in.

Now, sitting in a cold gray cell, she thought of what that hope had cost her. Lily had left her in this place, and Lily had not even tried to provide her with an alibi, because Lily was protecting her dad.

"We need to call Raven," Belle whispered to Jack. "Lily hid the *Recipe for the Perfect Murder* in the orchard, and if she mentioned the location to her dad, he must've gone looking for it. Maybe he left evidence out there. A strand of hair or a piece of his jacket."

"It's a long shot," Jack replied. "And if Lily told her dad where to find the recipe, she'd *have* to know he poisoned Evelyn. Maybe he overheard her talking about it."

"Where? She's been at the facility for the past three years, and the walls there are thick. It's not like at Raven's house, where you can hear people talking through the vents." Belle frowned, her brow furrowing. "I went over there the day Evelyn died, you know. To search Raven's room."

"Raven told me," Jack said, taking a deep breath. "They got you on camera entering the estate. I assume you wouldn't have gone through the front gate if you were planning to murder someone."

Belle huffed, shaking her head ruefully. "I wanted to check for cars in the driveway. To make sure no one was home. Once I knew the house was empty, I went up to Raven's room, but I kept thinking about the vents. How he could hear his parents arguing back when Arianna was alive. How I'd put a pillow over his vent when we wanted privacy—" Belle broke off at the sound of the cell clattering open. A broad-shouldered woman stuck her head inside, gesturing at the girls. That was what Belle thought. But when both of them stood from the bunk, the woman held up a hand, saying, "McClain, you're being released."

"What?" Jack's eyes went wide as she stumbled toward the guard. "How? Is my mom picking me up? Did she back up—"

"Not your mother," the woman said, muttering something into a radio and getting a crackling response. "Stefan Holloway."

18

The Secret That's Been Crushing You

Raven Holloway was not a liar. But these were desperate times. It took about an hour to convince his father to go along with his plan, and another hour and a half before they tracked down the detective and fed him their story. By the time Raven arrived at the juvenile detention center, he felt as if winds were kicking up dust in his chest, rustling leaves and knocking down branches. He hadn't wanted to lie to the police.

But he needed to rescue Jack.

Now he sat patiently in the passenger seat of his family's sedan as Dr. Holloway went to check Jack out of the detention center. He couldn't stop tapping his fingers on the dash. The clock blinked back at him, flashing 9:13 p.m., and he wondered what horrors Jack had already endured inside that hideous orange building.

To curb the panic inside his chest, he slid out of the front seat, climbing into the back, where Jack could meet him. She would be exhausted from her time in the detention center. If she needed a shoulder to rest on, Raven could provide that for her, and maybe, over the course of the ride home, her hand would slide into his.

And he'd never let her go.

Seconds turned into minutes. When the door finally opened, Raven half expected an officer to duck into the car, cuffs in hand. Instead, he saw a familiar tuft of auburn curls, and the breath rushed out of him. She was here, sliding into the seat beside him, her bright green eyes filled with wonder and awe.

"How—?" she began, as Dr. Holloway opened the driver's side door. He settled into his seat, closed the door, and turned to look at her.

"You don't have to worry. Everything's taken care of." He was wearing a freshly pressed suit, and his face was clean shaven. His dark hair, combed and styled. All of this had been Raven's idea, because they'd needed to sell their story to the police. "Your brothers are sleeping in our guest rooms, along with Flynn's new friend, while the police track down your mother."

Jack looked from Dr. Holloway to Raven. "But I don't understand. How did you get me out?"

"Raven told me you broke into Evelyn's office." Dr. Holloway pulled out of the parking lot, easing the sedan onto the street. "He explained that you were looking for a suspect, so you could clear Belladonna's name. You copied the files of her clients, and when the police arrived, you tried to burn them before you were found out."

"I . . . yeah, that's what happened." Jack's face was tomato red. Her gaze was on her feet. "You aren't mad?"

"I wasn't thrilled when I heard about what you did," Raven's dad said, signaling to turn left. "But we're all trying to make sense of what happened to my wife, and I understand why you did what you did. The police asked me if I wanted to press charges, since I'm leasing Evelyn's office. I said no."

"You did?" Jack stammered, looking to Raven in shock. "But the police aren't going to let this go. They think—"

"I know what they think," Stefan said gently. "That's why I sat down with the detective and explained that you couldn't have had anything to do with Evelyn's death. You were with me at the airport the entire time."

"What?" The curve in Jack's frown made Raven's stomach hurt. He wanted to trace his fingers across those lips, teasing a smile out of her. He couldn't help but notice that their hands were far apart. If he wanted to brush his pinkie against hers, he'd have to cross an ocean to reach her.

"My original flight was canceled," Raven explained, inching his hand closer. Just a little. "But my dad didn't get the message about it, so he thought I was getting in at eleven thirty. The camera on the front gate captured him leaving the house at ten o'clock. Since the airport is two towns over, it takes an hour and a half to get there. He was five minutes away when he thought to check his phone, and that's when he realized I wouldn't be getting in until the next day. So he went home."

"And he found . . ." Jack didn't speak the word *Evelyn* aloud.

She must've suspected it would feel like a knife in Dr. Holloway's heart. It would probably always feel like a jagged blade had lodged itself there, making it difficult to breathe. Speak. Sleep. Raven knew that feeling well, and his heart surged with warmth when Jack's fingers found *his* across the wide expanse of the car.

"Evelyn died between eleven and one," Raven said, hitching in a breath. He felt guilty for thinking of his mom when she wasn't the one who'd just died, but if *she* hadn't been killed, she'd be sitting in the front seat right now, her fingers twining with his dad's. Then again, if *she* hadn't been killed, Evelyn would've never moved into their house, and none of this would've happened.

The thought unsettled him.

"It would've been literally impossible for you to have poisoned her," Raven pushed on, ignoring the intake of breath from the front of the car. The tensing of his father's shoulders. He *had* to explain this part, in order for Jack to understand their deception. "You were in the car with my dad at the time, driving back from the airport. As soon as we explained that to the detective, he put in the call to let you out."

"But I told him I'd been with Belle," Jack blurted, almost as if she hadn't wanted to. Those words had a mind of their own. They slipped into the world, trickling around the quiet of the sedan. "I gave Belle an alibi."

"And the detective knew you were lying," Raven said calmly. "If you'd told him you were with my dad, it would've sealed Belle's fate."

"Didn't he think it was strange?" Jack's brow was furrowed,

her gaze shifting to Raven's dad in the front seat. "He interviewed you the night of the murder, right? Wouldn't you have mentioned me then?"

"I was in shock," Dr. Holloway said simply. "I hardly remembered the drive to the airport, let alone what happened after. The detective understood that, and he has me on camera leaving the house at ten. He has me on camera coming back after one."

Jack was silent a minute. They were nearing Holloway Manor, and the camera above the gate captured their progress toward the great stone house. The house that had felt haunted for years. The house that felt more haunted now. Raven hoped Jack would stay in his room that night. They could lie under his covers, all wrapped up together. They could protect each other from the storms raging in their hearts and the eerie quiet of the world outside.

When the car came to a stop, Jack finally spoke. "I don't understand why you did this. You know I wasn't at the airport that night. I was at home with my brothers, and if anyone finds out that you lied—"

"They won't." It was Dr. Holloway who spoke the words, his body twisted to look at Jack. His gaze was soft. Kind. "Ever since I've known you, you've looked after my son. I know you'd never do anything to hurt this family."

"I wouldn't," Jack agreed, wrapping her arms around herself. "Raven is my family."

"I know that, too," Dr. Holloway said. He put the car in park. "And I will never let anything happen to this family again." Here, he flashed a watery smile and climbed out of his seat. A moment later, Jack's door opened and his hand appeared in the doorway. Jack took it, letting Dr. Holloway guide her out of the car.

Raven followed, joining them in the driveway.

"You're welcome to sleep over," Dr. Holloway said, waving them toward the house. "The boys are settled into the guest rooms, but Lily's staying at her father's tonight, so her room will be empty." At the mention of Andrew Kane, Raven's stomach flipped. Getting Jack out of that detention center was only step one of his plan.

The next step was to rescue Lily.

For now, Raven led Jack into the house, ushering her toward the stairs. Jack could shower and change into something more comfortable. Once they reached the upstairs bathroom, he waved her inside. "We'll talk after," was all he said.

Jack nodded, relief loosening her shoulders. "Thank you. You didn't have to—"

"I know."

"Your dad didn't have to—"

"You heard what he said," Raven broke in, pulling a black, fluffy towel from the hall closet. One of his mom's towels. "You're family now. So you might as well use the amenities."

A hint of a smile, and then Jack was plucking the towel from his hands. She disappeared into the bathroom, closing the door with a click. Raven didn't wait around for her. Instead, he hurried to Lily's room, putting new sheets on the bed. He fluffed up the pillows, then raided Lily's closet, but she must've taken her entire wardrobe to her dad's.

The closet was empty.

Twenty minutes later, Jack slipped into Lily's bedroom to find a white collared shirt and jeans laid out on the bed. She closed the door behind her, clutching the towel to her chest. "Raven."

"I want you to wear them," he said. "I mean, if you want to."

"You can't give me your clothes. Not after I stole—"

"I didn't even miss them." He tossed her a smile, striding toward the door. "I'll come back in a few minutes, after you're dressed, and we can talk about everything that's happened. All right?"

Jack nodded numbly. Her eyes were brimming with tears.

Raven gave her ample time before knocking on the door. He opened it slowly, peering inside. Jack was sitting on Lily's bed, her curls damp and dangling over one shoulder. Raven's white collared shirt clung to her skin. She'd rolled up his jeans on the bottoms, so they didn't drag on the floor. She looked more comfortable than he'd seen her look since he'd come back from school, and he wanted to empty his dresser drawers and hand over his wardrobe.

Gingerly, he sat on the edge of the bed. "You don't have to tell me tonight," he began, tracing his fingers along the lace of Lily's white bedspread. His fingers ached to touch Jack. To trail across her chest until her heartbeat sprang to life and he knew, definitively, that she was all right. "We can talk about Belle, and the detention center, after you've eaten and gotten some sleep."

"I have to tell you now." She lifted a pillow from the bed, then placed it over the heating vent on Lily's floor. For years Raven had heard his parents arguing through the vent in his bedroom, because his vent connected to theirs. Lily's might've led somewhere different, but it was better to be safe than sorry. "Belle figured something out about me," Jack said, returning to Raven's side, "and I want to tell you before she does."

"I think I know."

Her head snapped up, swiveling to look at him. "You know? How could you—"

"Why do you think I gave you my clothes?"

Silence. It was the kind of deep, oppressive quiet that left a ringing in your ears that you *knew* you were imagining, and yet . . . it filled everything. There was a keening in Raven's mind. A sharp, gutting fear that he'd said the wrong thing, or pushed her too hard. But he wanted to know her so badly. And if "her" wasn't the right word to be using, he wanted to know that, too.

"You don't have to tell me anything," he began, and he already felt like he was rambling. Like there were no right words for what he needed to say. "But I want you to know that I know who you are. Deep down. And nothing you could tell me—"

"Belle thought I murdered Evelyn. She accused me at the detention center. She knows that we kissed the night before you left for school and . . ." Jack swallowed, fingers tightening on the hem of her shirt. She always grabbed on to something when she felt like she was falling. Raven knew this, and he wanted to reach out his arms and catch her, but he couldn't do it.

Not unless she let him.

"Belle thought I murdered your stepmom and framed her so

that I could have you all to myself. But I'd never do that, Raven."

"I know that. I know you—"

"You don't," she snapped, and she sounded angry. Defensive. "You make guesses, and you're trying to be a good person, but that's not the same as knowing me. There are things I've done . . . things I *am* that you couldn't understand."

"That's fine. That's fair," he said quickly, ignoring the storm in his chest. The crackle of thunder. The sizzle of lightning. "I'm not trying to tell you I understand. But I want you to talk to me. I want you to know that you *can* if that's something you want. It's okay to be scared and it's okay to protect yourself. But don't keep something from me because you think I can't handle it."

Jack took a slow, deep breath, and he wondered if torrential rains were raging inside her, too. If she was drowning in them. "The week before you left for boarding school, I stretched a vine across the attic stairs and tripped the man my mother was seeing. He'd been sneaking up to the boys' room, hurting them when no one was around, so I hurt him back. I did what I had to do."

Raven stared at her, unblinking. "What else?" he managed, his voice cracking. A moment ago, he'd been in the midst of a storm, but now the winds had died down completely, leaving him to pick through the rubble.

"The detective found a note in the kitchen the night your stepmother was killed. 'One petal of belladonna. One petal of poppy. Drop into a teacup and stir three times.'" Jack looked up, her lip trembling. "Belle called it the *Recipe for the Perfect Murder*. She wrote it three years ago."

"What?" It was the only word Raven could muster. The only sentence his lips could manage to form.

"We *were* planning to kill your stepmom," Jack said softly. "Belle came up with the plan a month before you left town. It was supposed to happen the night before the Apple Blossom Festival, because half the girls in town would be wearing flower garlands."

"And some of the boys." It was a curious thing to stick on, in that moment. But Raven's mother used to nestle roses in his curls. While the girls in town sported blossoms of pink and white, Arianna Holloway would weave a garland of crimson roses and crown him with it each year. It was one of his favorite memories of her.

Those garlands had been sacred.

Jack tilted her head, a soft smile on her face. "Half the girls, and some of the boys," she corrected, and Raven saw a tear slide down her cheek. "Lily found the recipe in the orchard, and she hid it so she could use it as blackmail."

"Blackmail for what?"

Jack cringed, swallowing audibly. "She wanted to be included in the plan. She suggested we weave poisonous flowers into our garlands so it looked like an accident when a few petals fell into Evelyn's tea. She was going to weave lilies into her garland, and I was going to weave poppies. With Belle, you can guess."

"Belladonna from her garden."

A nod, as she wiped away the tear. In spite of everything she'd told him, Raven's fingers twitched at the movement. He wanted to soothe her suffering. To find any wounds she might be hiding and kiss them with gentle lips. "As we got closer to the night of the murder, Belle started to hint that we should each drop a few belladonna berries into Evelyn's tea along with the petals. Just to make sure the plan worked. But after Mom's boyfriend fell down the stairs, I realized I couldn't go through with the poisoning. I knew how it felt to take someone's life in my hands. And if you'd ever found out that I'd killed your stepmom, you wouldn't have been able to look at me."

A beat, as Raven exhaled. "But you didn't do it."

"I came close. And I almost killed that man because of what he was doing to my brothers. I wanted to kill him, Raven."

He nodded, his eyes never leaving her face. "If I ever found the man who shot my mom, I would wrap my hands around his throat—"

"You wouldn't."

Raven's face broke into a grin. It was the kind of sharp, jagged grin that Belle had flashed a hundred times, before threatening someone with the flowers from her garden. That smile held no compassion. Only malice. "I would do what I needed to do." He scooted toward her, across the bed. "Do you want to tell me the other secret you've been keeping? The one that's been crushing you?"

Jack lowered her head. Her lips didn't part. Her eyes didn't find him.

But his fingers laced through hers, tightening until she squeezed back. "Why is this secret worse than almost killing someone?"

"It isn't."

"Then why does it scare you more?" He lifted his free hand and tilted her chin toward him, finding her nervous gaze.

She glanced at him, then looked down. "Don't make me do this."

"I won't. I promise. But I need you to know something." Raven slid off the bed, kneeling before her. He took her face in his hands. "There is *nothing* about you that will make me love you less. Do you understand?"

Tears slid down her cheeks. "You love me?" she whispered, as Raven fought to catch the tears before they fell. His fingers brushed her lashes, dancing across her cheeks. She leaned into his touch, and it made him feel brave. Bold. Reckless.

"I've loved you since the first day we met. You found me in the trees, and you rescued me from all my fears. All my sadness. You felt like a part of my family, and I thought I knew what that meant for a really long time. Then I looked up at you from that glass coffin and I knew you were the only one who could wake me from the nightmare I'd been living in."

Jack inhaled sharply, her forehead dipping toward his. "I couldn't look at you in that coffin. Not until you opened your eyes. You stared up at me, and I felt like you saw me so clearly . . ." Jack pulled back, arms wrapping around herself. "I don't know how to do this, Raven. I don't know how to say this without it changing everything. I'm probably going to lose my mom over it, and if I lose you—"

"You're not going to lose me," he said, taking the edges of her collar in his hands. The shirt had been his, but it was definitely,

definitely Jack's now. "You could never lose me, because you're my family."

"Your dad is your family," Jack replied. "He still thinks of me as Poppy, and if he finds out who I am, he could treat me differently. He could treat you differently for being with me."

"My dad?" Raven huffed, shaking his head. "The guy who tossed me aside when it wasn't convenient to keep me around? I'm not going to hide how I feel to make things easier for him. And I would *never* ask you to hide who you are." A nod in the darkness. Raven wanted to see Jack's face, so he reached over and flicked on the lamp beside Lily's bed. "If you want me to know, you can tell me. If you don't, it's all right. We'll eat dinner. We'll get some rest and—"

"Sometimes I don't feel like a girl. I mean, I'm *not* a girl." Jack swallowed, looking down. "I'm a boy."

"You're a boy," Raven repeated, his fingers still wrapped around Jack's collar. Brushing the skin beneath. "How long have you known?"

"Honestly?" Jack glanced up at him. "I think I've known since I was a little kid. I remember asking my mom for boys' clothes when I started *preschool*. I remember asking for a different name after Flynn was born. A name more like his."

Raven raised his eyebrows, taking a breath. "I had no idea. I mean, you never mentioned anything."

"My mom got really mad when I said those things. She told me girls didn't dress like little boys, and she said my name was perfect for me. She'd braid my hair and tell me I was beautiful. I *hated* it,

Raven. But I think her saying those things made me want to hide inside myself, you know?" Jack's voice was shaking a little, his fingers toying with a thread on his jeans. "If my own mom thought it was wrong to want those things, what would the world think?"

"So you hid inside yourself."

A nod. "For years. Then I met you, and you let me rescue you, and you let me be your knight and . . . it felt so right. I told myself maybe there wasn't anything wrong with me. Maybe the *world* was wrong about what girls could be."

"Because girls can be knights."

"Yes."

"And girls can wear whatever clothes they want, and girls can be named Jack."

"*Exactly.*" Jack smiled, and Raven was struck by the light in his eyes. How bright would Jack burn if that light was finally allowed to come out? How happy would he be if he actually got to be himself?

"I decided I didn't have to change myself. Or *become* myself, all the way. I could change the world, and I could be a girl who rescued princes and climbed towers and called herself Jack. But every time I got closer to making the world how I wanted it to be, I felt this twinge in my stomach, like I was missing something. Rewriting a fairy tale instead of admitting the hero wasn't a girl named Jack. He was a boy." Jack sucked in a breath. He wasn't crying anymore, but Raven would stay close, just in case tears spilled over his cheeks again.

Raven would stay close because he'd *always* wanted to be close to Jack. "What changed?" he asked, taking Jack's hands. "Did you realize something while I was away at boarding school?"

Jack shook his head. "It was almost the opposite of that. You went away to boarding school, and Belle stopped talking to me. I thought maybe she'd figured something out. Maybe she suspected there was something different about me, and she didn't want to be around me anymore, and if that was true . . . well, I could lose my mom next. I could lose my brothers, because my mom would try to keep me away from them, so I couldn't be a boy." Jack pulled his hands away from Raven, curling them into fists. "I couldn't be a boy, because I would lose everything, so I pushed myself away instead. I lived in denial and I didn't look anyone in the eye for years. Then you came home and . . ."

"You looked me in the eyes."

"Yes."

Raven smiled softly. "And you wanted me to know."

"No." Jack chuckled, a sharp, brittle sound. "No, I was terrified of you knowing. I retreated into myself even more until that officer came and slid cuffs around my wrists. He locked me in a cell and he told me I could be there for a long time. And suddenly I realized . . . I was going to lose everything anyway. I was going to lose *everyone*, and I'd never even found myself. I'd never even faced myself all the way."

"So you did."

"I'm trying." Jack's head dipped down, his fingers digging into the blankets. "I'm trying, Raven, but I'm so scared. Everything's going to be different now."

"You're right." Carefully, with the most delicate of movements, Raven cupped Jack's face. He trailed his fingers across Jack's lips. "Everything's going to be so much better. You get to be who you really are, and I get to know you, so just . . . keep talking to me, all right? Keep letting me know you."

Jack shook his head, finally meeting Raven's gaze. Gripping it. "The time for talking has passed," he said, a soft smile on his lips.

"Has it, now?" Raven was smiling too. Grinning, actually, as gardens bloomed inside him. There were petals strewn across his heart. He wished he'd had time to trail petals across the bed, but then again, this wasn't his room. "Should we go—"

"No time." Jack guided him up from the floor, where he'd been kneeling, reverently, and then they were falling backward onto the bed. "I need you now. But, Raven?" A pause, as Jack's gaze evaded his. "Did it change anything, what I told you? Did it make you love me less?"

Raven leaned in, brushing his lips across Jack's forehead. His nose. His chin. Before his lips found Jack's, and he lost himself in a kiss that he would remember for the rest of his life, he whispered into Jack's mouth, "More."

19

I Can't Do This Without You

Jack woke to a thrumming in his heart. Raven's limbs were entangled with his, and he thought he'd do anything to stay in this warm, dark place. But his bladder protested. And so he lifted Raven's pale brown arm from where it was draped over his body and climbed carefully off the bed.

His footsteps were silent on the carpet. The bedroom door opened with a barely audible click. Out in the hallway, the hardwood floor met Jack's feet with a soft slapping sound, and for that he was grateful. There was something unsettling about this eerily silent house.

Something foreboding.

Jack was in and out of the bathroom in a couple of minutes. When he heard a voice coming from the first floor, he stopped to listen. Dr. Holloway was downstairs, talking to someone on the phone. That was what Jack believed at first. But when a voice *responded*, cutting through the silence like a knife slicing through steel, Jack went stock-still, his heart tumbling over itself.

He knew that voice. He'd heard it ringing across the orchard on evenings when Raven had pulled himself into the trees, trying to block out the sound of his parents fighting. This time, the voice coming from downstairs was anything but angry. It was pleading.

"Please," Raven's mother called out, causing the hairs to rise on Jack's neck. "I can't do this without you. I need my baby boy."

Jack found himself at the top of the stairs. One step after another led down, down, down to the pitch-black first floor. He made his way through the hall, where new portraits had been hung since he'd last visited the house. New, but old. Over the past three years, all evidence of Arianna Holloway had been shoved into the guest rooms, until no trace of her remained in the common areas. Now her smiling face was back on the walls. If given enough time, red roses might be planted in the garden, replacing the white.

Then *Evelyn* would be erased.

Jack rounded the corner on silent steps, veering toward the living room. He could see a flicker of light coming from inside. Could see the silhouette of a man sitting on the couch, his shoulders hunched over with grief. But this time, Raven's father was not watching scenes of his family's breakfast table. This time, Arianna Holloway stood in the center of the Rose

Hollow Community Pool, clad in a crimson bathing suit and calling out to her son.

"Come on, baby," she cooed, striding toward the lip of the pool. Over on the deck, a toddler with big dark eyes stood, waffling. He dipped in a toe, then scurried backward.

"Jump into my arms and I'll carry you," Arianna promised, holding her arms out to her son. Raven hesitated. He was wearing black swimming trunks and his curls were shorn close to his head. The sight of him, so small and unsure, made Jack's heart squeeze. Raven sucked in a breath, tightening his hands into little fists.

Then he leapt into his mother's arms.

There was a splash. Arianna shrieked with joy, and Raven shrieked with her, kicking out his legs. She spun him around. Bounced him on her knee. Leaned in and said, "See? It's always better when you're with me."

Jack froze at the back of the sofa. He kept sucking in short, shallow breaths, telling himself everything was okay. He hadn't known Raven the year this video had been taken. There was no reason to recognize this scene, but deep down, in the recesses of Jack's memory, he did.

"Dr. Holloway," he choked out, and when Raven's dad twisted around, he looked like Jack felt. Gutted. Bereft. "I need to ask you about this video."

Raven's father narrowed his eyes. He was wearing the same suit he'd had on when he picked Jack up from the detention center, but he appeared to be shrinking into it. The dark gray fabric was a mess of wrinkles. Deep circles lined his eyes. "Did I wake you? I'm sorry."

"No, you didn't wake me." Jack sat on the edge of the sofa. Perched on the arm, just so, he could steady his trembling legs without sinking into the fat, white cushions like Raven's father had. He needed to be able to leap up at any moment. Needed to get back to Raven.

But first he needed to solve a three-year-old mystery.

"I know you were seeing Lily's mom while you were still married. I know she was your therapist," Jack went on before Raven's dad could interject. Whether Dr. Holloway had been *seeing* Evelyn in other ways didn't feel relevant anymore. Both of his wives were dead. "Lily's mom was a marriage counselor, and sometimes she asked couples to bring in mementos of a time when they were happy."

"I . . . We shouldn't be talking about this." Dr. Holloway paused the video, as if to shield the memory from Jack. To keep it for himself. But it was too late for that, because Evelyn had already discovered this memory, and she'd used it to torture her stepson. To poison his mind.

"I know this is prying," Jack said, "but Raven started hearing his mom's voice in the months before he left for boarding school. You know that, right? The detective talked to you about it?"

A slow, careful nod. Raven's dad was being cautious with Jack. Too cautious. "I think you need to let this go. It's not healthy to fixate on Raven's delusions."

"They weren't delusions, and Raven's your son. You should've believed him." A sound from upstairs, like feet hitting the floor. Raven was awake, and Jack couldn't let him walk in on this conversation. Even now, he was desperate to protect Raven from the ugliness in the world. The ugliness in his family. "Does the detective know about this video? Does he know how Evelyn used it—"

"The video came from Detective Medina. He cleared out Evelyn's office this morning, and he thought I'd want the video back." Dr. Holloway swallowed, his gaze flicking to the woman on the TV screen. Raven's mother was grinning widely, holding her son in midair. Eyes bright. Hair fanning out around her. "One night, in the dead of summer, it was so hot that Raven couldn't sleep. I think he was nine or ten. Arianna convinced us both to sneak into the community pool that night, and we swam for hours. She was spontaneous. Nothing like Evelyn," he added, his jaw tightening. "That woman was like clockwork. She got up at the same time every morning. Took a shower at the same time every night, while she let her tea steep."

"She let it steep?" A chill rippled up Jack's spine. "Did you tell that to the police? The time of death was—"

"Between eleven and one," Raven's dad recited, swaying a little. But he was talking about the time that Evelyn *consumed* the poison. The belladonna could've been stuffed into her teakettle half an hour earlier.

Before Lily got to Belle's. The words rang out in Jack's mind, as loud and garish as the silence had been upstairs. It was still silent upstairs, but he could've sworn he'd heard the sound of feet landing on Lily's bedroom floor.

"I have to check on Raven," he stammered, backing away so quickly, he banged his leg against a mahogany end table. Another piece of furniture that had been shoved into a guest room during Evelyn Holloway's reign. Suddenly, Arianna was *everywhere*. Smiling from the walls. Whispering on the television. Jack wondered how long it had taken Raven to bring out his mother's old things, and when, exactly, he'd had time to redecorate the house. The place had been crawling with cops his first day back. After that, Jack had appeared on the scene, and he'd hardly left Raven alone, except for when he'd been down in this room, watching Raven's father come undone.

The last time it had happened, Raven had been sleeping sweetly in his own bedroom. This time, Jack had left him wrapped in Lily's covers, and Jack hadn't even considered that someone might slip in through the window and creep up to the bed. Someone who had access to Evelyn Holloway's keys. Someone who knew the security code to her office.

Jack barreled down the hallway, rounded the staircase, and took the stairs two at a time. He told himself Raven had woken up of his own accord. Planted his feet on the floor and then realized he was far too scantily dressed to come downstairs. Jack had taken off his shirt hours earlier, along with his jeans, leaving Raven in a pair of silky black boxers. Maybe he'd had trouble finding his clothes in the dark. Maybe no one would be standing over him on the bed, a pair of gardening shears aimed at his bare chest.

Maybe, Jack told himself.

Definitely, he promised.

But Jack had always been a storyteller. He'd written himself into fairy tales in order to survive the darkness in his life. As he entered Lily's bedroom to find her leaning over the bed, Jack realized that darkness could be deceptively bright. Lily's hair was luminous in the moonlight. Her skin looked eerily white as she brushed the curls from Raven's face.

"Please." Jack took a single step toward the bed. "I'll give you anything you want. I'll disappear. I'll take Raven with me. Just don't—"

"You know I can't let you go," Lily replied. Her purse was slung over her shoulder, and Jack had no doubt that the rusty gardening shears were tucked inside. "Not after you stole my father's file. Not after you tried to pin the murder on him," she added, as Raven opened his eyes, blinking up at her. He had the brightest eyes of anyone Jack had ever known. The softest hands. The sweetest heart.

"Jack? What's happening?" he murmured, his voice heavy with sleep. With confusion.

"Everything's fine," Jack said softly. "Lily and I are just having a chat, right, Lil? Isn't that what your dad calls you? But he isn't the person who poisoned your mom."

"No, he isn't." Lily sat down on the bed. She was looking at Raven with the detached fascination of a house cat who doesn't need to hunt for food, but still has the wiring of a hunter. *That* was why cats played with mice after all, and didn't bother to eat them.

They were natural killers.

"Tell us about the night your mother died," Jack said, eyeing the distance between them. "After you stole the flowers from Belle's garden, you came here and found your mom's teakettle on the stove. Right?"

The moonlight sliced through the window, illuminating Lily's face. There was no blood in her cheeks. No curve in her lips. When she opened her mouth to speak, Raven reached out, placing a hand on her cheek. "I don't want to hear how you killed your mother," he said, his voice startlingly gentle in the quiet room. The quiet night. "That part's easy. That part, anyone can guess."

Lily shuddered as he found her gaze. "Don't tell us how you killed your mother. Tell us why you wanted her dead."

PART 3

The Truth According to Lily

I was ten years old when I found the old photo album in my mother's closet. I'd been sneaking into her bedroom for weeks, trying on her vintage lace slips and elegant costume jewelry. My first impression of my mother, from when I was very young, was that she was strikingly lovely, and I wanted to be like her.

The photo album was tucked behind her shoes. I'd been trying to pull a pair of ivory Ferragamo pumps down from a high shelf when it toppled into my arms, almost knocking me over. I was small back then. I'd always been a bit smaller than my peers, and for years I would believe this was a bad thing, until my mother explained to me that small was good.

The smaller the better.

But in that moment, my smallness caused me to stumble against the closet wall, and the photo album sprang open, revealing a picture of a family. Everyone smiling. Everyone blond. But in the places where the parents' eyes should've been, someone had taken a pair of scissors and hacked until no irises remained, no eyelids, no pale lashes brushing against cheeks.

I should've closed the album then, but I didn't. Instead, I sat down beneath the satin and the lace, and I turned page after page. Those eyes were scratched out everywhere. My heart raced at the sight of them, and I couldn't understand why my mother had done this to her own parents.

I wanted to ask her the minute she got home. It would take her a few minutes to close up her office, and half an hour to drive across town to our little apartment, which meant she'd walk through the door around a quarter to six. By the time she got home, I was waiting for her in the living room. The album in my lap. She took one look at it and yanked it from my hand, stomping toward the kitchen. With a flick of the wrist, she opened the garbage can and dropped it inside. Turned around. Wiped her hands on her white pantsuit.

"Shall we call in for dinner?"

"Who were those people?" I asked, though I already knew the answer. They were my grandparents. Her mom and dad.

"They're nobody, baby. What do you feel like? Popcorn shrimp? How about tapas? We haven't done tapas in—"

"Why did you scratch out their eyes?"

She came and sat next to me on the couch. We didn't have money then, but she'd managed to scrounge up a decent living room set from a nearby thrift store. The sofa and love seat were the softest, cushiest white. The tables and chairs, as bleached as the bones of a whale. This was a home where shoes were taken off the second one walked through the door, and beds were made before breakfast. Cleanliness and godliness and all of that.

"I was angry when I did that," my mother said simply, running her hand through my hair. She loved to toy with the pale blond strands. For years, we'd slept in the same bed every night, and she'd stroked my hair until I'd fallen asleep. Read me stories. Sang me songs. She was my favorite person in the world, and I was hers.

"Why were you angry at Grandma and Grandpa?" She tensed the second I said those words. Those names, which I'd rarely spoken. "Were they mean to you? To me?"

"They never met you." Her hand caught on a tangle in my hair. "They never touched you, and they never will."

"Not even for a hug?"

Her fingers tightened, tugging uncomfortably at my scalp. I slithered out of her grip. And I watched her, cautiously, breathlessly, as she strode over to the garbage can and pulled the album out.

She returned to my side.

"What have I told you about my family?" she asked, flipping through the album. Page after page sped by, revealing widely grinning smiles and impeccable clothing. Hands clasped. Eyes slashed.

"You lived in a beautiful mansion. You wore beautiful dresses, and your parents took you to lunches and dances and parties. But when you started sneaking out to meet Daddy, they got mad."

"Your daddy was wild. Reckless. He loved putting poison in his veins, and my parents threatened to disown me if I kept seeing him." She turned a page too quickly. The page tore, and her lips twitched up, as if the destruction pleased her. "I didn't listen. I didn't think they'd actually throw me out, but when I got pregnant with you at sixteen, they told me I'd made my choice. A few days later, I came home from school to find my dresses on the lawn. My shoes. My photo albums. They'd changed the locks to the house! I pounded on the door, sobbing, but my parents passed by the window like they couldn't see me. I thought . . ." She slid her fingernail along the photograph, scratching at her mother's eyes. "They didn't deserve eyes if they wouldn't look at their own daughter. I picked up a rock and threw it at the glass, hoping it would shatter. Hoping shards would make a home in their eyes. But the glass barely cracked, and nothing happened to them."

"So you stabbed their pictures instead."

She nodded, closing the album. "I stabbed their pictures, and I moved in with your daddy, and for a few years, I had a family. Until he left me too."

I frowned, reaching up to touch her face. "You still have a family," I promised. "You have me."

She smiled, and then she went to the bathroom to fix her mascara. We ate tapas while sitting on the living room floor. We laughed and told stories about finding your true family, and it was one of the best nights of my life.

For the next few months, I was happy. My mother and I felt closer than ever. Sure, she was buried in loan debt, and she was struggling under the burden of raising me alone, but we had each other. It was us against the world, and nothing could touch us. Hurt us. Tear us apart.

Then my mother started seeing a man she knew from college, and we didn't eat dinner together anymore. She got dressed to the nines, wearing her heels and her pearls, and she went out every night. She swore it was only temporary. The "honeymoon period," where they wanted to see each other every second of every day. Soon, those fluttery feelings would settle into comfort, and she'd bring him to meet me. Then we could be a family.

But things didn't go as planned. Two months into the relationship, my mother asked her new beau to come and see me, and he grew skittish. Distant. Based on snippets of phone conversations I overheard, he wasn't ready for the responsibility of raising a ten-year-old child, and that wasn't his fault.

She hadn't told him about me.

Over the next couple of years, my mother dated six different men, each of whom disappeared at the mention of me. It didn't matter if she told them on the first date or the twenty-first. Her adolescent daughter sent them running for the hills. She'd had me when she was sixteen, she insisted to them. She was still young, and they only had to be as involved in my life as they wanted to be. They didn't have to be my father. They didn't even have to be my friend. But no matter what spin she put on the story, the second they learned she had a daughter in middle school, they vanished.

Then, halfway through the seventh grade, she started dating Troy. She'd met him on some dating app or another, and he was a bright-eyed dental student with an easy smile. I watched through my bedroom curtains when he picked her up, and hurried to look out the window again when he brought her back home. He opened doors for her. He held his jacket over her head when it rained. He seemed nice! Maybe he would be the one!

Inevitably, it came time for me to meet him, and I could tell my mother was nervous about introducing us. He knew about me, but she'd talked about me so casually over the phone, I sounded more like an old sofa in the corner than a child. And maybe I wasn't a child anymore. Men looked at me like I wasn't. They held doors open for me, and though no one had covered me with a jacket when it rained, I thought it was only a matter of time, and so . . . I decided to introduce myself to Troy. I put on one of my mother's smallest dresses, which almost fit me, if I belted it very tight. I curled my hair like she curled her own, and when he came to pick her up that night, I raced outside to meet him.

My mother was aghast. She gaped at me with a horrified look

on her face, as if I'd hurled her over the side of a mountain, but she didn't understand what I was doing. I wasn't a little girl. The men she dated didn't have to be scared of taking care of me, because I was just a smaller version of my mom, and I could take care of myself.

Troy looked at me.

I looked at him.

His face broke into a grin. "You must be Lily," he said, holding out an arm and looping me into an embrace. "It's so good to meet you. You look just like your mother, wow. When you told me . . ." He turned to my mom, shaking his head in wonder. "She's so beautiful," he said.

I beamed.

My mother cringed, but a blush was spreading across her cheeks. Troy wasn't stumbling away. He wasn't stammering excuses about getting up early in the morning or needing to focus on work or going through a selfish period in his life. He liked me. I liked him.

Our problems were solved.

For the next few months, Troy and my mother got closer, and we had movie nights together, eating popcorn and laughing through ridiculous comedies. We made elaborate dinners. We went for walks in the rose garden in the middle of town. I never really thought about the fact that they were taking me on all their dates, because it didn't feel that way at first. It didn't feel bad, or wrong.

Then one night, my mother went away to a conference one town away, and Troy showed up at our door with takeout from Paradise Gardens. My favorite. We sat on the living room floor and ate with our hands. At the end of the night, Troy led me to the bed that I shared with my mother and he tucked me in. He said it was very adult of me to stay home on my own without a babysitter, but maybe he should stay with me to make sure I was all right. And I said sure, because . . . it made sense. I was a thirteen-year-old in a bad part of town, and the locks on our door were questionable at best.

Nothing happened that night. Nothing I could put my finger on, because he fell asleep soon after, and so did I. I remember dozing off to the sound of him snoring. But I woke up the following morning to the sound of my mother's screams. She dragged Troy out of the apartment and into the hallway. She all but pushed him down the rickety stairs to the building. Then she hurried back to me, sobbing and telling me she was sorry. I promised that nothing had happened. I told her he'd only wanted to stay with me, because I wasn't old enough to stay home alone.

Over time, her sobs softened to rasping breaths. I cleaned the mascara from her eyes and made her some tea. She always liked drinking tea when she couldn't calm down, the caffeine-free kind that slowed the heart rate instead of quickening it. "I will never let anyone hurt you," she told me, over and over again, lifting her cup with a trembling hand. "I will never bring another man into our home."

And for several months, she didn't. It was the two of us against the world again. But my mother didn't seem to enjoy being alone with her daughter anymore. She was lonely. I could see it. When she started dating a widower named Stefan Holloway, she came up with a way to keep me safe without sacrificing her own happiness.

She was going to hide me in plain sight.

"Some girls develop early," she explained, pulling out the sweaters she wore when she was pregnant with me. The oversize jeans. The layers of T-shirts. "It isn't your fault, but if we don't cover you up, men might think inappropriate thoughts."

"I'll wear all the layers," I announced, pulling on T-shirt after T-shirt. She giggled at the sight of me, like we were coconspirators. Spies, sneaking into the house of a king. It felt like a game. But after she married Stefan Holloway, and we moved onto the estate, my mother worried he might glimpse me changing after a shower. He might try to sneak into my room at night.

My bed.

And so, she suggested we monitor my meals. We were coconspirators again, plotting to keep Dr. Holloway from looking at me the way Troy had. Over the next few months, my curves withered like flowers drying in the sun. My ribs pressed against my skin. I looked more like a skeleton than a child, but even then, she jumped every time Dr. Holloway glanced at me. She jumped every time he glanced at Raven, who had his mother's eyes and his mother's laugh.

I started to worry that she wasn't protecting me at all. She was protecting herself. She'd lost her parents because of me. My father. Troy. When Raven started hearing his dead mom's voice in the middle of the night, I realized how far she would go to keep Dr. Holloway's attention. She'd torture Raven. She'd starve her own daughter. She'd kill us both, and pretend it had been an accident.

Unless I killed her first.

I hadn't even acknowledged how angry I was until I found Belle's recipe in the orchard. I'd been hurting for so long, and I'd been afraid to admit it. I blackmailed my way into the murder plot. Then Jack went behind my back and told the police Raven was in danger, and instead of getting my mother away from him, they sent him to a boarding school where he would be safe. I was left alone with the woman who'd been tormenting us both.

And I knew what would happen next.

One night, three months after Raven went away to boarding school, my mother laid out my nightly salad, and I just . . . refused to eat it. I wanted her to see what she was doing to me. I knew, by then, that I would never be small enough to make her feel safe around me. I would shrink and shrink until I disappeared entirely.

I wouldn't let her do that to me.

I pushed my chair back from the table with a screech. I looked into her eyes as if to say: Choose your daughter. Choose me. *Her jaw hardened and she grabbed me by the arm, pulling me out to the orchard where we could speak in private. "You're being reckless," she hissed at me. "Everything I've done over the past year, I've done for you. If you had any idea what it took to get into this house—"*

"You didn't do it for me! You did it for yourself!" I was crying, hunched over between the trees. I caught sight of Dr. Holloway's pruning shears in the dirt, and I thought of bringing them to my throat, showing her where all of this led. "You're going to kill me."

"I would never hurt you." A shadow crossed her face, her fingers still encircling my arm.

"You hurt Raven. You hated him because he had his mother's eyes, and every time Stefan looked at him—"

"Baby, you're delirious. You need to eat. Why don't we take a look at your diet plan, and see if we can't add—"

"I'm not eating until you listen to me!" I jerked out of her grip, landing in a pile of leaves. The pruning shears glistened at me from the dirt. They winked at me, as if sharing a dirty secret.

An ugly secret.

I lifted the shears to my hair. "You say you want to keep me safe, but that isn't what you're doing." One chunk of hair fell away, then another. My beautiful blond locks, decimated like the eyes in her photo album. Hacked. Slashed. "You want to hide my beauty so Stefan won't want me. You want to make me ugly."

Moment by moment, strand by strand, I took my beauty away. I left it lying in the dirt. That's how Dr. Holloway found me. Crouched over in the orchard, a pile of discarded locks at my feet. Bone thin and shivering in the wind. When my mother said, "She's refusing to eat," he didn't ask for an explanation.

He simply sent me away, just like he had with Raven.

For the next few months, I lived in the Rose Hollow Wellness Facility, eating and sleeping to my heart's content. I learned that I didn't have to hate my beauty. I didn't have to cower in the dark. Hidden away from my mother's clutches, I was able to do all the things she'd never let me do:

Play. Relax. Care about myself.

I reconnected with my birth father and learned the truth of my past. He had left me as a baby, but only to protect me from the addiction that had ripped through his life like a tornado. He'd spent years getting clean. More years trying to find his way back to me. Only one *thing stood in the way of us finally being a family, and if we could eliminate that obstacle, we could be together.*

And so, last Saturday night, I snuck over to Belladonna's yard, where I wrapped my hand around a clump of flowers. I quietly liberated them from the dirt. Then I went to see my mother.

20

The Delicate Art of Poisoning

Lily's breath came out sharp and fast as she finished her story. She could still feel the belladonna wrapped around her fingers, leaving little lines of red after she'd yanked it out of the ground. Petals had stained her skin. Juice from the berries had slid under her fingernails, making her terrified of biting her nails in the days to come. She'd washed her hands over and over.

But the fear had remained.

Now, as she looked up to find Raven gaping at her, she tucked those hands into her lap. She was wearing her gloves. She'd been wearing them for days, so no one would notice that she'd scrubbed her hands raw. She *should've* worn gloves the night of the murder, but she'd never intended for her mother to get hurt.

"I got to the house around ten o'clock," Lily explained, and

Raven's brow furrowed. Jack cautiously joined them on the bed. "I sat in a chair and dropped the belladonna on the kitchen table. She found me like that on the way to her nighttime shower. Her hair was pinned in curls and she was wearing her white silk robe. Everything was exactly like it had been three years earlier, including the teakettle on the stove. I could've stuffed the flowers into it while the water was coming to a boil."

Raven winced, and Jack reached for his hand. But neither of them spoke, because they'd waited too long to hear this story.

"She almost screamed when she saw me," Lily confessed, and it had hurt to see her mother react like that. As if Lily were a ghost risen from the grave. Or a killer, broken free from an asylum. "She went for the phone immediately, and she'd dialed the facility's number by the time I spoke. I only said two words: *I wouldn't....*"

"Did she hang up the phone?" Raven asked in a whisper-soft voice.

"She put it back in the cradle," Lily said, remembering the sound of the click. Her mother had listened to her. Her mother had been scared. "She came and sat at the table, glaring at the flowers like I'd brought her a clump of weeds. But that disgust turned into horror when I told her about our plan to murder her. I described the blossoms we were going to weave into our garlands. The kitchen table, strewn with petals. By the time I'd finished, my mother was white as her roses. That's when I plucked a berry from the belladonna and dropped it into her empty cup. I told her that I was going to move in with my dad, and if she tried to stop me—"

"You'd poison her," Jack said, and Lily nodded.

"She wouldn't know when. But if she ever tried to starve me again, or hurt Raven, I'd drop a poisonous berry into her soup, or her cider, or her wine. I'd get to her, and she wouldn't be able to stop me."

Light flashed in Jack's eyes. Was Jack horror-struck . . . or a little impressed? Lily couldn't tell. But Raven was unmoved by her story, and he peered at her, his dark eyes narrowed into slits. "If you found a way to beat her, you didn't have to kill her. You could've left—"

"You did leave," Jack realized, just as Lily opened her mouth to speak. "I talked to Belle at the detention center. She said you were together at the time of the murder. If you didn't stuff those flowers into the teakettle before you left, that means . . ."

"Someone else did it. But it couldn't have been my dad," Lily said. "I know what you're thinking, and it makes sense to you, because you don't know where he was that night. *He* checked me out of the facility. He left me when he was a teenager, and my mom didn't think he was coming back, so she never filed for full custody. He's still one of my legal guardians. Since the doctors knew I was doing better, they left me in his care, and he took me back to his house. We spent hours decorating my bedroom, and then we sat on the couch and ate ice cream. He fell asleep around nine thirty, and that's when I snuck out. When I came back, hours later, he was *exactly* where I'd left him, snoring on the couch. He couldn't have killed her."

"Lily." Jack spoke softly this time, and that gaze was kind. Gentle. It stoked the fires in Lily's chest, making her angry.

She would *not* be pitied. "He couldn't have done it," she nearly shouted, not caring if Raven's father heard her through the walls. "The next morning, I woke up to hear him talking to someone at the front door. The police were there, asking about my mother, and he told them I'd been with him the entire night. They had no reason to suspect us. No evidence linking us to the crime. Besides, once that detective found the *Recipe for the Perfect Murder* in the kitchen, and the belladonna missing from Belle's yard, he figured he'd found his killer." Lily scowled, fingers tightening to fists. "I would've given her an alibi if I could've, because I was with her for hours that night, but after my dad spoke to the police, it was impossible."

"Lily," Jack said again, a warning this time. "He gave you an alibi so that *he'd* have one. I know you don't want to believe it. That's why you followed me around and took the video of me burning Raven's clothes, right? You were desperate to blame someone else."

"You don't understand," Lily said, her voice cracking. "After the police drove away, my dad turned to me and started to cry. He said he understood what I'd done to my mother. He knew she'd been hurting me for so long. But he wouldn't let anyone arrest me. He'd lie for me, and he'd say we'd been together the whole night, so no one would know that I—"

Raven jerked out of Jack's grip, inching toward Lily. "He thought you killed her? He said that?"

Lily nodded, a tightness in her chest. Her father had looked so frightened as the police drove away. He'd clutched her shoulders, fingers digging into her skin. He'd bruised her. And he'd promised that no one would ever know that she'd poisoned her mother.

No one would ever take her away from him.

"He must've been playing you," Jack said, looking bereft without Raven to care for. Lily understood that feeling well. In order to get Belle back, she'd have to give up her father. How could she choose between them? How could she sentence either of them to life behind bars? She'd brought the belladonna to her mother. She'd given the killer the idea, and no matter what happened after that, she *was* complicit in the murder.

"I can't turn him in." Lily shook her head. "Not after everything he's done for me. Not unless I know for sure."

"You turned me in," Jack snapped. "You forced me to burn your father's file, and then you called the cops, and they dragged me—"

"Belle said you were obsessed with Raven! She said you kissed him behind her back, and then you stole his clothes. After he got cleared to come home, Belle thought you killed my mom to keep him safe, and then you stole my dad's file from my bedroom so you could frame him for the murder." Lily looked up, her eyes laced with red. "It made sense. I knew where my dad was the night my mom was killed, but you don't have an alibi."

"I was home!" Jack swallowed, cheeks flushing with heat. "And I stole Raven's clothes because I missed him. I started wearing them because . . ." Jack trailed off, looking at Raven.

"They made you feel close to him," Lily whispered, her gaze flicking between them. "And maybe . . . they made you feel closer to yourself?"

Jack's head snapped up, his green eyes narrowing. "Why would you say that? Did you hear—"

"I wasn't trying to listen!" Lily held up her hands. "I came over here a few hours ago. I knew you'd been arrested, and I wanted to explain to Raven what I'd done. I wanted to explain *why*, but when I got to the house, I noticed the light was on in my room. I crept up the stairs quietly so I could listen outside my bedroom door. I thought you'd be confessing to murder. I didn't know. . . ."

Jack's shoulders hunched, and Raven looped an arm around him, so easily. As if it were instinctual. "You had no right to do that," Jack whispered, his voice hoarse. Shaking.

"I know. I'm sorry! But after I heard your story about the vine you trailed across the attic stairs . . . after I knew why you'd called off the murder of my mom, I realized I had everything backward. You're not the villain, Jack."

Lily crouched on the floor in front of the bed. She wanted to take Jack's hands, but she knew it would be invasive after everything she'd heard. Everything she'd done. "I don't expect you to forgive me for calling the police. I'd just lost my mom, and I thought you were taking my dad away from me." She swallowed, blinking back tears. She would not cry. She would not think about the life she was going to live if she lost both parents. The only family she'd ever had. "And I'm so sorry for stealing that secret from you. Ever since I met you, I wanted to be your friend, and if you'd told me who you are, I would've been so happy. But I should've let you come to me. And I should've come to you instead of calling the police."

"I don't forgive you," Jack said, still avoiding Lily's gaze. "You shouldn't have turned me in and you shouldn't have . . ." A slight shake of his head, and then Lily found herself seared by those bright green eyes. That piercing gaze. "You have to get your father to confess. If we record his confession, we can get Belle out of juvenile detention. Will you help us?"

Lily opened her mouth to speak, but Raven cut her off, rising from the bed. Nervous energy was emanating from his pores. Every cell, a vibration of terror. "Her father is dangerous. If he thinks she's going to turn him in, he could lash out."

"I'm not afraid of him." At that, Lily pushed to her feet. But instead of joining Raven in the center of the room, where he was pacing, she strode to the window, looking down at the roses below. "I haven't been hiding the way Jack's been hiding," she told Raven, "but I have been cowering in the dark for years, trying to keep my mother from hurting me." She turned, opening her pale pink purse. The movement was innocuous. Innocent. But Lily Holloway was neither of those things, and she pulled the rusty gardening shears into the light. "I'm not cowering anymore."

21

Blood in the Snow

They had three hours to put the details into place. Lily's father didn't get off work until four in the morning, which gave Lily and Raven time to track down the perfect rose. Jack, in the meantime, snuck into the guest rooms to check on the boys. Conner and Dylan were wide awake, turning their four-poster bed into a fort. Meanwhile Diego buzzed the sides of Flynn's hair in one of the guest bathrooms, so that only the curls remained on top. Jack took one look at the end result and asked, "Can you do that to my hair?"

The answer was a resounding yes.

Three hours later, Jack felt more like himself than he had in years. No, scratch that. Jack felt more like himself than he *ever* had, and it wasn't just the hair. It wasn't just the white collared shirt and jeans, gifted from Raven and topped with the long green jacket that made Jack feel like a conqueror of giants. It was the *power* he felt as he slipped out of Andrew Kane's back door. It was the feeling of taking control of his life without resorting to poison, or panic, or pain.

They were going to win this. Jack knew it definitively as Andrew's truck turned into the driveway. Everything was quiet, the deep breath before the scream. The silence before the confession. Lily had set up a camera in the kitchen, where she was planning to meet her father. But unlike the last time, when she'd greeted her mother with belladonna, she came bearing an elegant rose.

No poison.

Just thorns.

That was Lily, Jack thought, as he took up his post in the backyard. Raven was hiding in the living room closet. After Andrew stepped into the house and strode toward the kitchen, Raven would slip out of the closet and block the front door. Jack would block the back.

Then Lily would go in for the kill.

When the front door opened, Jack's heart started to thump. It felt too heavy in his chest. Slamming and slamming like the footfalls of a giant. He told himself to breathe, to *trust* Lily, because she could play innocent better than any of them.

Andrew Kane strode across the living room. Within seconds, he'd passed through the entryway to the kitchen. All the lights were out in the house, and when he flipped the switch in the kitchen, nothing happened.

Lily had removed the bulb.

"The light went out," Lily said, as her father flipped the switch again. There was a window over the sink, cracked just enough, and Jack could hear the conversation perfectly. "I didn't know where you kept the bulbs, so I figured I'd wait until you got home."

He turned to her, slowly. Could he tell something was wrong? She was sitting at the kitchen table at a quarter after four, caressing the petals of a rose. That rose was pink. She'd stolen it from the gardens in the center of town, because white roses reminded her of her mother, and red ones reminded Raven of his.

They lived in a town of roses and ghosts.

"I've been thinking," Andrew said, reaching across the table to take her hand. His fingers came close to the thorns of the rose, but no skin was broken in that moment. No blood was spilled. "After the trial is over, and the dust settles, how would you feel about getting a fresh start somewhere else? I have a lead on a job in Wood Haven—"

"You want us to move?"

He nodded, his eyes narrowing against the darkness. The sun would rise in two hours' time, and they needed that rose to scratch him before the world was filled with light. It was the only way to ensure that the neighbors didn't see what they were doing.

When Lily tilted her palm upward, Jack held his breath. Any second now. The slightest movement, and the thorns would kiss Andrew Kane's skin.

"Lil, you don't want to stay in town," her dad told her, his voice soft in the dark room. "Everywhere you look, you'll see reminders of your mom."

"You want us to run." This time it wasn't a question. Lily's voice was hard, and her gaze was too. Jack could see her through the opening in the window. "You sounded so believable, the day the police came knocking at our door. I honestly thought you were covering for me."

"I . . ." Andrew ran his hands through his messy brown hair, and Jack saw that only half of his face had been shaved. Clearly, he hadn't been sleeping since the murder. Unfortunately, things were only going to get worse from here. Sleeping in a quiet house might've been difficult, but that was nothing compared to curling up on a cot in a cramped cell.

"It's so funny, isn't it?" Lily pressed on when her father didn't speak. "Jack gave a false alibi for Belle. Dr. Holloway gave a false alibi for Jack. Everyone's been lying for everyone, but only because we're *innocent*. You lied to cover your own ass."

Lily's dad reached for her, but she yanked her hand away at the last second, and then there was only the rose. Pale pink petals. Sharp curving thorns. Andrew's hand wrapped around it, and he pulled back, cursing.

Lily leapt from the table. Without a single word, she hurried to the hall closet and pulled out some Band-Aids. On the way back to the table, she grabbed a rag from the counter and handed it over. "Clean the wound," she instructed, as if she were the parent and he were the child.

So thoughtful. So nurturing.

Andrew did as she requested without a moment's pause. Then Lily was plucking the rag from his hand, passing him the Band-

Aids. As he wrapped one around his wounded finger, Lily strode to the window over the sink and inched the screen open. She handed the rag to Jack.

Andrew might've missed the entire thing. He *would* have missed it, if Jack hadn't spoken from the other side of the window, saying, "Thanks, Lily. I'll take this to the police. Once they match it with the evidence they found at the scene of the crime, they'll make their arrest."

This part was a bluff. The police had found no physical evidence at the scene of Evelyn's murder. No fingerprints, except Evelyn's and Dr. Holloway's. But Andrew could've easily left a strand of hair on the kitchen table, and he wouldn't know that he hadn't until it was too late.

Jack waited, breath held.

Lily waited too.

Andrew's brow furrowed at the sight of the figure standing on the other side of the window, dressed in a long green jacket and holding a bloody rag. "What's going on, Lil?" he asked his daughter, rubbing at his eyes. "Who is that?"

He didn't sound scared. Jack couldn't make sense of it. But Lily, bless her hardened little heart, didn't falter at her father's confusion. She simply returned to the table, picking up the rose. "You thought you could kill a person and no one would suspect you, because you left no evidence at the scene of the crime. But all it takes is a single fingerprint or a few drops of blood."

Andrew pushed away from the table. He kept sliding his jaw back and forth, as if he were chewing on a particularly tough piece of steak. "You don't know what you're talking about. You weren't there."

"But you were," a voice said at his back. Andrew spun to find Raven standing in the entryway to the kitchen. "I got there after she was dead. Lily was with Belle, and Jack was home the whole time. That only leaves you."

Andrew swallowed, darting a glance at the back door. "I never meant to hurt anyone. The gun was supposed to be loaded with blanks. By the time I realized she'd put real bullets—"

"What gun?" Jack asked, opening the back door. Andrew's head whipped toward him, then back to Lily. Then to Raven.

"The gun. None of it was supposed to be real! I was only trying to scare her, and once we had the pills, we could sell them and pay off Evelyn's debt. No one was supposed to get hurt, but she tried to wrestle the gun away from me. She scratched me, and the gun went off. It was so loud."

"What are you talking about?" Lily demanded, her cheeks drained of color. Dawn was still two hours away, and yet Jack could see everything in the kitchen. The cracked countertops. The rusty faucet that dripped every few seconds. And the unhinged man stumbling toward Lily, his legs trembling beneath him.

"Your mom said we could be a family. She said I had to prove that I could look after you, and if I did this one thing, she'd know that she could rely on me. The Holloways were Rose Hollow old money. Their ancestors had helped found the town. If I cleaned out their pharmacy, I'd have enough money to take care of you, and she'd let me see you again. She'd let me be your dad."

The world swayed at Jack's feet, and he told himself that everything was not sliding into place. Andrew had fled the scene of *Evelyn's* murder. He had not been at the pharmacy the day Arianna had been shot. He had not carried the gun that killed her.

"No." It was Lily who spoke the word, her eyes widened in shock. "No, you aren't making any sense. You followed me to Raven's house the night of Mom's murder. You heard us talking in the kitchen."

"That isn't what happened." Andrew reached Lily's side, and in spite of everything, he took her face in his hands. In spite of everything, she let him. In the seconds that followed, Raven crept up behind Lily, guiding the shears from her purse. There was no time to stop it. Jack was disoriented, and Lily was mesmerized, staring into her father's eyes for what could be the last time.

Men could fall so easily. Jack knew it as Raven passed Lily, nearing Andrew Kane's back. When Raven lifted the shears, Jack felt all the breath rush out of his lungs, and out of the room.

"You didn't just kill Lily's mom," Raven whispered, bringing a blade to Andrew's throat. "You killed mine."

22

Snow White

It was the first snowfall of the season. Flurries drifted down from the sky, landing on Raven's lashes. He loved the snow. Loved the cold. He loved getting bundled up in sweaters and spinning in circles in the school parking lot as the blue sky turned black.

It was four forty-five. He'd just finished his violin lesson, and he was supposed to meet his mother at the pharmacy on the north side of town. This time of year, she'd be brewing hot cider for her customers, and when he burst through the door, teeth chattering and limbs shaking, that cider would warm him up.

If it didn't, she'd pull him into a hug.

Raven hurried across the parking lot of Rose Hollow Middle School. His black Schwinn was locked up on the rack by the sidewalk, and he struggled to unlock it with gloved hands. He'd seen

Belle come to school with a pair of black lace-up glovelets the other day, and he thought he might mimic her and take a pair of scissors to the fingers on his gloves. That would be practical, wouldn't it?

Finally, the bike came unlocked. Raven swung his leg over the seat, pushing off the ground. This time of year it was dangerous to race down the road, and his heart hammered as he narrowly missed a patch of ice on Main Street. He was nearing the rose gardens in the center of town. There was something about the thorny bushes, stark and lovely against the backdrop of snow, that made him want to climb off his bike and wander through the empty rows. Lately, his home life had become hectic. School had become hectic too, the classrooms overflowing with students.

In the rose gardens, the entire world slowed to a stop.

Raven slid off his bike, wandering in the quiet. It didn't take long for his heartbeat to calm. His ragged breathing grew even, and the tension in his shoulders gave way. There in the cold, quiet darkness, he felt his entire being exhale for the first time in *months*.

Raven breathed in, then out. He felt peaceful. Calm. He didn't know that a man was nearing his mother's pharmacy, boots trailing snow and breath heavy against the quiet. He didn't hear the bell chime above the pharmacy door. By the time he climbed back onto his bike, the man had revealed a gun in his jacket, the fat black barrel pointed at Arianna Holloway. By the time the pharmacy was in sight, the shot was already ringing out.

The silence was obliterated. In the minutes that followed, Raven told himself all manner of stories about engines backfiring and fireworks being set off in the dead of winter. Anything but a gunshot in his mother's pharmacy. Anything but a wound in his mother's chest.

Nothing was supposed to lodge itself there. Nothing except her fierce, beautiful heart. This was the woman who'd taught him to ride a bike, and nestled roses in his hair. This was the woman who'd chased him around the kitchen with a wooden spoon, pretending it was a wand. As he sped through the parking lot, he could see her through the glass door of the pharmacy. She was wearing a long white jacket, but something was staining it.

Raven skidded to a stop at the door. But the latch had a habit of sticking and his stupid, bulky gloves couldn't yank it open. The door was stuck. Raven was stuck, staring at his dark-haired, bright-eyed mother on the other side of the glass as she crumpled to her knees.

No. He would not watch her die. He had a phone in his pocket, and after he pulled it out, he would dial 911. Medics would arrive on the scene. They would save her, and everything would be fine.

Raven's hand slid into the pocket of his jeans. Miraculously, the phone came out easily, and he realized his glove had fallen into the snow. Good riddance to it. He would never wear those stupid gloves again, because they had kept him from getting to her, and she *needed* him. An operator came on the line. Raven mumbled something about an emergency and managed to give the pharmacy's address. After that, the phone fell into the snow. First the glove, then the phone.

Nothing else would fall. Raven swore it to the heavens, and

he swore it to his mom, and then he jerked open the door. A body pushed past him. He hadn't even seen the tall, lanky man in the ski mask, because he must've been hiding between the rows of medication. He must've realized he was trapped, the minute Raven arrived outside the door, and he must've been skulking through the pharmacy like a half-starved dog.

"I'm sorry," the man choked out, tossing a glance in Raven's direction. His voice was low and scratchy, as if someone had wrapped their fingers around his throat. Or maybe he'd been crying. Raven didn't know. None of this made sense, because none of this was possible.

His mother was crawling toward the pharmacy door. She must've been trying to get to her son, and Raven reached for her, the sound of footsteps retreating at his back. "The ambulance is coming," he promised, gathering her into his arms. "Just give it a couple of minutes, okay, Mom? Stay with me."

The man with the gun had disappeared. Even his footsteps faded as sirens rang out in the distance, the snow falling harder now. Raven had always loved the snow. He'd always loved the cold. Now he desperately longed for the warmth of his mother's embrace, which he feared he'd never feel again.

The life was bleeding out of her.

He could feel it as she clung to him. He could see it, as the snow darkened beneath her body. Farther off, in the direction where the man had been, there were three crimson drops in the snow.

But they weren't hers.

23

Ensnaring the Huntsman

Slitting a throat came easily. All you needed was a single rusty blade. Jack watched his oldest friend bring the shears to Andrew Kane's neck, and for a moment, all the air leached out of the room.

No one was breathing.

An instant later, Andrew gasped, and Jack gasped too. Lily's hands flew to her mouth. Only Raven seemed perfectly calm as he tightened his grip on the man who'd murdered his mom.

"You shot her. You left her for dead."

"I'm sorry," Andrew choked out, but it wasn't enough to sway the boy standing behind him. It was far too little and far too late. Raven's mother was dead, and this man could've stopped it.

He could've admitted to it.

But he hadn't. And now a blade dug into his skin, drawing blood. "Raven, stop," Jack began, but Raven cut him off.

"You don't get to say that. You, of all people, should understand—"

"You're right." Jack eyed the distance between them. The table. The chairs. "I almost killed someone, and I'm so glad that I didn't. I know what it would've cost me."

"I have nothing to lose."

Those words, damn. They were shards of glass sliding into skin. They were slivers making a home in soft fingers, and Jack wondered if he'd ever get rid of the sting. "Are you sure about that?" he asked Raven.

Raven looked up for a moment. Their eyes met, and there was a charge between them. Something intangible reaching across the air. "I can't let him go after what he did. I can't let him live."

"It was an accident," Lily stammered, her gaze glued to her father's throat. A thin trail of red was nearing his collarbone. But when she stepped toward him, Raven shook his head, and Lily froze. "The gun was supposed to be loaded—"

"With blanks. Yeah, that's what he claims," Raven snapped, his voice cold and clipped. He'd never sounded like this before. Not after his mother had died in the snow. Not after he'd climbed into a coffin and pretended to be dead.

"Raven, it's over," Jack insisted. "Evelyn must've tricked Andrew into killing your mom so she could marry your dad. Now she's dead too, and killing him won't make any difference."

"It will make a difference." Raven's breathing was shallow, his dark curls heavy with sweat. "He doesn't deserve to live. He killed them *both*."

"No," Andrew sputtered, his legs buckling beneath him. "I didn't kill—"

"When someone hands you a gun, you check it for bullets," Raven spat. "You don't hold it to someone's chest and then feel *sorry* for yourself when it goes off. You don't get to pretend you're innocent."

"You're right." Jack was eight feet away from him. A universe unfolded between them. "Andrew killed two people, not because he was forced into it, but because he made those choices. Lily brought the belladonna to her mother's house. I hurt somebody because I didn't know how else to stop him. All of us are guilty, Raven." A beat, as Jack held his warm, brown gaze. "Except you."

"Stop."

"You're the kindest person I've ever known." Jack took a single step, then two. "The best person."

"And what has kindness ever done for me?" His face contorted, tears welling in his eyes. "My mom bled out in my arms. Nobody even *tried* to find her killer, and instead of being there for me, my dad threw me away. Because I was kind. Because I was weak."

"You aren't weak," Jack said, as Lily backed toward the living room. She mouthed *Dr. Holloway* to Jack, slowly pulling out her phone.

"I am weak," Raven murmured, his gaze trained on Jack. "That's why you always tried to protect me. You thought I couldn't protect myself."

Jack took another step, his heart hammering. His stomach clenching. "I didn't protect you because you were weak. I protected you because I wanted you in the world."

Raven's face crumpled, tears spilling freely down his cheeks. "*Why?*"

"Because the world is better with you in it. And I have always loved you, Raven. Just like you've always loved me." Jack took three more steps, his arm outstretched. "You don't have to do this. Your mother wouldn't want this."

"My mother is gone."

Jack's fingers grazed Raven's cheek. He trembled at the touch, leaning forward, and the shears slipped a little. "We'll replant her roses in the garden. We'll make her spiced cider in the fall. We'll fill the house with her memory, just like you already started to—"

"I didn't do that," Raven interrupted. "That was my dad."

"Fine, then we'll help him," Jack said, unfaltering. "We'll put all her pictures back in the frames. And every time I look into your eyes, I'll see the same light I saw in hers."

"You will?" he said reverently, a whisper.

"Yes." Jack cupped Raven's face in his hands. Raven shuddered, silent tears giving way to a sob. "But that light will go out if you don't let go."

The shears clattered to the floor. So did the man, gasping and rolling onto his side. Raven slumped into Jack, and Jack's arms encircled him, holding him close as Lily returned to the room. Her eyes were dry. Jack knew she was trying to be brave. Maybe she would wait until she was alone to break down, or maybe she would wait until Belle had been released and they were wrapped in each other's arms. But sooner or later, the rage would come. The anguish. The grief.

Pain couldn't be outrun. It was a wild, snarling creature in the forest, indiscriminately stalking its prey. There was only one way to survive it. You had to call out for other voices in the tangled woods. You had to reach for careful hands and let them pull you to safety, away from gnashing teeth and curling claws. And then, when you were strong enough, you had to reach out your own trembling hands and pull other people out of the darkness.

That was the only way to weaken the pain. The only way to defeat a monster that left no footprints. And now, as tears slid down Lily's cheeks, Jack and Raven pulled her into their embrace.

24

The Beauty of Bolt Cutters

Belle was free of her prison, but she didn't feel free. The elegant Tudor cottage should've seemed enormous after spending three days in a cramped cell. She should've spun around in the library like a girl in a storybook, arms outstretched and fingers never brushing against the walls.

Instead, she stood before the door to the attic, a pair of bolt cutters in her hands. She'd learned some things in juvenile detention. A plastic utensil could be used as a weapon in a pinch. The sharp blade of a knife could slide a lock out of place. And if you found yourself in front of a chained attic door, the average garage would hold the tools you'd need to break through them.

Belle broke through the chains in five minutes flat. They

clanked on the floor, lifeless and dull. Then she was stepping over them, opening the creaking attic door. A dusty staircase led to the top.

One step followed another, and soon Belle was passing through a smaller door. The ceiling jutted up at a slant. She had to hunch over as she moved toward the center of the room. Then she just stood there, heart hammering, as she took in the contents of the attic.

There was a bed shoved into the corner. The lavender lace covering had lightened to gray, and bits were eaten away by moths. The pillows looked misshapen, as if they'd been slept on by trolls. A smattering of pale, faded stuffed animals sat beside the bed, but the most interesting part of the bedroom was the board strung up on the wall. Belle's fingers vibrated as she reached out to touch it. Breathing came with great difficulty. Her adoptive father had to be a serial killer, because why else would he have pinned this little girl's face on his wall over and over again? Why else would he have tacked up articles about her disappearance? The only things missing were red bits of string connecting one article to the other.

With this thought came clarity. Edwin Drake wasn't celebrating a murder. He was trying to solve a mystery, Belle realized, as her eyes scanned the headlines. Almost two decades earlier, a little girl had gone missing while walking home from Rose Hollow Elementary. Reporters speculated on what had happened to her. Someone could've pulled up in a windowless van. Someone could've dragged her into the woods. A number of horrifying scenarios flooded Belle's mind until her vision started to glaze.

Edwin's daughter had been stolen.

In the twenty years that followed, the police had never found a trace of her. Not a single lock of hair or a fingernail. Not a tooth or a piece of clothing. One day she'd been in this room, cradled in her father's arms, and the next she'd ceased to exist in his world.

Belle slumped onto the bed, lifting a faded blue tiger from the floor. Half his stripes were gray. The other half, cornflower blue. Had he been vibrant once? Sapphire and white until someone had smothered the color right out of him? Had the girl been smothered too? Belle couldn't help but wonder as she stared down at the toy. These kinds of thoughts, well, they had a way of burrowing into your mind. And Edwin had spent a decade alone in this grand house, envisioning all the ways his daughter had been killed.

A sob welled up in Belle's throat, not only for the girl that had been stolen, but for the life that had been stolen from *her* as a result. She'd never walked home from school alone. She'd never ambled through the rose gardens in the center of town, leaning in to whisper in a friend's ear. *Better safe than stolen,* Edwin had told her when she'd wanted to go to a birthday party in the sixth grade. *Better hidden than gone.*

There was a creaking on the stairs. Belle's breath fluttered, the sob stopped up inside her like a bottle stopped up by a cork. Her gaze flicked to the turning doorknob. Edwin was supposed to be at the store, gathering ingredients for a celebratory dinner. If he caught her in his daughter's old bedroom, she didn't know how he would react.

She braced herself for the worst.

Then a girl stepped into the room, and Belle rose to her feet, stumbling forward. Lily met her in the center of the attic. Strong arms encircled her, and Lily's breath was warm on her cheek.

They held each other tightly and didn't speak.

Slowly, they pulled apart, and Lily looked down at her hands. "I know you've heard everything by now. That I stole the flowers from your garden. That I brought them to Raven's house. If you hate me, I would under—"

"I could never hate you," Belle said. Without a word, she led Lily back to the stairs, and they descended together, following the hallway to Belle's room.

Lily sat down on the bed. Meanwhile, Belle began pulling clothes out of her drawers, piling them on the floor. Soon, the pile was up to her knees, and she strode to her closet, removing a suitcase from the highest shelf.

"What—" Lily began, but Belle cut her off.

"You're free of the facility," she said, folding a black lace dress and setting it lovingly in the suitcase. In spite of everything, she appreciated what Edwin had given her. A wardrobe worthy of a princess. A bedroom fit for a queen. And a house that had felt like a castle in a fairy tale, until she'd realized how easy it was to be trapped inside those walls. Beautiful doorways held no value when you couldn't walk through them.

"Raven's free too, because with Evelyn gone, he and his dad can actually be happy. So can Jack, since Jack and Raven have always looked after each other. Even before I came along," Belle added with a sad smile, because maybe, deep down, she'd known their story would end without her. She'd never really belonged with them, like she'd never really belonged in this house.

But she belonged with Lily.

"I can't stay here anymore," she pushed out in a rush, piling clothes into the suitcase. "I'm not going to disappear on Edwin. I would never do that. But as long as I'm here, he's going to do everything he can to keep me safe, and I don't want you to have to sneak over in the middle of the night. I don't want to sneak out—"

"You want me to sneak over?"

A twitch in Belle's lips. She turned to see Lily looking at her, a light in those blue eyes. "Correct me if I'm wrong, but you *have* snuck over," Belle pointed out. "It didn't end well. The cops showed up at my door."

"It *began* well," Lily reminded, lying back on Belle's bed. "You held me all night. And even though there wasn't time for much else, it was the best night of my life. Until the arrest."

Belle turned to look at her. The suitcase was full, and she could join Lily on the bed if she wanted to. Lily's blond locks were splayed out on the pillow. She was wearing a bulky sweatshirt, not unlike the ones that had been handed out at the detention center, and Belle wanted to guide it off Lily's body slowly, seeing her girlfriend for the first time. With nothing between them. They *had* done more than hold each other the night Lily had slept over, but that had mostly included kissing and very timid touching. Lily had kept her clothes on. After a lifetime of being hidden, it was difficult for her to let herself be seen.

That was something Belle could understand. Edwin had taught her to hide her vulnerabilities, until it looked, to the outside world, like there was no softness inside her. She threatened people with the flowers in her garden and kept her fingernails sharpened to points. Everything about her was a weapon.

Everything but her heart.

Belle walked over to the bed, but instead of reaching for Lily, she reached for the hammer in her bedside table, the one Raven had given her in middle school. It took mere seconds to pop up one of the floorboards. Then she was pulling out the letters she'd stolen after Raven had gone to boarding school. Letters from Raven. Letters from Jack. She knew what she was risking, showing these letters to Lily, but she didn't care in that moment.

She wanted to be seen.

"I started stealing these on my lunch break," she admitted, handing Lily one of the letters. "Edwin drives me to school and picks me up, so lunch is the only time I have to wander during the day. I never go very far, but one day, after Raven left town, I noticed the mailwoman at the end of Jack's block. I don't know what came over me, but the next thing I knew, I was creeping up to Jack's mailbox, pulling out a letter to Raven. Then I just . . .

hung around until Raven's letter had been delivered. I did this every day for weeks, until they stopped writing to each other. It was easy."

"See also: illegal."

Belle shrugged, ignoring the heat in her cheeks. "We were going to kill a person, and you're worried about mail fraud."

"We were never going to kill my mom." Lily pushed onto her elbows. "We were just scared of her, and we didn't know—"

"I knew what to do." Belle slid one of Jack's letters out of the envelope. Together, they read the large, messy handwriting that Belle had committed to memory until she could imitate it:

> *I don't think you want to hear from me at this point. I think you want to forget what happened between us, because it was too much. Or too soon. I'd never touched you before, and I wanted to make up for lost time, before we had no time left.*
>
> *I'm sorry for that.*
>
> *But I'm not giving up. Tonight, I snuck over to your orchard and I climbed into the tree where we first met. I sat there so long, the day darkened to evening, and I thought I saw you in the distance. I thought I caught a glimpse of your curls and it startled me so badly, I almost fell out of the branches. But it wasn't you. It was your dad, holding his pruning shears and wearing his pruning gloves. He was halfway up a tree, trimming branches, and it broke my heart to see him doing what we used to do together. I was so angry in that moment, and so disappointed it wasn't you. . . .*

Belle turned the page over for Lily, so she could keep reading. This next part was important. It was the crux of her plan. The fruit of a year-long labor, of practicing over and over again until her hand cramped up. She held her breath as Lily read the backside of the letter:

> *I thought he deserved to suffer for sending you away. I thought his new, beautiful wife deserved to die on the kitchen floor, a cup of poisonous tea swimming in her veins.*

Lily sat up, the blood draining from her face. "Jack was planning to kill my mom? All this time, I thought Jack was the noble one."

"Lily."

"My dad swore he didn't do it. Even after Dr. Holloway called the police, and I admitted that I was with *you* at the time of the murder, my dad swore he didn't poison—"

"*Lily.* Jack didn't write this." Belle turned over letter after letter, revealing no writing on the backs. "Jack only wrote on one side of the pages. After I'd learned to imitate Jack's handwriting, *I* wrote the part on the back." Carefully, she procured a packet of poppy seeds from beneath the letters. "I was going to poison your mom with poppies, and then I was going to plant this letter in Jack's room so the police could find it. Jack would be arrested. Raven's heart would be broken. And you would get out of the facility."

Belle glanced up to find Lily peering at her, a soft look in her eyes. No hatred. No disgust. "Don't look at me like that," Belle warned, her voice low and hard. "Don't look at me like I'm a savior. I almost *poisoned* a person."

"So why didn't you? No one stopped you this time."

Belle shrugged, looking down. Tears sparked in her eyes. She was determined not to let them fall, *until* Lily's hand slid over hers.

A tear slipped from her cheek, landing on the letter below.

"Why did you decide not to frame Jack?" Lily pressed, squeezing Belle's hand. "Why did you decide not to break Raven's heart?"

Because you gave me back mine. Because you gave me a family, when I never thought I'd have a family again. Because Raven and Jack may have stopped loving me, but I never stopped loving them. I just told myself I had, because it hurt too badly to lose them.

"Because I'm not a killer," Belle said finally. "I don't want to poison people to feel protected. And I don't want to live in a cage of my own making." A pause, as she met Lily's gaze. "I want to let someone in."

"Then let me in."

Belle swallowed, wrapping her arms around herself. "What if something goes wrong?"

"Something will definitely go wrong. But we'll find our way back to each other, if that's what we want. Is that what you want?"

"Yes." No hesitation this time. No pause. Belle's body was racked with fear, her breath coming out sharp and fast. But this time, the fear wasn't strong enough to keep her from doing what she wanted.

Carefully, she guided Lily onto the bed. Lily's body was languid. Her back arched as Belle crawled over her. "I will never let anyone hurt you," Belle whispered into Lily's mouth, just before she kissed her.

Lily looked up, a light in her eyes. "And I will always protect your heart."

Then, a kiss. Belle tasted Lily's lips, her fingers sliding into Lily's hair, and there was nothing sweet or tentative about it. Lily was hers in that moment. Belle was Lily's. And they would *find* each other, over and over again, because it was what they wanted.

Belle wanted this.

Her hand slipped under Lily's sweatshirt, as if to lift it. Lily pulled back. "I can't," she whispered, her body gone rigid. "Just leave it on. Okay?"

Belle nodded, working around the fabric, because she would always give Lily what she wanted. But an idea occurred to her, just as her fingers neared Lily's heart, and she pulled back. "Wait here a minute."

Lily nodded, too breathless to do much else. Her hair was disheveled. Her sweatshirt, bunched up on the left. She watched with curiosity as Belle strode across the room and riffled through the suitcase.

"Here it is," Belle said, returning to the bed. She held a bright amethyst slip in her hands, the exact color of the belladonna in her garden. She'd bought it to wear *for* Lily, but now she thought it might serve a greater purpose.

"Put it on. If you want to," she added, because Lily was eyeing the satin fabric with suspicion. "You'll be covered, but you won't be hidden."

With that, she turned around, facing the wall on the far side of the room. There was a mirror there, but she angled her gaze away from it. She could hear rustling at her back. A minute later, Lily's soft voice trickled into her ear. "Okay. You can look."

Belle turned to find Lily half covered by blankets. She was wearing the bright amethyst slip, and she looked . . . more than beautiful. Honestly, there wasn't a word for her, and Belle wanted to gather Lily in her arms so badly, kissing every inch of her body.

Instead, she held out a hand. "Come here."

"Why?" Lily's eyes narrowed. She hadn't let go of the blankets.

"Just come here for a minute. Please? I want to show you something."

Lily rose from the bed. She crossed the room shakily, and Belle positioned her in front of the mirror. "Do you know how beautiful you are?" Belle asked from behind her, wrapping an arm around Lily's waist.

Lily shook her head, gaze dropping to the floor. "I don't want it. People will try to hurt me."

"They'll try to hurt us if we're beautiful. They'll try to hurt us if we're ugly. But you know what, baby? They're the ones who are ugly. It doesn't have anything to do with us."

She lifted Lily's chin. "And you are crushingly, stunningly beautiful. You're also sweet. Clever in a way that scares me. Braver than anyone—"

"I'm not."

"You can be. We can be, together. Come here." Belle led her back to the bed. They crawled under the covers. For a moment they just watched each other, Lily's shoulders peeking out from the blankets and Belle's hair falling in waves over the pillow. Then, in the slow, careful way of two people who've been waiting an eternity to touch each other, they found their way to the center of the bed. Limbs entangled. Hands entwined. Lips pressed against lips, and hearts pressed against chests, until they were both so breathless, they pulled back, gasping.

The pile of letters fell to the floor.

Belle leaned over the bed, gathering them in her hands. Lily came up behind her, trailing kisses along her neck. "That was smart, hiding them under the floor," Lily mused as Belle set the letters on the bedside table. "If I'd hidden the *Recipe for the Perfect Murder* under a floorboard, my dad would've never found it."

"How did he find it?" Belle asked, turning to face her. "Did you tell him where it was hidden? You never even told me."

"I didn't tell him anything about it! But he snuck onto the Holloway estate *for me*, to steal that red rose. He must've found the recipe then."

"How? The guy steals a rose from the garden and then decides to climb a bunch of trees for fun?" Belle huffed, tapping the stack of letters. "That doesn't make any sense. The only person climbing trees was Jack—"

"Wait." Lily snatched the letters from the table. After a minute of shuffling, she retrieved the one that Belle had altered. "Jack wasn't the only one climbing trees while Raven was gone. Someone else was going into the orchard, holding pruning shears and wearing gloves."

"Dr. Holloway," Belle whispered, her heart thrumming like the wings of a hummingbird. Her lungs constricted, and she could barely speak the words, "We have to get over to Raven's house. Now."

25

Holy

Raven was hosting a sleepover in the orchard. He knew it sounded childish, but after everything he'd been through over the past four years, he wanted to indulge in some innocent fun. With his father's permission, he'd draped old white sheets over the trees, creating an elaborate fort. There were blankets and pillows hidden inside, and by the time Jack arrived, Raven had strung tea lights across the lowest branches.

Jack's jaw dropped at the sight. "Raven. This is—"

"It's too much, isn't it?" He felt silly. Sheepish. But then Jack stepped closer, squeezing his hand, and he felt his entire being exhale.

"It's perfect." Jack crouched down, swinging his backpack off his back. He was wearing another one of Raven's button-down shirts, forest green this time, and his jeans brushed against the ground as he dug a potted plant out of his backpack. "For you."

Raven took the rosebush reverently. Its single blossom was just starting to open, and there was a light dusting of crimson petals peeking at him from Jack's backpack.

Jack scooped up a handful, nestling them in Raven's hair. "I figured we could plant this in the garden. I see your dad's already torn up the white roses. Did he do that for you?"

"I don't know." Raven glanced toward the back of the house, his gaze finding the empty plot of land where the roses had lived. First red, then white. But Raven wasn't certain he wanted to fill the fresh, upturned earth with crimson roses. "For most of my life, my mom was everywhere. Her roses were in the garden. Her portrait was in the hall. Then Evelyn moved in, and *she* was everywhere, and my mom was just gone. If we put everything back the way it was . . ."

"It'll be like none of this ever happened."

Raven nodded, a twinge in his chest making it difficult to breathe. "But it did happen. They're both gone, and my dad thinks he can just bring back my mom's memory by hanging up pictures and changing the furniture. Maybe he is doing it for me, but I don't want it." He turned the potted rosebush in his hand, fingers brushing the barely opened bud. "Maybe I'll just keep it in my room."

"We could put a planter's box outside your window. The roses could grow there, and maybe they'd climb up the side of the house. She'd still be here, but it would be different. We wouldn't be pretending she'd never left." Jack stepped closer, brushing Raven's cheek with the back of his hand. "Your dad has old home videos of your mom. I saw him watching them in the middle of the night, and I'm pretty sure you haven't seen all of them, because Evelyn—"

"Can we talk about Evelyn when the girls get here?" Raven asked, setting the rosebush on the ground. "I want to show you what I've done."

Jack nodded, a soft smile on his lips, and Raven's desire for an innocent sleepover drifted into the air. The orchard was filled with apple blossoms. They fluttered down to the ground, pale petals blending with elegant white sheets. There were a dozen fluffy pillows under the fort Raven had created, and Jack settled into them, looking up at the sheet billowing above their heads. "What time are the girls coming over? It's already after seven."

"I haven't invited them yet."

Jack blushed, eyes catching Raven's for the briefest of instants. He ran a hand through his recently shorn hair. The tea lights in the branches were flickering through the pale white sheets, and when the light reflected in Jack's eyes, they glowed like emeralds. "We have some time then," Jack murmured, and then his blush deepened. "I mean—it's not like we're going to—"

"I knew what you meant." For years Raven had been certain that joy was a brief, fleeting thing. An enchanted stag you spotted in the forest. You could search for him for years, until your skin was bloodied by branches and your heart was heavy with longing, and still, you'd never stop hoping for another glimpse of him.

For the possibility.

Now, as Raven crawled into Jack's lap, it seemed as if all his searching had been worth it. His limbs weren't aching anymore. His heart sprang to life as Jack rose to meet him. Then, in one elegant movement, Jack had flipped Raven onto his back, and was crawling over him, and the *rightness* of the moment seared Raven like a flame.

Jack's lips were warm and delicate, at first. Then hungry. Then feral, as they sought to devour him. Jack's lips were his religion. Jack's hands were holy. Jack's body was his temple, and Raven had come to worship like he'd never worshipped anyone before. He was helpless against this feeling. He liked being helpless, completely at the mercy of someone who'd never try to hurt him. Someone who'd always tried to protect him. Save him. Heal him. And as much as he liked seeing those clothes on Jack's body, he wanted to see them on the orchard floor.

"Can I?" he asked, fingers lingering over the buttons of Jack's shirt. Jack nodded, biting his lip, and a tremor of anticipation shot through Raven. Of longing. Of *reunion*. He'd never felt so much like himself as he did in that moment, looking up to find Jack leaning over him.

One button came undone, then another. His fingers trailed down Jack's chest, lingering over the jeans that had once been his. "Can I?" he began again, and Jack shuddered, leaning into him.

"Yes."

Raven was in heaven. He knew he'd never tire of the ritual of asking and being told yes. Soon, Jack's jeans and collared shirt were reunited, crumpled together on the ground, and it didn't take long for Raven's own clothes to join them. Two shirts and two pairs of pants. Four socks and four shoes. Off to the right of the clothing, two friends became so much more than that. Their limbs entangled like vines. Jack's fingernails trailed down Raven's back and Raven brushed his fingers over Jack's body, memorizing him inch by inch. Soon, he had almost reached Jack's center, had almost done the thing he'd been longing to do since that first fumbling night in the garden, when they hadn't known what they were doing.

Raven knew better now. He'd been too shy to ask questions at fourteen, but he wasn't shy anymore, and he'd done a lot of reading while away at boarding school. Separated facts from fiction. Now, as his fingers trailed along Jack's thigh, he asked, "Do you want me to . . . ?"

"Yes." Jack's voice was as soft as a leaf touching down in the dirt. Raven could barely hear him, and he *wanted* to hear him.

Desperately, he wanted to. "You don't have to be so quiet," Raven teased. "My dad can't hear us through the vents out here."

"The vents." Jack sat up so suddenly, Raven gasped at the loss of him. "Belle mentioned the vents when I was at the detention center."

"She did?" Raven furrowed his brow. He had *not* planned on having this conversation. He hadn't planned on having any conversation, unless he was asking what Jack wanted and what Jack liked. "What did she say?"

"She used to hear your parents arguing in their room." Jack

reached out absently, pulling on the green collared shirt. "She used to put a pillow over your vent, to muffle the sounds of you—"

"That was a long time ago," Raven said, following Jack's lead. Moment by moment, piece by piece, their clothing returned to their bodies. This time, Raven's shirt felt too tight, and his jeans didn't fit the way they had before. It was impossible to be undressed with Jack and ever want to wear clothing again.

But the time for undressing each other had passed. Raven could sense it as Jack pulled him to his feet. Together, they ducked out of their fort, emerging beneath twinkling branches. The lights shone brighter now that the night had gone dark, and Raven wanted to stay in the orchard forever. "We don't have to muffle the vents if we stay out here."

"This isn't about us," Jack said, leading Raven toward the house. "Evelyn had a home video of your mom teaching you to swim. You were little and she was trying to get you to join her in the pool. She said she couldn't do it without you."

"She said that?" Raven's breathing quickened. Blood rushed through his ears, blocking out the memory of his mother's voice. "Show me."

Jack nodded, jogging up the porch steps. He was still holding Raven's hand, but Raven could hardly feel it as they stepped into the pitch-black house. Their footsteps creaked on the hardwood. Shadows twisted, making his pulse spike. When Jack pushed open the doors to the living room, Raven held his breath, expecting his father to be sitting there. Ever since Evelyn's death, Dr. Holloway had planted himself in the living room, surrounded by photographs. Memories. Ghosts.

The room was empty.

Jack plucked the remote from the coffee table. All he had to do was push two buttons, and then the TV was on, the home video playing. Raven's dad must've left it in the player so that he could stumble in here at any time and hear her voice. See her face.

Raven slid to his knees. His mother was before him, her eyes brighter than he remembered. For years, those eyes had been his favorite sight. That laugh, his favorite song. She was holding him in the video, and he pressed his fingers to his mouth, trying to remember the feel of her as she twirled him around in the pool. But the memory was buried in the recesses of his subconscious, too old to conjure.

It was lost to him.

Raven's eyes stung as Jack rewound the video, stopping it when Arianna started calling to him. "Please," she pleaded, her arms outstretched. "I can't do this without you. I need my baby boy."

The little boy in the video leapt, and Raven's heart leapt with him. When her arms encircled him on the TV screen, Raven swore he could feel her embrace. He looked up to find Jack holding him. Watching him with soft eyes. "This is what you heard in your bedroom," Jack said gently. "Isn't it?"

Raven nodded, tears sliding down his cheeks. "Why did Evelyn have this? Did she find it after she married my dad?"

Jack shook his head. "Your dad brought it to her office when she was counseling him. She asked him to bring in mementos of a time when he and your mom were happy, and after she moved into your house . . ."

"She played the video in my bedroom at night." Raven frowned, glancing toward the hallway, and the stairs beyond. "But that doesn't make sense. I got up and searched my room a dozen times. I looked outside the window."

"She wasn't getting to you through the window, and she wasn't sneaking into your room," Jack said, brushing a tear from Raven's cheek. "She was getting to you through—"

"The vents," a voice responded, and Raven spun around to see a figure approaching in the darkness. He caught a glimpse of familiar black hair and deep, dark eyes. A smile that could cut you to pieces or bring you to life.

This time Belle's smile was grim as she drew near. Lily was beside her, and Raven realized their fingers were entwined. "The day Evelyn was killed, I came close to figuring out how she'd been torturing you," Belle said, her gaze trailing up to the third floor of the house. "But the answer wasn't in your bedroom, Raven. It was in your dad's."

26

Two Kinds of Girls

The day of Evelyn's murder, Belle couldn't stop shaking. Raven was coming home. Her first boyfriend. Her once-upon-a-time true love. She didn't love Raven like she once had, didn't feel a crushing weight at the thought of him kissing someone else. But her fear of losing him completely was like a fire that had been waiting to be stoked, embers burning and smoke curling inside her. One mention of him coming back to Rose Hollow, and Belle was aflame.

She had to protect him. It didn't matter that he'd sounded stronger on the phone, like the scrawny-limbed, stoic child had grown into a man. Raven was not vicious enough to survive Evelyn Holloway. He was not wicked, and while Belle's time with Lily had taught her that she had sweetness inside her, she would never be an innocent girl.

She would keep her loved ones safe. Belle took her phone out of her pocket, pulling up the calendar she'd synced with Edwin's years ago. She'd needed to know when he'd be out of the house. Needed to know when he'd be attending a charity auction or a town luncheon, so she could slip off to visit Lily at the facility. According to the calendar, Edwin would be out of the house between five and seven that evening, and the second he left, Belle would sneak out after him.

But she wouldn't be going to visit Lily.

Day bled into evening. Belle followed Edwin to the door, and he kissed her on the forehead before leaving, just like he had when she was eleven. She waved him out the door, locking it behind him.

Then she snuck out the back.

She could hear Edwin's car pulling out of the driveway as she passed the little patch of belladonna on the side of the yard, and a few seconds later, she was heading for the street. She'd gotten alarmingly good at sneaking out of places. She'd gotten alarmingly good at sneaking *into* places too, but that day she headed to Raven's front door, because she needed to know which cars were in the driveway: Stefan's, Evelyn's, or both.

Miraculously, the driveway was empty.

No one was home. If she hurried, she could search Raven's room, and maybe the master bedroom, before anyone got back. Three years had passed since Raven's departure. Evelyn could've destroyed any and all evidence in that time, but Belle couldn't help but feel there was *something* hidden in a drawer or stuffed into the bottom of a box. Something to prove Evelyn had been torturing Raven.

Sneaking into his room brought pleasure and pain. So much had happened between these four walls. Soft whispering. Sweet, innocent hand-holding, and then, as they'd gotten older . . . kissing. They'd tumbled around on his black satin sheets, clueless and fumbling. They'd spoken in breaths, fingers tangling into hair. Raven had been surprisingly gentle, considering the warnings Edwin had passed down about boys, and every touch had been a revelation. Maybe that was why it had hurt so badly to see Raven kissing someone else. She'd found a way to trust him, in spite of the fear festering inside her.

And he'd broken her heart.

Belle lay down on Raven's bed, trying to breathe through the tightness in her chest. She'd come so far since losing Raven. She'd started to trust someone again. But every time she came close to letting Lily in, she saw a flash of Raven kissing Jack in the garden, and she shut down completely.

She shut Lily out.

Belle hugged a pillow to her chest. Being here wasn't helping to calm the clamor in her head, the harsh, ringing voices that told her to *trust no one, let no one in, keep your heart protected*. She wished she could muffle those thoughts the way she'd muffled the voices of Raven's parents when they fought in the master bedroom. All she'd had to do was press a pillow to the vent on Raven's floor.

The vent.

Belle twisted to the side, leaning over the bed. Raven's vent connected to his father's bedroom. To *Evelyn's* bedroom, where his father slept soundly each night, under the influence of sleeping pills. If Evelyn had found a way to imitate Arianna Holloway's voice, she could've used the vents to make Raven think he was being haunted.

Belle raced out of the room. It took very little time to reach the master bedroom, and one glance out the window told her the driveway was still empty. She knelt beside the bed. The pale, elegant four-poster rose up beside her, with a white gauze canopy and matching sheets. It looked a lot like Lily's bed—not that Belle had spent any time in it. She'd only been able to steal moments with Lily at the facility, little touches here and there. Soft kisses. Secret smiles. She felt a thrill at the thought of spending the night in Lily's room, wrapped up in Lily's arms, but that would never happen if Evelyn kept Lily locked away. *Nothing* would happen if Evelyn was allowed to reign.

Belle needed to steal her crown. She pulled her little master tool from her pocket, the one with tiny scissors and a tiny screwdriver tucked inside. Edwin had given it to her when she'd started high school. He'd encouraged her to bring it to class, even though she could've been expelled if anyone found out. He'd taught her that each of those tools could be a weapon, and if she had to hurt someone in order to get away from them, well, the ends justified the means.

Belle shivered as she flipped out the screwdriver. For a very long time, she'd believed the world was split into two kinds of girls: fighters and victims. Brutal, vicious witches and delicate damsels. There was no in-between. But as she guided the screws out of the vent covering, she felt a sharp, visceral pain at the choice she'd been given.

Assault or be assaulted.

Kill or be killed.

There had to be another way. There had to be another *choice*, Belle thought, lifting the grate from the floor. Then she was lying on the ground, sliding her arm into the vent. Her fingers met with dirt and dust bunnies. There was no evidence here. No hidden secret. No proof.

She pulled her arm out of the darkness, frowning at the layer of filth coating her skin. In her pocket, her phone was chiming, warning her that Edwin would be heading back from his engagement soon. And out in the driveway, she heard a car pulling up.

She needed to run.

Still, she hesitated. If she left now, both Raven and Lily would be at the mercy of Evelyn's cruelty. She had to find something. She had to try. And so, in spite of the dread unfolding in her stomach, she lay back on the hardwood floor, lowering her phone into the vent.

Light cut through the darkness.

She saw the things she'd felt before: grime and dirt and dust. A long, narrow channel, which would eventually lead to Raven's bedroom. But there in the distance, farther than her fingers had been able to reach, she saw a little rectangle, coated in gray and nearly hidden in the dark. It could've been a piece of garbage that had fallen into the vent years ago.

Or it could be the answer to all her questions.

Belle pushed to her feet, her eyes scanning the space. Through the crack in Evelyn's closet, she could see a hint of white, cascading fabric. She darted across the room. It took a couple of seconds to hurl open the closet doors, and a couple more to yank a white satin dress from its hanger. The dress billowed to the floor as the front door opened.

Belle froze, the wire hanger in her hand. She could hear someone closing the front door, and a moment later, she heard heels clacking on the stairs. Evelyn was home. Evelyn was coming upstairs. Frantically, Belle unwound the hanger, creeping across the room. She knelt in front of the vent. Guided the hanger inside.

Evelyn's heels hit the second-floor landing.

It took a moment to hook the end of the hanger around the rectangular object, and then Belle was guiding it toward the opening in the vent. She almost had it. But Evelyn had reached the third floor now, and when Belle's head jerked toward the sound, the hanger clattered into the vent.

She cursed under her breath. The smart thing to do would be to get the hell out of there and come back another time. She and Raven could investigate together. They could solve the mystery of Evelyn's deception *without* incurring her wrath.

Belle placed the lid over the vent. There wasn't time to replace the screws, so she nudged them under the bed. Just as Evelyn's hand twisted the doorknob, she bolted toward the window, knocking into a bedside table in the process. A bottle of pills toppled to the ground. There wasn't time to retrieve them. Belle climbed over the windowsill, channeling her old friend Jack, and used the vines to guide her body toward the ground.

"Later that night, Evelyn was dead," Belle whispered now, in the quiet of Raven's living room. "And the police never mentioned the vent, so I figured they didn't find anything down there."

"Or they were saving it for the trial," Jack muttered.

Lily shook her head. "That isn't what happened," she said, her eyes finding Raven's. "I searched your room after my dad's file went missing. I searched your dad's room too. In his bedside table, next to his bottle of sleeping pills, I found a tiny tape recorder. But it was empty, so I didn't think anything of it."

"That doesn't prove that he . . ." Raven swallowed, pushing to his feet. "The police could've found the tape recorder in Evelyn's bedside table. Everything got shuffled around while they were here. They could've put it back in the wrong one."

"There's more." Belle dug around in her purse. When she revealed the stack of letters she'd stolen, Jack reached for them first, knocking half the pile to the ground. Belle crouched down, pulling out the letter she'd shown to Lily earlier that night. *"Tonight, I snuck over to your orchard,"* she quoted, looking at Jack. *"I thought I caught a glimpse of your curls and it startled me so badly, I almost fell out of the branches. But it wasn't you. It was—"*

"Your dad." Jack's mouth dropped open, and he glared at Belle. "You stole the letters."

"Yes, and you can hate me for that tomorrow. But tonight you have to think about what you saw in Raven's orchard. Dr. Holloway was up in the trees, and he was wearing gloves. He was pruning the branches. If he found the *Recipe for the Perfect Murder* in a tree hollow—"

"No," Raven broke in, voice shaking. Hands shaking too.

"He would've already known how to poison Evelyn. He just wouldn't have known why, until he found the loose vent the day I snuck over to your house." Belle reached for Raven's hands, but he jerked away from her.

"*No.* He would never—"

"He must've found the tape recorder," Jack said, "and recognized your mom's voice. He must've realized you'd been telling the truth about hearing her in the middle of the night."

"Do you realize how ridiculous this sounds?" Raven clutched his head in his hands, taking a step backward. He looked like a fawn that had been cornered in the forest. Shaky limbs. Glittering eyes. "Lily's dad killed my mom in cold blood, and then he came back here to keep Evelyn from taking Lily away. We *know* he's a killer."

"My dad was home that entire night," Lily said. "And he never knew anything about the recipe I'd hidden in the orchard. I didn't tell anyone where it was, not even Belle. The only person who could've found it was your dad. Then, three days ago, it was sitting on your kitchen table, and my mother was lying on the floor beside it. Whoever killed her had to have planted it there."

"This isn't true. This isn't real." Raven leaned against the wall, taking long, slow breaths. "I lost my mom. I lost all of you for three years. Please don't take away my dad."

"He let me get arrested," Belle snarled. "He would've let me rot for *years*—"

Jack held up a hand. Cautiously, he stepped forward, cupping Raven's face. At first Raven flinched, but then he leaned into Jack's touch, letting himself be cradled. Letting himself be held. "You don't have to do anything you don't want," Jack whispered, forehead touching Raven's. "We won't take your family away from you. Whatever happens, you get to choose—"

"You're my family." Raven's head snapped up. His voice was calmer than before, though his legs still trembled. "You've always been my family. And I think . . . I need to know the truth."

Jack nodded, wrapping an arm around Raven's shoulders. "We'll confront him together. Maybe we're wrong, and there's an explanation for—"

"No." Raven strode toward the door, and the others followed. The hallway was dark, but there was a hint of shuffling coming from the study next door. Raven's father was awake. As Raven turned to face the three of them, a terrible feeling blossomed in Belle's stomach. A feeling of warning. A feeling of loss. "I have to do this alone," Raven said.

Then he was gone.

27

The King of the Castle

Raven's father was sitting in the study, drinking whiskey in the dark. *Three fingers, no fat.* Raven smiled at the thought, remembering the first time he'd heard his father order whiskey at a party. Raven had spent the rest of the evening joking about *sipping giggle juice* and feeling *three sheets to the wind.*

He'd been five.

He was seventeen now, and that meant, in the eyes of the state, he was almost a man. When he entered the study, his father rose from his desk and walked over to the bottle of whiskey on a corner table. Poured Raven a drink. A moment later, Raven was holding the glass in his hand, swirling the liquid around nervously.

When his father sat, he did the same. They stared at each other across the wide expanse of the desk. Dr. Holloway's office had been stolen from an era where assistants were called secretaries and sexual harassment law hadn't been invented. The chairs were leather. The desk, a dark mahogany wood. As Raven leaned forward, his elbows resting on the edge of the desk, he asked himself how well he really knew the man in front of him.

His mother had made him omelets. His mother had taught him how to swim. But his father had always been there, hovering in the background, offering encouragement when he wasn't working at the hospital. He'd supported his family, and he'd helped plant a garden in Jack's backyard. He couldn't have done what Raven suspected.

"How's the sleepover?" Dr. Holloway asked, taking a sip of his drink. Raven did the same. Even now, he couldn't help but want his father's approval. His love. "I don't think I've had a good night's sleep in the past four years."

Sleep deprivation, Raven thought, taking another sip. That could explain some things. It could explain a lot. Prisoners of war were kept awake for days on end because their captors believed the lack of sleep would break them.

More often than not, it did.

"I couldn't sleep after Mom died." The whiskey burned in Raven's throat. His eyes stung, and he told himself it was because he wasn't used to drinking alcohol. He wasn't about to break down. "I couldn't sleep and I couldn't eat, and you sent me away instead of helping me."

"I didn't know how to help you," his father said quickly. His throat sounded like it was constricting too. "I thought I was doing the right thing."

"Do you feel that way now?"

A pause, as Dr. Holloway swirled his drink around. "I've made a lot of mistakes. But everything's going to be different now." He reached out, clutching Raven's arm across the desk. His grip was fierce, his gaze desperate.

Raven's heart cracked. "I don't want to be mad at you," he confessed, sliding his arm out of his father's grip. "I know what losing Mom did to you. You lost yourself, and every time you heard me laugh—"

"I will never leave you again. You and I are family, and no one's going to take you away from me."

"No one's trying to take me away from you," Raven answered, and it was the truth. At least for the moment. But maybe his father knew what was coming, because he downed the rest of his drink in one gulp. "Why don't we go and visit your mother tonight?"

"What?" The room swayed a little. Raven thought it was the oddness of his father's suggestion, but something was rising in his stomach. He set his drink down. "I can't leave. I have friends over." Those friends were waiting for him in the living room. He'd needed them to wait there, because he'd had to do this alone.

And he'd known his father wouldn't hurt him.

"Your friends will understand." Dr. Holloway swept around the side of the desk, his black slacks brushing against the edge of the wood. He was wearing a matching jacket and a shirt that hadn't been properly buttoned underneath. Shoes but no socks.

Raven's stomach clenched at the sight of him. "Just get into the car with me—"

"No." Raven jerked out of his chair as his dad lurched toward him. His shoes slid across the heating vent on the floor, and he wondered if his father had heard him talking in the living room. Blood rushed through his ears. "I'm not abandoning my friends. That's the difference between us."

Dr. Holloway sucked in a breath as if Raven had punched him. "My son was sick. I wanted to help him."

"Don't talk about me like I'm not here! You always do that. You decide things without asking me. You married that woman and you never even talked to me about it."

"That was a mistake." Dr. Holloway slid an arm around Raven's shoulders, guiding him toward the study door. "I told you, I wasn't seeing clearly before, but I know the truth now."

"Because of what you found in the heating vent the day Evelyn died."

"I don't know what you're talking about," Dr. Holloway said calmly, and Raven told himself he might be wrong. He *must* be wrong. The past four years of his life had been a waking nightmare, and his mind had become a mess of paranoia, giving life to monsters where only shadows should live. Andrew Kane was guilty.

His father was innocent.

Still, Raven glanced back at his drink. The closer he'd gotten to the bottom of it, the more the world around him had started to sway. Had his father put something in his whiskey? "Dad? I don't feel so good."

"You need to see your mother." His father opened the study door, then ushered Raven outside. "We both need to get out of this house, and then we can—"

"I'm not going anywhere." Again, Raven jerked away from him, but the carpet was bunched up in the hallway. He stumbled, landing on his knees on the floor. According to the police, Evelyn had been found sprawled out on the kitchen floor, her limbs at odd angles and her hair falling out of its curlers. Raven was glad he hadn't found her like that. Finding his mom had been traumatizing enough.

"After Mom died, I started hearing her voice at night." Raven pushed to his feet, using the banister to pull himself up. "The police told you that, right? Before you sent me away?"

"You were suffering delusions." Dr. Holloway yanked open the front door, and Raven's eyes traveled back to the living room. He was certain those double doors would open at any second. No one burst into the hallway. No concerned faces stared back at him, and no arms reached out to clasp his fingers.

I could call out to them, he thought, his heart slamming against his ribs. *I could race out to the orchard and hide there like a kid.* But if he ran from his father now, he'd never be able to ask the questions he needed to ask.

He'd never learn the truth.

"I wasn't delusional," Raven insisted, striding out the front door. He plodded down the porch steps beside his father. "Evelyn had a recording from when I was little. Mom was teaching me how to swim."

"You loved swimming together." Dr. Holloway smiled softly, pulling his car keys out of his pocket. A few seconds later, he was opening the passenger-side door and guiding Raven inside. He was so gentle. So loving. Raven wanted to cry. Why had his father waited until this moment to be tender with him? Why couldn't he have been this person all along?

They were both in the car within seconds, the doors closed and locked. No one could see them. No one could hear them, and maybe that was why his father started to talk. "She took you every summer. You'd stay in the pool until your fingers were shriveled. I had to beg you to get out. And even after you did, you'd cling to her." He lowered his head, and Raven reached out, touching his father's arm. "When Evelyn asked me to bring old videos into the office, I'd completely forgotten about that first day at the pool. I got choked up, watching it. Evelyn listened without judgment." Dr. Holloway shook his head, sliding the key into the ignition. "Then I lost your mom, and Evelyn was the only one who kept calling when the weeks turned into months. She was the only person who'd look at me without tears filling her eyes. I got *so sick* of everyone's pity."

"Me too," Raven said, subtly reaching for his door's handle. He just needed to know that he could bolt out of there if necessary. But the door wouldn't budge, and it took him a second to realize his dad had enabled the childproof locks. He'd done it quietly, without Raven noticing. "I lived in that same place, Dad. We could've gotten through it together. But you chose her."

"I didn't know who she was! How could I have known that

she'd . . ." Dr. Holloway swallowed audibly, steering the car down the long, twisting driveway. Raven turned around, peering back at the house. No one was watching him from the windows. No one was coming for him. "The week before you came home from boarding school, I couldn't sleep. You were so thin when you left. Half-starved, like something was eating you from the inside out. You'd looked like . . . *her*," he whispered, "after she was found in the snow. Cold and lifeless, and I didn't know what you'd be like when you came home. I didn't know if you'd hate—"

Dr. Holloway broke off, pressing his hand against his mouth. He didn't cry. He didn't sob. But his eyes were closed for an instant, and Raven inched his phone out of his pocket, pulling up his latest text. The one asking Jack to come over. He hit the call button just as his father looked up, veering the car toward the front gate. "I was exhausted the day you were scheduled to return. I wanted to get some rest before picking you up at the airport, so I came home in the evening. I found Evelyn in our bedroom getting ready to have dinner with some friends. She left soon after."

"And you went to get your trusty sleeping pills," Raven muttered, his stomach tightening in anger. His chest tightening in fear. No one was answering the phone. "But they weren't on the table where you'd left them, so you went looking for them under the bed. Right? And you found the loose screws to the vent."

A slow, careful nod. "I retrieved the bottle of pills, but the unscrewed vent bothered me. I didn't understand why someone would go tinkering around in there. So I lifted the vent, and that's when I found—"

"The tape recorder," Raven said, his mouth so dry, he thought he was going to be sick. He realized something in that moment. His father hadn't drugged his whiskey. Raven felt ill because he was terrified of learning the truth about the night Evelyn died. His vision was blurry because he was trying so hard not to cry.

"I must've listened to that recording a hundred times in the span of an hour," Dr. Holloway said, his voice thick with anguish. "Your mother's voice *haunted* me. And it brought me to life. I hadn't heard her speak in years, and in that moment, I realized I'd been living in a fog. I'd kept myself in a fog so I couldn't see what was right in front of me."

They were nearing the gate now. Beyond it, the world spread out, wide and infinite, and if the car reached the road, Raven wouldn't be able to escape. He inched the phone out of his pocket again. This time his father caught the movement. He reached out, snatching the phone from Raven's hand.

Then he was lowering his window and tossing the phone into the darkness. "Please. Just listen," Dr. Holloway said, closing the window again. "When I left to pick you up at the airport, I was planning to *divorce* Evelyn. I didn't want to hurt her. I swear, son, I never wanted to hurt anyone. But I saw a figure darting across the lawn as I was leaving the estate, and I just . . . pulled the car around to the side of the road. Snuck in through the back gate, like you kids had done for years. I heard everything Lily said to Evelyn because I was listening outside the window, and once I realized Evelyn had been hurting both you kids . . ."

"You snuck back into the house."

"While Evelyn took her shower, yes. She liked to let her tea steep." He twisted to the right, finding Raven's gaze. "It was easy to pick up the flowers and stuff them into the kettle, but I swear, Raven, I wasn't thinking about what I was doing. I must've been in shock."

"You killed her." Raven wrapped his sleeve around his fist. He would punch his way out of this car if he had to. He would try, because his father wasn't taking him to visit his mother. He was kidnapping him. "You killed Evelyn, and then you framed Belle for the murder. You must've found her recipe out in the orchard while you were pruning the trees. And you kept it all these years."

"I wanted to ask you about it when you came home! I tucked it away in the garage, and forgot about it, until . . ." Dr. Holloway winced as if he'd been struck. "Until Evelyn was lying on the kitchen floor. And you were on your way home. I knew the police would take me away from you if they figured out what I'd done, so I planted the recipe in the kitchen, figuring it would send them in another direction. I had no idea the flowers had come from Belladonna's yard. I had no idea she'd snuck over to the house earlier that day."

"You left her in a juvenile detention center! Anything could've happened to her in that place. And instead of letting her out, you gave Jack a false alibi and abandoned Belle—"

"Everything I've done, I've done to keep us together." Dr. Holloway fumbled with his key chain, looking for the button that would open the front gate. The car came to a stop as they drew near. "You're the only family I have left."

"I have a family," Raven whispered, staring at his reflection in the glass. He thought maybe he'd see his mother's eyes. Her warm, wide smile. But all he could make out were his own dark curls, and the curve of his father's jaw behind him. This was not his family. This would not be his life. Raven took a single, shuddering breath, and slammed his fist into the glass.

There was a sharp, sudden sound, like a blade puncturing a balloon. But it had come from outside the car. Cringing, Raven rubbed at the glass with his sleeve, trying to glimpse the outside world as his father hit the gas. The car stuttered forward unevenly, like the vehicle itself had been drugged, and then it stopped.

Dr. Holloway cursed, unhooking his seat belt. He unlocked his own door—only his own—then slid out of his seat, his body instantly swallowed by the darkness. The door shut and locked at his back. Raven scrambled into his father's seat. His knuckles were throbbing from where they'd slammed into the window, but there were noises outside the car. Voices he recognized. With trembling fingers, he pushed the lock up, yanked the handle toward him, and then he was tumbling out of the car.

He looked up to find figures in the darkness.

"Don't touch them," he warned, because his father had poisoned Evelyn. He'd allowed Belle to be locked up in a cell.

Raven had to protect his true family.

But he'd forgotten who he was dealing with. As he pushed to his feet, he saw Belle standing in front of the car, blocking their passage. Lily was kneeling beside the front tire, her gardening shears stuck deep in the rubber. Jack stood nearby, his phone set to record in case Raven's father lashed out.

Dr. Holloway held up his hands. "I'm sorry," he said, tears streaming down his cheeks. "I don't want you to live in fear of me. I'll turn myself in."

A pang shot through Raven's stomach as his friends surrounded him. "Every time we call the police, it makes things worse. I don't want you locked up—"

But his father was already climbing back into the car. Before Raven could stop him, Dr. Holloway had sped through the open gates, disappearing into the darkness.

Raven raced after him, but the road spread out before him, silent and empty. "This isn't what I wanted," he said at the sound of footsteps approaching.

"I know." Jack touched his arm and Raven spun around, letting Jack enfold him into an embrace. "We don't turn each other in," Jack whispered. "We fight for each other."

"You fought for me." Raven pulled back, his gaze drifting to the house. "How did you get to me so quickly? You didn't answer your phone."

"I didn't have to." Jack leaned in, brushing his lips against Raven's cheek. "I heard you talking through the vents."

28

Happily

They didn't sleep in the orchard as planned. Instead, Raven and Jack curled up together in his third-floor bedroom, while Lily and Belle settled into Lily's room on the second floor. Hours passed, and the sun started to rise. As Raven slept fitfully, Jack snuck downstairs and tracked down a planter's box in the garage. Raven awoke to find a single crimson rose greeting him from outside his window.

He blinked at the sight of it, then smiled. "You did what you promised."

"I always will," Jack said, coming to sit on the bed. There was dirt on his hands and cuts on his fingers. It almost felt like a normal day.

But it wasn't.

"Do you want to talk about last night?" Jack asked softly. He was aching to toy with Raven's hair. Aching to cup Raven's face in his hands. But with dirt on his fingers, the best he could do was grip Raven's gaze.

Then Raven reached out, entwining their fingers. "My dad locked me in the car. I tried to get out, but I couldn't, and the whole time, he was telling me—" He broke off suddenly, the way the car had staggered to a stop after Lily had punctured the tire. That had been a stroke of genius, and Jack was thankful for Lily keeping those rusty shears in her purse the entire time. He was thankful for Belle's idea to listen to Dr. Holloway through the vents. No matter how many times the people around them had tried to destroy them, abuse them, or tie them up in knots, none of them had stopped fighting back.

It was the only way they'd survived.

Now Jack was looking forward to quiet nights beside the fire. Toasting marshmallows with his brothers. Reading stories. Someday soon, their mother would come home, and their lives would be cast into upheaval once again, but for the briefest of moments, the world was peaceful.

The breeze filtered in through the window, rustling the dark curtains. Raven untangled his limbs from his sheets. Jack could tell that he was still exhausted from the previous night, because his usually graceful movements looked a bit sloppy. His eyes were red from crying. Still, he managed to swing his legs over the side of the bed, testing his strength. "He said we were going to see my mom. I thought, maybe in the quiet of the cemetery, he'd tell me the truth. I kept hoping we were wrong about things. Maybe he'd only meant to scare Evelyn, or maybe Andrew really was the killer."

"Andrew's a killer too. He killed your mom, and he doesn't get to pretend he's innocent because Evelyn tricked him into it. He could've checked the gun. He could've said no to her." Jack studied Raven's eyes, expecting to see devastation. "Now he'll be going to prison along with your dad."

Raven huffed, shaking his head. "Maybe they'll share a cell."

"Raven."

He turned to look at Jack then, truly peering into his eyes, and Jack expected to see devastation. Fury, bleeding into heartache. But Raven's gaze was strong. That little boy who'd jumped at every shadow was gone, replaced by someone Jack recognized but didn't really know anymore. Not as much as he wanted to.

Maybe, if he was very lucky, Raven would let him in, like he was letting Raven in. Jack's heart swelled at the thought. He guided Raven to his feet. "The girls are outside taking down the fort in the orchard. We've been talking, and we think it would make sense for you to stay at my house until my mom comes home."

"I have a better idea," Raven said. His voice was clear and unwavering. He took a shaky step, then two. After that, he was striding toward the door, pulling Jack along with him. Jack had to hurry to catch up. Together they made their way through the hallway, where Raven's father had hung up portraits of his first wife. Arianna smiled back at them all the way down the stairs. The foyer was free of her, but only because it was sparsely decorated. Two end tables framed the ebony door. Two vases sat, emptied of roses. Raven opened the door and led Jack out of Holloway Manor, with its jagged gray stones, into the orchard where the girls were waiting.

They were supposed to be taking down the fort, but it was clear they'd gotten a little . . . distracted. Lily brushed apple blossoms from her hair, struggling to smooth her wrinkled clothing. Belle, on the other hand, did nothing to hide the fact that they'd been up to mischief, and she pulled Lily close as her friends approached. "You're up," she said to Raven.

He nodded. "I'm glad you're here. I wanted to talk to you about your time in foster care."

Belle flinched, and Lily stood on her tiptoes, brushing a kiss against Belle's cheek. "We're not letting them place you in some home," Belle said fiercely. "We've already been talking about it—"

"I'm not going anywhere," Raven agreed. At least, Jack thought he was agreeing with their plan, until he said, "I wanted to know how long it took to place you in a home. I'll be eighteen in a year, and it seems like a waste of time for them to spend months pairing me up with some family, just to have me turn around and leave a few months after that. Better to let me get emancipated. Then I can stay here."

He gestured to the estate around him, and suddenly, Jack started to understand. With Raven's father in prison, and his mother buried six feet under the earth, this estate could legally be his. But not unless he was an adult.

"I don't know how quickly they'll set the trial. How quickly they'll convict. But if I can prove that I can take care of myself between then and now, I wouldn't have to move in with any of you." A pause, as Raven flashed an impish grin. "You could move in with me."

"What?" It was Lily who spoke the words, because Lily had lost as much as Raven had. A father and a mother. She had nowhere to go. There was no way she'd be allowed to live in Andrew Kane's house alone, and going back to the facility couldn't have been a palatable option. She needed a home and she needed a family.

Jack wanted that for her.

But things were more complicated for Jack. "You should live here," he said to Lily, forcing a smile to hide the heaviness in his chest. "But I have my brothers to take care of. I can't just pack up and leave."

"They can stay here too," Raven said swiftly. "You know those boys are my family, just like—"

"It isn't that simple. My mom's going to come back someday soon, and she won't be okay with them living somewhere else. Not unless *she* gets to live here too." Jack gestured to the beautiful estate, the twisting branches, and the house that rose up like a castle in the early morning mist. "Plus, we have Diego to think about. He's started to patch things up with his parents, but nothing's settled yet. Flynn won't send him back home until he's sure it's safe."

"He can stay here too." The words came easily. Raven didn't even blink before he offered them, and Jack's heart squeezed as if Raven had cradled it in his hand. "There's room for everyone."

"You don't have to do this."

"I know I don't have to," Raven said. "If I *had* to, it wouldn't be nearly as fun." A soft smile then, the kind that rounded his cheeks and brightened his eyes. Jack wanted to accept his offer. He wanted to believe he could, but he'd been so certain, for so long, that he didn't deserve this.

A family.

True love.

"Things are really complicated, Raven, and if people find out we're all staying together, they might try to tear us apart."

A shrug, so casual. Raven didn't seem the least bit concerned. "Let them try. If we all get emancipated, we can take care of each other, and if they try to take away the boys, we'll prove this is a safer environment—"

"Raven, stop." Jack shook his head, tears welling in his eyes. Raven wanted to take care of him. Jack understood that. He wanted to take care of Raven, too. But Raven had lost his last remaining parent, and he was probably feeling really unsteady right now.

Jack couldn't take advantage of that.

"Why don't you focus on getting emancipated? Once the house is yours, you can decide who you want living here with you." Jack smiled softly at Lily, who was watching the encounter with bright eyes. "You and Lily were a family once. You can be a family again, and I can take care of—"

"Don't you get it?" Raven stepped up close, dressed in the black satin pajamas Jack had helped him into hours earlier. Jack was still wearing his clothes from the previous night. Green shirt. Rolled up jeans. They were exhausted and disheveled. They were unstoppable and wild. "I could live in a castle or I could live in the trees. It doesn't matter, as long as you're with me. *You* are my family, Jack. *You* are my home. All of us can live here together. Lily can have her old bedroom—"

Lily tilted her head up, taking in the sight of the white, billowing curtains. "I'm redecorating *everything*. I can do that, right?"

"Of course." Raven nodded at her, smiling. "Belle can have the guest room next door, unless she wants to stay with Edwin. Do you?" he asked tentatively, and Belle let out a bark of a laugh. It startled some blue jays from a tree. But down below the branches, nobody jumped.

"I was already planning to bail." Belle gestured to a suitcase tucked under the fort of sheets. "I can't stay there anymore. I'll never be free if I'm living with him."

"Then it's settled." Raven's fingers slid into Jack's hair. He guided Jack closer to him, until their foreheads were touching. "We'll live on the estate together. The house will be our home, and we'll plant vegetables where the roses used to grow. You'll never be hungry again," he whispered, so that only Jack could hear. "You'll never be alone."

It sounded like a fairy tale. A story to whisper to a child who was too terrified to sleep. But Jack had separated the world into heroes and villains long ago, in order to survive a life that shouldn't have been so wicked, and he wanted to believe there was kindness to battle the cruelty. Glittering light to cut through the darkness.

He wanted to believe that love was stronger than hate, and as his eyes met Raven's, love surged in his chest, beating back the pain that had threatened to swallow him for so long.

Raven loved him, and he loved Raven. The four of them could be a family, and no matter what the world tried to throw at them, they would survive it together. It wouldn't be easy, but it never had been. They could've given in to the darkness years earlier, and become like the monsters around them. Grown claws. Cut out their own hearts. Instead, they'd chosen to fight for one another, and maybe they wouldn't live happily ever after, because life wasn't a fairy tale.

But they would live happily.

Acknowledgments

To Mandy Hubbard, my unstoppable knight of an agent, for constantly fighting on my behalf. You make my work stronger, fiercer, and bolder every time. Thank you.

To Kate Prosswimmer, my talented weaver of an editor, who helped tie all my dangling strings into a tapestry. I am indebted to your brilliance.

To Nicole Fiorica and the magical staff at Margaret K. McElderry Books, for all the spells you cast behind the scenes. Thank you for your time and your creativity.

To my family, both blood-related and chosen, for the million little ways you've supported me on this path. Love this journey for us.

To my critique partners, AdriAnne Strickland, Phoebe North, and Elle Cosimano, for always making me ground my fables in reality. You bring order to my chaos.

To Mindy McGinnis, Kara Thomas, and everyone in the Lucky 13s. We began as a debut group, seven years ago, and I am continually humbled and grateful that you've shown up for me in the years since. I can't wait to see what you do next.

To those of you who've always known who you were, in spite of what people told you. For those who found yourself along the way. For those still looking.

This book is for you.

Turn the page for a sneak peek at

This Lie Will Kill You

CLASS ACT

Juniper Torres woke with a smile. Today was the day. She knew it, though there was no particular reason to think today would be different. The sun wasn't shining. The sun was barely even up, but it didn't matter much. The universe was speaking to Juniper directly, lighting a fire in her veins and making her heartbeat thrum. It whispered to her in a soft, lilting voice:

Today is the day your life is going to change.

She sat up in bed. Kicking away her tangled sheets (and running a hand through her equally tangled hair), she crawled to the window, looking down. And there she was. The blond, bedraggled mailwoman was leaning over the mailbox, stuffing a host of envelopes inside. Juniper couldn't tell for certain, but she had a sneaking suspicion the envelope was among them.

She raced from her room. Down the hallway she went, past her baby sister's nursery, and the bedroom where her parents slept, their limbs entwined like the branches of neighboring trees. Soon the family would wake, and she wouldn't be able to scour the mailbox in secret. But if she was very quiet (avoiding this floorboard, and that creaky step), she could slip outside without anyone noticing.

So she did. Out of the olive Victorian she went, into the white, winter world. Overnight, the yard had been transformed. Icicles dangled from the oaks, threatening to impale Juniper as she passed beneath them. And at the end of the yard, the snow-frosted mailbox stood out like a sore thumb.

Juniper yanked it open. Her fingers danced over advertisements, brushing the edges of a coupon packet, and then she was pulling the envelope out of the darkness. She knew it was the envelope she'd been waiting for, even before she saw it. It was big, and it was fat, and the writing was . . .

Blood red? The envelope leapt from her hand. It fluttered slowly, like the snowflakes falling around her, and by the time it hit the ground, she'd registered two things: This was not the letter she'd been waiting for. It was an invitation.

She scooped it out of the snow. Someone had written, *You are cordially invited to a night of murder and mayhem!* on the back of the ebony envelope, and Juniper turned it over, confirming that it was addressed to her. It was. *Thanks but no thanks,* she thought, ripping it in half. She had zero interest in getting wasted with her classmates, and even less interest in pretending death was hilarious. The only reason she was stalking her mailbox was because she was expecting an acceptance letter from Columbia University. Their online system was down, which meant she'd be getting her news the old-fashioned way.

And so it went. Juniper raced to the mailbox on Monday morning, then Tuesday. By Wednesday, her confidence had started to ebb. Why was she so convinced she'd be getting an acceptance letter? Yes, her grades were mostly stellar, but last winter, after that party up in the hills . . .

Juniper shook herself. She'd only fallen off track for a month, and most of her teachers had let her make up the work. Even if she didn't get into the college of her choice, she had a couple of safety schools that would take her far away from this town. She'd still go to med school. Cure people. Save lives. Everything would go according to plan.

She was about to return to the house when a black envelope caught her eye, way back in the corner of the mailbox. A shiver skittered up her spine. She already knew what the envelope was. An invitation to "a night of murder and mayhem!"

They'd probably mailed two by mistake, she thought, rolling her eyes. But as she drew the envelope from the darkness, an undertow of guilt started tugging at her limbs. This was how it always happened. She'd be going about her day, not even thinking about Dahlia Kane's Christmas party, and out of nowhere, her limbs would get heavy. She'd feel herself sinking, the way a body sinks to the bottom of a swimming pool, while people stand by, laughing—

"Junebug!" Mrs. Torres appeared in the doorway, her face flushed from standing over the stove. "Breakfast, mi amor. What is that?"

Crap. Juniper's reflexes were dulled this early in the morning. Two hours (and three cups of coffee) from now, she'd never have let her mother see this envelope. But now she was trapped, and she couldn't very well shred the thing in front of her mom. She'd have to play this just right.

Forcing a smile, she jogged up to the doorway. "Just some dork's idea of a good time," she said, holding up the invitation. She wasn't offering it to her mother; she had a very good grip on the envelope. But Mrs. Torres must've seen *a night of murder and mayhem!* scrawled across the back, because she snatched it out of her daughter's hand.

"Ooh, a party. You should go."

"What? No." Juniper scrunched up her face. "It's probably on Saturday. I'm watching *Rudolph* with Olive." Olive was her baby sister, and now that the kid could walk, Juniper was pretty much on permanent call. She chose to think of it as practice for when she was actually on call at the hospital of her choice. Better get used to functioning on two hours of sleep, right?

"Junebug, she's my kid." Her mother disappeared into the hallway, and Juniper followed close behind, plotting to retrieve the invitation. "Believe it or not, I like spending time with my kids."

"And yet, you're forcing me out of the house."

"I'm just making a suggestion." Her mother pulled out a chair at the kitchen table. Olive was in her high chair, giggling and dancing in that I-can-see-invisible-fairies way that babies had. "Don't you want to have fun with your friends?"

"They aren't my friends. They probably sent one to every senior at school."

"All the more reason to go," her mother said, swooping in with the old, chipped coffeepot. "Just think about it, okay? It wouldn't kill you to go to a party."

It might, Juniper thought, her hands starting to shake. She took a gulp of coffee, hoping her mother wouldn't notice her jumpiness. Luckily, Mrs. Torres was busy fussing with the tostadas on the stove. But somebody did notice, and when coffee sloshed over Juniper's fingers, her baby sister frowned, reaching for their mother's purse. Two years old, and she'd already decided makeup was the cure for sadness. Juniper wasn't sure where she'd learned it. This wasn't exactly a beauty pageant house. But wherever the lesson had come from, Juniper didn't mind being her sister's living dolly. Olive's eyes got so bright and her mouth got so smiley.

"Tip-sick!" the baby announced, pulling out a vibrant burgundy gloss that would make Juniper look like she'd been eating berries. Or drinking wine. It was kind of pretty, and Juniper was okay with looking kind of pretty, as long as it didn't eclipse her other accomplishments. She felt a pang as Olive dabbed the gloss on her lips, wishing she could stay in town and teach her sister about making people better, rather than beautiful. But she couldn't stay after everything that had happened—she couldn't—and besides, nothing she could say to Olive would be as influential as becoming the doctor she'd always wanted to be. She'd do everything she'd set out to do, and one day, she'd whisk her family out of this creepy little town, away from all of its secrets.

Its ghosts.

After the lip gloss was on, Olive clapped her hands, squealing, "Pretty!" and Juniper felt the cracks in her heart close.

"You are, baby girl," she said, as tiny fingers encircled one of her own. Meanwhile, their mother had gone completely silent by the stove. Juniper turned, goose bumps rising on her arms, to find Mrs. Torres leaning against the counter, staring at a single page.

"What? Mama, what?"

Her mother didn't answer, so Juniper snatched up the invitation. She made no attempt to be sly about it. One second the paper was fluttering in her mother's fingers, and then it wasn't. One second the breath was filling Juniper's lungs, and then it was gone.

Dear Miss Torres,

Due to your achievements in ACADEMIC
EXCELLENCE, you are cordially invited to a murder

mystery dinner! Prepare to be challenged as you,
and five of your esteemed classmates, fight to unravel
the mystery and apprehend a killer!

The world will become a stage!

A friend will become a foe!

Costumes will arrive later this week!

And, of course, the winner will take home the
coveted $50,000 Burning Embers Scholarship, to be
used at the school of his or her choice.

Your humble benefactor,
The Ringmaster

"It's a scam." The words were out of Juniper's mouth
before she could stop them, and even after she'd spoken them,
she felt no desire to take them back. Even after her mother
sank into a chair, studying the invitation in shock.

"You were right, it is on Saturday," Mrs. Torres said. Her
voice was breathy, and Juniper hated the thought of disap-
pointing her. "They must've had a last-minute opening—"

"Mom, it's a scam. Real scholarship offers don't sound like
this." She'd never even heard of the Burning Embers Scholarship. She'd never heard of it, and she didn't like the sound of it.

"It isn't an offer," her mother said calmly. "It's a contest."

"Real scholarships don't make you compete," Juniper
insisted. "Not like this. Not at a *murder mystery dinner*."

"Misery dinner!" Olive shouted, and Juniper cringed. She
did not want her sister repeating that.

"Calm down, baby girl. Eat your Cheerios."

But it was an exercise in futility. Juniper's own breakfast
sat, forgotten, on the stove. Even her coffee cup couldn't entice

her now. "Look, I'll do some research," she said, plucking her mother's phone from the table, "but I'm pretty sure scholarship foundations don't sign their letters 'The Ringmaster.'"

"They're trying to make it fun."

"They're trying to make money off me." She typed *Burning Embers Scholarship* into the search engine, waiting for zero hits to come up. "Just wait. The day before the contest, I'll get a second letter, asking for an entry fee. If there isn't a website . . ."

Juniper trailed off, clicking the first of several links. Not only did the Burning Embers Foundation have a website, it looked legit. There was an "About" page that highlighted the project's aims (*finding unique and exciting ways to reward students who excel in academics, fine arts, and athletics*) and a "Contact" page with a phone number, an email address, and a physical location. Juniper made a vow to contact them in every way possible before Saturday's event, to prove that real people worked at the foundation.

Or rather, to prove that they didn't.

She wasn't certain why she was being contrary at this point. A fifty-thousand-dollar scholarship would change her life. Hadn't she spent the past six months applying to every scholarship she could find, hoping for one-fifth of that amount?

"I never applied for this," she mumbled, her last-ditch effort at logic. "I would've remembered—"

"Sometimes teachers submit you. Guidance counselors. You're such a good student, and you were going to be valedictorian."

Yes, I was going to be valedictorian. Then I went to a party, last December . . .

"Wait, let me see that." She smoothed out the invitation on the table. It didn't take long to locate the date of the event: December 21. One year *exactly* since Dahlia Kane's Christmas party.

"Mom—"

"This money would be a big deal for us," her mother broke in softly. "Your father could use the good news."

"I know." Juniper glanced at his empty chair. After fifteen years of teaching music at Fallen Oaks Elementary, a recent round of budget cuts had left Mr. Torres jobless. Now Juniper could hear him milling around upstairs, choosing the perfect tie for another set of dehumanizing interviews.

"Are you going to tell him you're passing up fifty thousand dollars?" Her mother fixed her with a stare. "After everything he's been through?"

"Of course not." Juniper swallowed, her chest tightening. "I just don't understand who would submit me for this sort of thing. I'm the world's worst actress."

"Maybe Ruby did it."

Juniper blinked. She could see her mother staring at her, could see her baby sister bouncing in the periphery, but she felt completely displaced. Like she was floating outside of space and time.

"I'm just saying, she has quite the flair for the dramatic. This sort of thing is right up her alley," Mrs. Torres explained. "Why don't you give her a call and ask about it?" Then, almost too quietly for Juniper to hear, she added, "I miss that girl."

I miss her too. Juniper's vision blurred as she thought of Ruby's smile, Ruby's laugh, Ruby's touch. She pushed off from the table, her chair screeching behind her. *Too bad she doesn't miss me.*

+ + +

Juniper slammed her bedroom door, leaning against it. She knew she was overreacting, but she didn't know how to stop it. It was like being in one of those dreams where you *are* yourself, and *see* yourself from outside your body. Like being God and Jesus at the same time.

She shook her head, crossing the room. If she was any kind of religious, it was casually Catholic with atheistic leanings. She just wasn't sure she believed in anything anymore. Still, she'd always been fascinated with the idea of being God and Jesus at the same time. Of being inside your body and watching from high above. Maybe that was what it meant to have a body and a soul, to be at one single point, and everywhere, all at once.

Juniper dug her phone out of her purse. She told herself these thoughts were random, the musings of a girl who still desperately needed her morning caffeine, but deep down, she knew the truth. After everything she'd done to Ruby, she wanted to believe in the possibility of redemption.

She wanted to believe she had a soul.

With trembling hands, she typed out the message, **Did you submit me for the Burning Embers Scholarship?** Ruby's number was still in her phone. She couldn't bring herself to erase it, which was definitely ironic, considering the thing she'd erased from Ruby's life.

The person.

She hit send, then dropped the phone onto her bed. She absolutely would not wait by the phone like a sad little girl on prom night, hoping and hoping while her heart sank to her knees. But maybe *Ruby* had been waiting for *her*. The phone pinged almost instantly, and she found herself scrabbling to pluck it from the bed, her eyes scanning the message frantically: **No.**

Juniper started to laugh. It was the cold, brittle kind of laughter, like twigs snapping underfoot. Of course Ruby hadn't submitted her for the scholarship. Of course Ruby wasn't looking out for her from behind the scenes. Their friendship was over. It had been over for a long time.

She sank down to her bed. When her phone lit up again, she was surprised to feel her heart leap. How could she still have hope after everything that had happened? Her heart was a bruised and bludgeoned thing. A Pandora's box filled with grief and regret. But somewhere, hidden in the darkness, hope was glittering. It caused her breath to falter as she read Ruby's text.

I didn't submit you, Ruby wrote, **but I'm going to the party. Maybe we can solve the mystery together?**

Juniper didn't trust herself with words, so she sent back a smile.

TELL THE TRUTH OR FACE THE CONSEQUENCES

Will the truth set these teens free? Or will their lies destroy them all?

"The fear is palpable. . . . Part high school drama, part suspense, the fast pace will keep readers on edge from start to finish."—*Kirkus Reviews*

PRIVATE NUMBER:
Wouldn't you look better without a cheater on your arm?

AMANDA:
Who **is** this?

PRIVATE NUMBER:
I'm watching you, Sweetheart.

ROSALIE:
Who is this?

PRIVATE NUMBER:
You shouldn't have ignored me. Now look what you made me do . . .